Stress Fractures

Kevin Markinson Series

Book 2

J.E. Seymour

Somersworth Public Library
25 Main Street
Somersworth, NH
www.somersworth.com/
departments-services/library/
(603) 692-4587

Barking Rain Press

This is a work of fiction. Names, characters, places, and events described herein are products of the author's imagination or are used fictitiously. Any resemblance to actual events, locations, organizations, or persons, living or dead, is entirely coincidental.

Stress Fractures (Kevin Markinson Series, Book 2)

Copyright © 2014 J.E. Seymour (www.jeseymour.com)

All rights reserved. No part of this book may be used or reproduced in any manner whatsoever without written permission, except in the case of brief quotations embodied in critical articles and reviews.

Edited by Brenda Morris
Proofread by Robin Layne Wilkinson (www.writingthatsings.com)

Barking Rain Press
PO Box 822674
Vancouver, WA 98682 USA
www.barkingrainpress.org

ISBN Trade Paperback: 1-941295-03-7
ISBN eBook: 1-941295-04-5
Library of Congress Control Number: TBA

First Edition: July 2014

Printed in the United States of America

9 781941 295038

Dedication & Acknowledgements

This book was a very long time coming, and there are many, many people who believed in it from the beginning. Sonia Pilcer was the first to encourage me to send it out. Gareth Esersky was my first agent with an early draft of *Stress Fractures*.

As usual, my long-suffering husband and first reader John deserves a big thank you. Sean McCluskey, Deputy United States Marshal, deserves a mention for his general insight into the world of the US Marshals Service.

Many thanks to the folks who beta read this manuscript for me: T. Kollas, Cindy Amrhein, Jim Clark-Dawe and John M. Urban.

My thanks to all of you, but especially to Barking Rain Press and my editor, Brenda Morris, for finally bringing this book to publication.

Chapter 1

Kevin let go of the boxcar and jumped, hitting the ground hard, then tucking and rolling down the steep bank. His arm throbbed and his head felt light. It was still too dark to see the blood, but he could feel it running down his left arm to his hand, dripping off the fingers. Fighting the dizziness, he got to his feet and looked around. He should have stayed on the train, but he knew he couldn't hold on any longer. Bad luck or bad planning had handed him a line of closed boxcars instead of the open and empty ones he'd expected. Because he couldn't get into the train, he'd ridden this far by hanging on the outside of one of the cars. Better to jump and have a controlled landing than to pass out and fall under the wheels.

His plans had involved getting off in the state park near Staatsburg around two a.m. It wouldn't be that time yet, because he'd jumped off early. A look at the sky showed no sign of the sun. *No kidding.* Nothing there but the clear black sky, blanketed with the pinpoint lights of the stars, a few white clouds, and a hazy ring around the half-moon. Something in the recesses of his brain told him that meant rain. Perfect. Then he'd be wet and cold as well as hurt and tired. He shrugged it off. If it happened, he'd deal with it.

He scrambled back up the bank and began to walk along the tracks, following the long-gone train. He twined the fingers of his left hand into the fabric of his tee shirt and grabbed the open wound on the arm with his right hand, applying direct pressure. That brought renewed pain, but he fought it, keeping his head above the rising tide of black nothingness, and forcing himself to keep going.

He'd been alternating between resting and walking when he realized he could hear and smell running water. He took a deep breath, and then slid down the embankment off the railroad tracks, pushing through the brush and wading into a stream. The water came over the tops of his boots and filled them. He cupped his hand and splashed some of the cold water on his face. He gritted his teeth and tried to wash his arm without touching it; there was still a persistent ache from his earlier attempts to stop the bleeding. Then he began to walk in the stream. His feet slipped on the smooth rocks once in a while, but he managed to keep his balance, despite the dizziness and steady ringing in his ears. He was still losing blood; he could feel it oozing around his fingers. No way of knowing how bad it was, but it didn't matter anyway.

The sun was just starting to cast slivers of light across the sky to his left when he spotted the concrete drainage pipe running under the tracks. It looked like a good enough place to rest. He knew he had to stop for a while, or he would drop, and he didn't want to rest in the open. Besides the danger of being spotted by someone—as unlikely as that seemed out here in the middle of nowhere—the mosquitoes were becoming intolerable every time he stood still. He studied the culvert for a second or two, then, without thinking, reached out with his left hand to grab the side of the pipe. He had to bite his lip as the pain screamed at him.

He swore out loud, lowered the arm, and closed his eyes for a second. As he clamped his teeth even harder on his lower lip, a fuzzy blackness tried to overtake him; approaching with a loud ringing and making his head feel as though it would float off his shoulders. This time he reached out with his right hand and caught the side of the pipe, steadying himself. It took a few minutes for his surroundings to stop spinning; then he scrambled up into the pipe and collapsed. As he leaned back against the concrete walls of his sanctuary, he could just make out some blankets, water bottles, and a flashlight. That would come in handy after he had a bit of a rest; he could check on his arm. He gritted his teeth and closed his eyes, just for a second.

Sally Barnard parked her Volvo in the garage at the Federal Courthouse in southern Manhattan. She looked around as she walked into her office, a large open expanse of desks ringed by filing cabinets set against the wall. The room was empty and dark; most people who worked for the Marshal's Service didn't have to be here at this ungodly hour. The smell of coffee was strong though, which meant somebody was here.

"Thomas?"

A young man with curly brown hair walked into the room with a stack of files. "Right here."

"How you doing? What've we got?"

"New York State Police have asked us to help out on a fugitive task force. The FBI has been called, too." He handed her a grainy photo. "Blond hair, blue eyes, late forties, broken nose—nasty looking." Thomas continued. "This guy escaped from an upstate medium security correctional facility this morning just after midnight."

"Who is he, and why do we care?"

"His name is Kevin Markinson. He's a cop killer. This is his third escape."

"But what about Northern District? Why didn't they call them first? They're closer, right?"

"It's on the border. Hudson is in Columbia County, which is in the southern part of the Northern District. The prison officials say he hopped a train headed south, and we're going on the assumption that he's actually in Dutchess County at this point."

"Okay then. Let me put a team together, and we'll hit the road."

"I'm right behind you, boss."

She glanced at the clock. It was nearing five hours since their man had broken out. The State cops were already looking for him. Probably county, too. Yet it would be her responsibility to pull all of the agencies together, start a serious investigation, figure out where the man would be heading, and make sure he was caught. She was in charge here—the veteran of this crew—which meant she was responsible. They were part of the new plan on the part of the US Marshal's Service to reciprocate help to the State and local authorities that had been helping them for years. They would help, when asked, with violent fugitives or drug related cases. Sally figured they were called in on this case because the fugitive in question had a history of violent and repeated escapes.

Sally looked up from the fax as Elizabeth Doucette walked in. "God, Sally, what the hell are we doing here at this time of the morning?"

"Hey, Liz. Fugitive task force. Upstate. You want in on it or not?"

"I'm in. I just don't understand why these guys can't break out in the middle of the day instead of the middle of the night. Did Thomas make the coffee?"

Sally nodded, sipping at a mug of what could only be described as thin mud. She would add a packet of hot chocolate mix to every cup, but even that wouldn't help.

Craig Wallace walked in as Elizabeth was pouring some of the suspicious brown liquid into her mug. He was a few years older than Liz, who was in turn a few years older than Thomas. Craig was a former Marine, who still wore his blond hair super short, and still worked out. He had a neck like a tree trunk, but a wide, easy grin. Craig's area of expertise was communications—radio and computer stuff, electronic surveillance—things Sally didn't understand or want to.

He spoke to Elizabeth. "You're not really going to drink that stuff?" His coffee was from Dunkin' Donuts.

"Too cheap to buy my own," responded Liz.

Craig turned to Sally. "What've we got?"

She tossed the fax from the state onto her desk as her team gathered around, all of them taller than she was, bending over to scrutinize the material.

Craig scowled. "Medium security? What do they need us for?"

"He's a cop killer with a history of violent escapes."

"Yeah, but he's old."

Sally frowned up at him. "He's a couple of years younger than I am."

Craig grinned. "Like I said."

She shook her head. "Y'all ready to move?"

"Absolutely."

Her team followed her out the door and down into the garage, where they all threw their gear into the back of a black Suburban.

"Thomas, you drive."

Thomas groaned, but climbed in on the driver's side. "You want me to run code?"

"Nah. He's already out; we're not in that much of a hurry. You get stuck in traffic, go ahead and use the lights. Otherwise, forget it." Sally pushed an Elvis Presley CD into the player and took one more sip of foul mocha, humming along with "Jailhouse Rock" as Thomas turned the behemoth north, towards Columbia County.

Danny Rutledge was having a bad Thursday. It started out all right, when his mother informed him she had decided to let him stay home alone for the weekend for the first time ever. But it began going south when he rode his new mountain bike into town.

The ride in itself wasn't so bad, mostly downhill, and he had a chance to talk to his friend Jessie Saxby, whose father owned the little general store in the center of town.

He found her putting cans of Coke into the glass-doored cooler in the back.

"Hi, Danny." She always spoke right up. He figured she wasn't as shy as he was.

He smiled at her, then looked away and chose a can of Sunkist. "Hi, Jessie. You working this summer?"

"Yeah. My dad wants me to start saving for college." She rolled her eyes. "Like I need to worry about that now. How about you?"

"I picked beans a while back, but that's mostly gone by. I figure to pick some drops this fall. Nothing serious." Danny's mother expected him to earn his own spending money, and there wasn't much a thirteen-year-old could do. Agricultural work was about it, aside from babysitting or yard work. Danny didn't have any neighbors to do yard work for, and he didn't really have an interest in babysitting. Most people seemed to want girls for that job anyway. That left working for the big vegetable farm and orchard up the road. He could earn a decent amount of money, picking by the pound, keeping his head down, and just doing the work.

She continued to transfer cans from the cardboard cases to the racks in the cooler. "You looking forward to fall?"

He started picking up cans and shook his head. Fall meant back to school, back to the constant teasing, the slow wearing down of what little self-esteem he might have left. It was easy for Jessie. She wasn't exactly the most popular kid in school, but she got along with everybody. Nobody ever picked on her.

She seemed to figure it out. "It'll get better. They're getting older. Everybody grows up sooner or later."

"Sure." Danny doubted it. "Listen, Jessie, I've got to get going. I'll see you around, okay?"

"Sure. Take it easy."

He paid for his soda and three Snickers bars and headed out the door, squinting in the sunlight. He almost ran right into a group of three boys, all bigger and older than he was.

"Well, look who's here. It's Danny the queer," taunted the oldest of the group, a boy named Eddie. He was heavy, with a mop of curly, greasy black hair and a face full of zits. He wore a ragged jean jacket covered with Harley patches. His pants were baggy and torn at the knees.

Danny backed towards his bicycle as Eddie and his gang pressed in on him. Fear rose in his throat, pushing its way up from his stomach, threatening to explode in a sudden scream, or even a whimper, neither of which would be smart in this crowd. He hated this reaction, even more than he hated Eddie and his gang. This was part of the problem, wasn't it? Why couldn't he just take it? Why did he have to be afraid?

"Whatcha doin', four eyes? Gonna ride your tricycle?" This came from Randy, a red-haired, freckle-faced kid with dirty hands. His outfit was the same as Eddie's, except his denim jacket had the sleeves cut off. His patches ranged from Anthrax and Metallica to Obituary and Megadeath.

"Will you take me for a ride?" Terry asked. He was Randy's younger brother, the only one in the group in Danny's grade, despite being a year older. Terry was wearing Randy's old clothes—which were too big for him—still covered in his big brother's grime.

"Leave me alone, you guys," Danny muttered, staring at the ground as he grabbed his bike and pulled it out of the rack. A foot appeared from nowhere and he fell, scraping his knees. He got to his feet, climbed on his bike, and started to ride away, wishing himself invisible. He realized the group had flattened both his tires, and he was forced to walk the bike the two miles home. He could swear he heard them laughing the whole way.

He spent the long walk plotting revenge. He thought about getting one of his dad's guns and shooting them from the bell tower of the Baptist church on the green in town. He could picture that in his mind. But he knew he couldn't do it. He was a good shot, but he still couldn't do it. Not just because he would never get away with it; nobody ever got away with stuff like that. No, the reason he knew he wouldn't do it was because it was wrong. He knew what he was—a straight arrow. He knew he was never going to explode and lose it. He was just like his father, carrying it around in silence. Just a sheep.

He'd been enduring the taunts of these kids and others like them since he was little. Ever since the day they'd moved into this small town, and he'd presented himself to Mrs. Robinson's first grade class and heard the snickers, the whispered taunts that became louder on the playground. As he got older the taunts turned to blows, smacks in the kidneys, kicks in the butt, rabbit punches to his stomach. His glasses made him a target, and his quiet nature made him even more attack-worthy. He wouldn't fight back, never had. He would just crumble inside, try desperately to fit in, and end up alone most of the time. He got along well with his teachers, did well at his schoolwork, stayed out of trouble. He never told anyone what went on, although teachers would question him on it. He had no desire to become a rat, no need to turn the other kids in. He accepted what he felt was his lot in life. There were some people in this world meant to be leaders, some meant to be followers, some sheep, some wolves. He knew he was a sheep, a follower, never one to break away from his place.

He found himself wishing he was a cop, or a spy, or someone who could do something. A detective from one of his books, or even a criminal. He just wanted to be a little bit braver, a little bit stronger, a little bit more of a wolf. His ears still burned with the laughter of the group when he got home. He sighed as he parked the bike in the garage, and decided to head out to his fort, a concrete culvert under the railroad tracks. In the spring it would drain water from the swamp on one side to the stream on the other, but this time of year it was dry. He spent a lot of time out there, just reading, hanging out, watching the birds in the swamp, and listening to the stream. It gave him a place to be, a place of his own. Along the way he pretended to track down and wipe out the bullies who had taunted him, making the town safe for democracy once more. He jumped down off the tracks, clambered up into the pipe, and froze.

Chapter 2

There was somebody there, hiding, betrayed by a quick movement of a dark shape. They were both surprised. Danny almost fell backwards out of the pipe. The man tried to leap to his feet and whacked his head on the concrete ceiling.

"Goddammit!" he growled as he dropped back down onto the blankets, shaking his head.

Danny just crouched in the opening with his mouth open and stared.

"What do you want?" The intruder's voice sounded like sandpaper.

"Uh… nothing… I was just, well, I…" Danny couldn't think of anything to say. As his eyes adjusted to the dark he took in the whole picture. The man was very tall, even doubled up in the pipe, and thin, with long dirty-blond hair pulled into a ponytail, a mustache of the same color, and a pale face with blue-gray eyes so cold they could have been made of ice. He wore dark green workpants and a green tee shirt, both of which were covered with mud and something darker that might be tar. He resembled a scarecrow folded up and jammed into the pipe.

"What are you doing here?" The man's voice was still no more than a low growl.

"This is my fort. You know, my hideout." That sounded stupid. Thirteen years old, and he still played in a fort. Danny wondered why he wasn't more scared, wondered why he hadn't turned tail and run. Why was he sitting here with this man, this stranger, having a conversation?

"Oh." The man answered as though this made perfect sense, leaned back against the side of the pipe, and fished a cigarette out of the pack in his shirt pocket. Danny watched as he inserted the cigarette into his mouth, using only his right hand, keeping his left arm folded tightly across his chest. He lit it, holding the matchbook in his left hand and striking with his right. In the glow from the match Danny could see a dark stain on the man's shirt, near the left shoulder.

It occurred to him it wasn't tar at all, but something else.

"Are you hurt?"

"Mind your own business."

"Okay, I'm sorry." Danny was feeling just a little braver now, starting to feel a little more indignant. After all, this guy was in his place. "How did you get here?"

"Beat it." Still a low growl, this time accompanied by a glare.

Danny shrugged and wondered if he should mention that those blankets were his, the water bottle was his. In the end, he decided discretion was the better part of valor and climbed down out of the pipe. He had no interest in getting into a fight with a man older than his father, a man who looked like he would just as soon cut your throat as look at you. After a quick glance back—where he saw the man lean back with his eyes closed, the end of the cigarette glowing in the dark—he meandered home, eating a Snickers bar and staring at the ground as he went.

Where had this person come from? Danny wondered. *He had to have jumped off a train.* There was almost no other way to get to this spot, unless he had simply followed the tracks. This particular place was a long hike from any road. Anyway, he looked like he was a bum, one of the homeless people who rode the freight trains. Were there still people who did that? There were certainly homeless people in the city, but there weren't so many in the country, right? And what about the dark stain on his shirt? He had to be hurt. That stain didn't look like sweat. But he also didn't seem to want help. Maybe, though, if he was still there tomorrow, he would accept Danny's help. *People are people,* Danny thought. *You have to help someone who needs it.* He planned the next day as he arrived home. Right after breakfast he would head out and see if the man needed something to eat. He could make a day's adventure of it. It would be cool.

Kevin was trying to focus on the pain in his arm. It had to be close to sixteen hours now, and it was hurting more than ever. He wanted to roll over and sleep. It was a real struggle against that temptation, knowing it would be dark soon and he should get moving again. He knew how to use the pain to his advantage—focus on it, sharpen the senses, and let it bring him awake.

But even if he could handle the pain, there was the food problem. If he didn't eat soon he wouldn't be able to go on. Close to twenty-four hours since his last meal. He'd found a bottle of water in the pipe and had been rationing it, not knowing when he would get more. The water would keep him alive, but he knew he wasn't going to last a lot longer. He was already getting lightheaded and dizzy from the pain. The lack of food didn't help. He didn't want to think about the problem. He didn't want to think about any of his problems. His head was getting fuzzy again.

The incident with the kid worried him. He debated the possibilities. The kid could have already called the cops. He should have done something with the boy; should have kept him here; should have prevented him from leaving, but he wasn't thinking straight. Even now he wasn't thinking straight. What could he have done? He wasn't going to kill a kid and he didn't think he had the strength to hold anybody hostage, not even a boy.

Everything had gone wrong. He should have been miles beyond here, and he shouldn't have gotten hurt. That wasn't part of the plan. To compound the problems, he heard helicopters. He knew what they were, why they were there, and it scared him. He hated the twinge of pain in his belly. He didn't like to be scared, didn't like to admit he could still be scared. Hell, he prided himself on having no fear. He wasn't afraid of anyone; he just didn't want to get shot again.

All right then, so he wasn't afraid. It was too risky to travel in daylight though, so he would have to take his chances and stay where he was. Okay, he told himself, a few more hours until dark; sleep a little while waiting, and then move on. Find a pay phone, make a couple calls, get somebody to come and pick him up, and get the hell out of this godforsaken jungle. Half his brain told him not to sleep; the other half convinced him he'd be able to wake up. Hadn't he always had an alarm clock in his head? He fell asleep as the first half of his brain tried to remind him the alarm clock didn't always work when he was hurt.

"This looks like the place," said Thomas, pulling off the road into the staging point, a large dirt parking lot with tents set up and a half dozen assorted cop cars parked around them.

"Great." Sally got out of the SUV and headed towards the man she assumed was in charge. He was in his late forties at least, on the heavy side, wearing the green uniform of a local sheriff's deputy, complete with the standard mirrored aviator sunglasses.

"What can I do for you, ma'am?"

She took off her sunglasses and offered him a hand. "I'm Deputy US Marshal Sally Barnard. These are my associates, Deputy Thomas Neelon, Deputy Craig Wallace, and Deputy Elizabeth Doucette." She waved a hand in the direction of her team. "You know the details?"

"Yes, ma'am. I'm with the Dutchess County Sheriff's department. Reggie Crandall." He shook her hand without taking off his sunglasses, which annoyed her. "I'm in charge here."

She squinted at his chest, trying to figure out if he was the actual sheriff or just a deputy. "Not anymore, Deputy Crandall. I'd appreciate your cooperation, but I'm afraid that the State Police have asked me to head up the task force. I'm going to have to take over the operation." The deputy sheriff reddened and nodded, looking down past his shiny black gun belt to his shiny black paratrooper boots. She continued, "Markinson went right out the front gate at the Hudson correctional facility just after midnight. He was shot on his way out. The warden thinks he hopped a train. The train got all the way to Poughkeepsie before anybody checked it. We need to set up roadblocks, and I need some trackers. I want to work backwards along this branch line until we pick up the trail. We should get people working this way from the other end as well."

"Beg your pardon, ma'am, but how the hell am I going to set up roadblocks over sixty miles of territory?"

She frowned at him. That was logical. "How about rolling checkpoints, try to cover the roads near the tracks?"

Deputy Crandall nodded and glanced at his watch. "How long has it been, about twelve hours?"

"Yeah."

"He's probably long gone." The man pushed his Smokey Bear hat back on his head, exposing his super-short haircut, and scratched his forehead. "He probably had somebody meet him with a ride."

"I don't think so. I guess it's possible, but I just have a feeling about this. He's hurt, and he knows we're out here looking for him. I have a feeling he's holed up somewhere. We haven't had any reports of stolen cars or hijackings, and he wouldn't have gotten far on foot, not hurt the way he is. I want to flush him out. We need to keep the search going day and night; I've already arranged for helicopters and dogs. We need to keep him unsettled; make sure he stays awake; not let him get any rest; keep him moving and scared."

"There's an awful lot of woods out there. The tracks run right through two state parks. Over a thousand acres of territory."

"Then we'd better get going." She started to turn away, and then stopped. "Can you point me to the person who would have the files on this guy?"

The deputy raised his hand towards the tent. Sally headed in that direction.

"Thomas, can you get the warden of that prison on the phone?" She browsed through the paperwork while she waited, looking for anything that would give her a clue as to what this guy would do.

The file was full of the standard stuff. A long list of aliases, descriptions of four Marine-related tattoos, and numerous scars, almost too many to keep track of. Old bullet wounds to the neck, left leg and chest, knife wounds to the stomach and right arm, that one fairly recent. Broken ribs, broken nose, broken jaw, broken leg, walks with a limp. God, this guy was a mess even before he took the slug this morning.

He was also on the run, injured, out of his element. She didn't like what she saw. When she finally got the warden on the phone, she got right into the problem. "So when was your last escape?"

"I've only had one escape from this prison before this—over a year ago," he replied. "It's not really that kind of population. You know, medium security, short-timers. Low risk for escape."

She looked down at the thick file in her hands. "Are we talking about the same man here, 'low risk for escape?' He's broken out before this."

"Yes ma'am, but he's forty-five years old; he's served more than half his sentence. His last escape was in 1984... that's like fourteen years ago. We need the beds in maximum, so the state moves them to medium when they've been in the system as long as he has."

"You've got an empty bed now, warden." She shook her head. "Well, thank you for your cooperation. He's our responsibility at this point." She hung up the phone. "Craig."

"Yeah?"

"You know anything about the Marine Sniper program?"

"A little."

"Our fugitive is an ex-Marine. He was a sniper. Did two tours in Vietnam."

"Way before my time. And there are no ex-Marines, unless he got a dishonorable discharge. He's a former Marine."

"Thank you for informing me." She rolled her eyes. "So what does that tell you about this guy? What kind of skills does he have?"

Craig sat down across the table from her. "He knows how to hide."

Liz snorted. "Lots of insight there."

"He'll have a background in the woods. They don't take city boys for sniper training."

"It says he grew up in Red Hook. In Brooklyn."

"Hell, I'm just telling you what I know." He closed his eyes for a second. "This program would have been brand new when he was in it. Maybe they just took whoever they could get, or maybe he's got some experience in the woods—hunting or something."

"Tell me more."

"I didn't do scout sniper, but I guess he'd be at least. . . oh. . . a staff sergeant. A non-com. He'd have some leadership abilities. He'll be used to working alone even though the snipers work in two-man teams. One scout, one shooter; they take turns. It'd be easier if I knew what you're looking for."

"Brainstorming is good, Craig."

Craig furrowed his brow. "Goes without saying he knows how to shoot."

"And he won't be afraid to if he thinks he has to," put in Liz.

Sally sighed. "We can only hope he's not armed."

"Right." Craig nodded.

Sally settled herself in a folding chair with a cup of coffee, pouring a packet of hot cocoa mix into it, and spreading the prison files on the table in front of her while she stirred. It was stifling in the tent; the fabric walls blocked what little breeze there was outside and it felt like she was trying to breathe in a pot of hot soup.

"Thomas?"

"Yeah?"

"Can we move to more permanent quarters? Someplace with air conditioning?"

"I'll see what I can do."

"Thanks."

As Thomas wandered off, she flipped through the pile of papers crammed into the manila folder. Kevin Michael Markinson was born in Brooklyn, November 15, 1952, the second of five children. Joined the Marine Corps in November of 1970, two weeks before his eighteenth birthday. Trained as a sniper, and went to Vietnam at the tail end of the war. The last Marines left in June of 1971. He was injured more than once and received two purple hearts and a bronze star. She skimmed past the details, wanting to know more about what he'd done once he got home. His first adult arrest came in 1973, in connection with a shooting in Queens. He walked away from that, but got a mandatory sentence for the handgun he was carrying at the time of his arrest. She flipped ahead again, looking for something that would tell her what he would do under these circumstances—hurt, running, alone.

Craig sat across from her, typing something on a laptop, cursing under his breath.

Sally looked up from the file. "What?"

He looked up. "Oh, sorry. I just installed Windows Ninety-eight on this thing and it takes some getting used to."

She raised her eyebrows.

"Anything I can do for you?"

"Can you find me contact information for the Mid-Hudson Forensic Psychiatric Center?"

"That's a mouthful. Why?"

"Markinson underwent a full psychiatric evaluation there in…" she looked down at the file. "Nineteen ninety-two. I want to talk to anybody there who knows him."

"Is he crazy?"

"He didn't meet the qualifications."

"Okay. I'll get the contact info for you."

"Thanks."

She went back to the file just as Elizabeth sat beside her. "Anything interesting in there?"

Sally poked through papers. "Let's see. He's a recovering alcoholic. Does AA in prison."

Elizabeth snorted. "He probably does that to look good to the parole board."

Sally took a sip of mocha and noticed some pages with lines of black marker through them. "What's this? It looks like he worked for the CIA."

Elizabeth sat up in her chair. "What?"

"He was a CIA assassin. Freelance. A kite."

"What does that mean, 'kite'?"

"It means they can cut him loose, disavow him if he gets into trouble. Which is what happened when he killed that cop." Sally set the file down.

"Wasn't your husband CIA?"

Sally nodded. "He might be able to give me a name, someone I can call."

"If they'll talk to you."

Sally picked up the file again. "Yeah."

"So how did he go from professional to cop killer?"

"He says he didn't do it."

"They all say that."

"I'm just telling you what I see in the files, Elizabeth. We need to think the way he does if we want to find him."

"So what else?"

"You know Charles Marconi?"

Elizabeth shook her head.

Thomas piped up from behind Sally's chair and she had to twist to see him. "Vincent Marconi's son. Nasty small-time mob boss out in Queens. The FBI would love to get him on a RICO, but so far, nothing. Nobody in that organization has ever turned, or if they have, they've disappeared."

"Who do you think makes them disappear?" Sally turned back to the file.

"Markinson?" Elizabeth leaned forward to try to get a look at the file.

"Rumor has it."

"Where do they get this stuff?" Elizabeth asked.

"I have no idea. I'd love to talk to the person who put all this together."

"Maybe nobody has ever looked at the whole thing before," said Thomas.

Sally nodded. "That's possible. It's been a while since he escaped."

"So where is he going to go? Where is he headed? What would he do, hurt and off course?" Elizabeth was making an attempt to pull them back on topic. Sally liked that in her. All business.

"Give me a little more time. I haven't gotten into his head yet." Sally looked over at Craig. "You have a phone number for me?"

Craig nodded. "Doctor Penelope Woodbury. You ready to copy?"

Sally nodded and wrote down the phone number. "Thanks."

"Are you okay, Danny?" his mother asked at dinner.

"Huh?" Danny looked up from poking a piece of pie with his fork.

"You haven't said a word all evening."

"I'm sorry. I was just thinking."

"You aren't worried about being left alone this weekend, are you?"

"No." Danny considered telling her about the man in the pipe, but decided not to. He knew she wouldn't understand. He didn't really understand himself. He just knew he didn't want anyone to know about the wounded man in the drainage pipe.

After dinner, Danny worked on the dishes while his mother sat in the living room, watching the evening news.

"There's been another escape from Hudson," his mother called out.

Danny heard the words and felt his stomach start the familiar clench, the same feeling he got when the bullies surrounded him. Coincidence, right? No connection to the man in the culvert. He dried his hands and moved closer to the door of the living room to watch the television.

She turned up the volume, taking in the information. The newscaster was describing the escapee. "Violent, serving time for killing a police officer, wife and family in the city, decorated veteran."

As his mother got to her feet, Danny hurried back to the dishes. She gave him a feeble grin. Danny turned back to loading the dishwasher.

"I'll finish up, Danny. Why don't you get ready for bed?"

"Okay." He nodded. He didn't want to ask her anything about the escaped prisoner. He didn't want to know any more.

He lay awake in his bed, staring at the ceiling, listening to the tree frogs, crickets, and train whistles. He'd never thought before about how noisy it was around here. He finally gave up and grabbed his book, so thick it was heavy, even in paperback. He turned on the crooknecked lamp on his nightstand and began to read.

Before he realized it, he could hear the footsteps signaling his mother coming up the stairs. He switched off the light.

She stopped in the doorway. "Are you still awake?"

"Yeah."

"Are you worried about being left alone with an escaped prisoner on the loose?"

He shook his head, and realized she probably couldn't see him in the dark. "No."

"Maybe I should ask Mrs. Warner if she can stay with you."

"I'll be okay."

She nodded and headed down the hall. Danny rolled over and stared at the wall, his mind going a mile a minute. What would happen if he told his mother about the man in the pipe, the man he intended to help? She'd cancel her trip. That would mean she'd be mad at him. Even if she didn't want to be mad, she would be. She'd tell him he was stupid for even talking to the guy to begin with. Maybe he was. Don't talk to strangers; wasn't that what he learned from the time he was just a toddler? He fell asleep with it ringing in his head… don't talk to strangers, don't talk…

Sally and her crew settled into a motel just south of Poughkeepsie around nine that night. She was exhausted, dragging her gear to her room.

"Hey, a pool," said Thomas.

"Like we're going to have time to swim," muttered Craig.

"I've got to do my laps every day. Can't live without it."

"Sure, Thomas, whatever. Sally, why do I have to share a room with this idiot and you get a room to yourself?"

"Because you're not the boss."

"Yeah, but Liz gets her own room too."

"That's right." Sally stepped through the door. The room was already cold, and she took a deep breath of the refrigerated air. Then she spread her paperwork on the table and sat down to try to figure out where her quarry was. It was ten-thirty before she picked up her cell phone.

"Hey, Bob."

"What're you doing up so late?"

"Just settling down for the night." She smiled. "How're the dogs?"

"They miss you."

"You going to take them running Saturday?"

Bob snorted. "No."

She said her goodbyes, folded up the phone, and stretched out on the bed, luxuriating in the cold, and trying to picture where the man she was chasing was stretched out. Back in the city? Inside or out? Fighting mosquitoes in the bush? Dead? She almost hoped it was the last. That would make life so much easier.

It was a bad afternoon for Kevin, stretching into a bad night. He could hear the helicopters in his sleep. That and the heat combined with the pain made it almost impossible to get any real rest. He was on edge anyway. His mind played tricks on him, transporting him back about thirty years ago, to another hot, steamy night.

The helicopters pounded in his brain, mixing with the sound of artillery fire. He could almost smell the gunpowder, taste the tinned food. His stomach burned, and he would have given anything for one bite of lousy canned cheese. Why hadn't he brought more food? Not supposed to be out here this long, that's why. The food is too heavy, too hard to carry. Isn't it enough you had to carry four canteens? Always needed more water. The food you could live without—not water, though.

Dust-off, right? That's what the helicopters were for. They were going to take him out of here, get him to help. All he had to do was get to the LZ, get out in the open where they could pick him up. He began to crawl, trying to get out of the hole he was in. He poked his head over the edge, looking for tracers. He felt his pockets for a smoke canister, tossed aside his cigarettes. Where was his pack? Pulling himself up to the edge of the hole, he started to climb out, and then for some reason he was falling. He ducked, tucked and rolled, and fell into the water. That woke him up.

It was daylight. The next morning. With all the trouble he'd had falling asleep he hadn't expected to sleep through the night. He stood up, shook the water off as best he could and climbed back into the pipe. He allowed himself another sip of water as he considered his options. He didn't want to travel in the light. Too risky. As he lit a cigarette he could hear the echoes of his buddies, telling him to lie low, keep his head down, and stay safe.

Chapter 3

Danny made his way down the stairs and glanced over at his mother, who was scooping leaden oatmeal into a bowl. He sat down at the table and stuck a spoon into the cereal. The utensil stood straight up. Once upon a time, his dad would have been here; he would have rolled his eyes or laughed. Her cooking had been a private joke between them, neither of them having the heart to tell her how bad it was.

Danny forced down as much oatmeal as he could, pushing aside thoughts of his father. Then, while his mom was upstairs getting ready for work, he made four tuna sandwiches. He packed them and some bottled water and juice boxes into his backpack, along with a radio, a flashlight, a couple of books, and what he could scrounge up for first aid supplies.

When she came back into the kitchen he said, "Mom, I'm going to be gone all day. I've got some exploring to do. Okay?" He knew that would please her. She was always trying to get him to go outside more. He preferred to read or play video games.

"Be back by four; I want to take you grocery shopping. We'll get some stuff for you for the weekend." She smiled at him as he headed down the back steps and towards the trees. "Hey," she called after him as he reached the edge of the woods. "Not too far from home, okay?"

"Okay, Mom." He waved at her.

He made good time on this trip, alternating between walking and running. He had spent the night trying to decide who and what the man in the pipe was. His thoughts ran the gamut from double agent to mob informer. He could be a simple bum, somebody without a job, hitching rides on trains, traveling across the country. He came up with a multitude of explanations. A Russian spy, operating under deep cover, gets shot by a United States agent who discovered his identity. Were there still Russian spies? He didn't think so. He could be an informer living in the federal witness protection program who was found by the mob and shot, barely escaping with his life. Or an escaping convict who was shot as he went over the wall at a state prison. Definitely not that one. Maybe a police officer shot by a pulled-over motorist who lost his memory and had been wandering around in the woods for days. A man shot by aliens! No, this was getting too weird.

Danny approached the pipe and peered around the edge to make sure the man was still there. He was there, lying on his right side, apparently asleep. Danny watched him for a minute as he waited for his eyes to adjust to the dark. He realized then that the man was not asleep. His eyes were open and he was watching right back.

"Hello," said Danny.

The man rolled over onto his back, and then sat up. What little color there had been in his face drained out of it. He leaned back against the pipe and squeezed his eyes shut.

"How you doing?" Danny asked, although he could tell just by looking.

"Lousy," the man whispered.

Danny climbed up into the pipe and set his pack down. "I can help you."

The man's eyes opened, and he stared at the boy. "What?"

"You need help."

"What's in it for you?" His voice was weak and soft, barely audible.

"Nothing." Danny moved a little closer. He noticed beads of sweat standing out on the man's forehead. It wasn't even hot outside yet, and it certainly wasn't hot enough in the cool of the pipe to account for that much sweat. "So, what happened to you?"

"It doesn't matter." The man closed his eyes again.

"How can I help you if I don't know what's wrong?"

The man was silent for a moment, opened his eyes again and said, "My left shoulder, upper arm, somewhere in around there."

Danny approached, bent over to avoid hitting his head. In the dim light he could easily see the stain on the man's shirt. There was a peculiar smell too, even above the musty concrete smell of the pipe, a coppery-sweet odor that nearly turned his stomach. The man's clothes were soaked. "How'd you get all wet?"

"Fell in the water."

"What, in the middle of the night?"

"No, just a little while ago."

Danny looked around the pipe and grabbed his flashlight. "Can you move your arm?"

"A little."

The boy aimed the light at the left arm. "My name is Danny, by the way." The light revealed a long furrow of open flesh just below the shoulder, with congealed blood stuck to the shirt, and dirt stuck on top of that. Danny swallowed the bile rising in his throat. "This looks pretty nasty; it's still bleeding. You probably ought to have a doctor look at it, mister. What's your name anyway?" He reached in his pack, looking for a jackknife, while trying to keep his mind occupied to avoid throwing up.

"Duke. You can call me Duke." He paused to take a breath, drawn sharply through his teeth. "No doctors. I can't afford it."

Danny used the jackknife to cut the shirt away from the wound. "This is going to hurt," he warned as he prepared to pull the fabric off of the wound.

The boy watched the remaining blood drain out of the already pale face. The man moved his lips and squeezed his eyes shut, muttering something Danny couldn't quite hear. He then gritted his teeth and clenched his fists.

Danny poured water onto a gauze pad, added a little Betadine, cleaned the mess up as best he could, and then applied some antiseptic with another square of gauze. To finish up, he wrapped a roll of gauze around the arm and fastened it with some tape. "Looks a little better now. How's it feel?"

"Lousy. Does it look deep?" Duke tried to crane his neck to look at the back of the arm without twisting it.

"Yeah. But if you can move it it's probably not broken."

"Good." He muttered something under his breath. Aloud he said, "Still bleeding though, right?" He closed his eyes and leaned back, then fished an antacid out of a roll in his pocket.

"Yes, it's still bleeding." Danny turned back to his backpack, rummaging through it. "You should drink some water. Are you hungry?" He handed the man a water bottle.

"A little," Duke replied. He sipped, as though rationing the liquid.

Danny unwrapped a tuna sandwich and handed it to him. "Here you go." He watched Duke eat. At the first taste, the man perked up, attacking the tuna fish as though he was afraid it would get away. "How long has it been since you ate?"

The man looked at him, blinked, and swallowed. It took him a minute to answer. "What day is it?"

"Friday."

"What time?" He looked out the end of the pipe. "Somewhere around ten?"

Danny glanced at his watch. "Nine forty-five."

"Forty hours, give or take an hour." He fell on the second sandwich.

"Forty hours?"

"Yeah, what is that, like a day and a half?"

Danny nodded, handed the man a juice box, and continued watching.

"You got nothing better to do than watch me eat?"

"How'd you go forty hours without eating?"

The man blinked again, as though he was surprised by the question. "I drank some water."

"Just water?"

"Yeah, what is this, a war crimes tribunal? So I can go without food. It's just one of those things you get used to." He finished off the second sandwich.

It occurred to Danny that this man had probably gotten used to a lot of things in his life. He shook his head and moved to the opening of the pipe to read one of his books.

After Duke finished drinking the juice, he moved to sit beside Danny and lit a cigarette. He held the pack of Camels out. "Want a smoke?"

"No, I don't smoke."

"Good for you. Nasty habit." He inhaled deeply and closed his eyes for a moment.

Danny looked at him. The man was sitting on his haunches, his right leg tucked under, supporting his weight, with his left leg bent only slightly. He wore heavy combat boots, black leather and nylon with deep lug soles. Even in the dim light he looked old, maybe close to fifty. His hands were callused, stained yellow from years of smoking. The fingers were long and almost delicate, and there was a plain gold band on the ring finger of the left hand. His face was almost skeleton-thin, the skin stretched over the skull. His nose looked like it had been broken—maybe more than once, from the lumps in it. A day's growth of beard was sprouting from his chin, and he had a carefully trimmed mustache. His long dirty-blond hair was pulled into a ponytail, bound with a red rubber band. The man opened his eyes and creased his brow, staring at the boy. Danny looked back down at his book, fighting a shiver. He'd never seen eyes like that. What was it his mother had said last night? Mean eyes.

"What are you reading?"

"*Les Miserables.*"

"Oh. Heavy reading for a kid."

"I've just started it. My mom thought I would like it; I'm really into detective stories, crime novels, mysteries."

"You reading it in French or English?"

Danny looked at the man and thought there might be just a hint of a smile there. "English."

"Like it so far?"

"It's a cool story, but you're right. It is heavy."

"I read it a couple of years ago." He cleared his throat and spit in the stream. "You ought to try *Crime and Punishment* next. Shorter, but still heavy. You probably want the English translation on that one, too." He took another drag on the Camel. "You read Poe?"

"Edgar Allan Poe?"

"Yeah."

"A little."

"What is it, *The Purloined Letter,* that's supposed to be the first detective story?"

"Yeah, I guess so." Danny shook his head. Literary discussions in a concrete pipe under the railroad tracks in the middle of nowhere. "I have another book here if you'd like to read."

"No thanks, I don't think I could concentrate." He crawled back into the middle of the pipe and made some feeble one-handed attempts at arranging the blankets.

Danny put the book down and looked at the man again. "So what are you doing here?"

Duke glared at him. "What difference does it make?"

"I'm just curious." Danny stared back out at the stream and slapped a mosquito on his cheek. "I'm not going to tell anyone."

"You don't know who I am, do you?" His tone was more matter-of-fact than questioning.

"Should I?"

"I don't know." The man pulled a blanket up over his chest and shivered.

"Are you famous or something?"

"No, not really."

"What are you running from?"

"What makes you think I'm running from something?"

"You're lying in a pipe, under some railroad tracks. You're hurt, but you won't see a doctor." He paused. "You not only don't want help, you're downright hostile. You must be running from something."

"Bright kid," Duke muttered under his breath, just loud enough for Danny to hear. Out loud he said, "It shouldn't make any difference to you one way or the other. You're so determined to be a good Samaritan, you shouldn't care whether or not I'm running from something."

But Danny did care. He wasn't sure if his good Samaritan tendencies carried far enough to help an escaped murderer. "How long were you planning on staying here?"

"I'll be gone by tomorrow."

"Are you sure you're strong enough to move?"

"I can't stay here. It's too damp. I'm just going to get sicker. I have to move." His voice was getting weaker. "Just waiting for dark."

Danny realized then that maybe he was willing to cross the line. Maybe he was willing to help the guy, regardless. "You could stay here for a couple of more days. I can bring more blankets, and I can bring you food every day."

"How do you know I won't hurt you?"

Danny didn't hesitate. "You're in rough shape at the moment. Besides, I just don't think you'd hurt me." He was fighting his own instincts as he said the words, ignoring the sinking feeling in the pit of his stomach. He knew, even though he didn't know. He knew, somehow, this was not an innocent man. But he wasn't sure he cared. He understood, even as he knew the man was dangerous, that he somehow wasn't a threat to him. He figured if the guy had wanted to hurt him he would have done it the day before.

"What about when I get stronger?"

Danny paused. "I guess I'll just have to trust you."

The man blinked and sat there with his mouth hanging open, eyes narrowed. "Are all kids as gullible as you?"

"I'm not gullible. I just have good instincts about people. I would know if you were dangerous. I don't think you're planning to hurt me."

The man shook his head and looked as though he wanted to scream, his mouth working, his eyes wide. "No. I won't hurt you. I won't… " His voice trailed off as he appeared to be struggling with something only he could see. He squeezed his eyes shut tight.

"Duke?" Danny moved closer and touched his forehead. It was burning hot.

The man snapped his eyes open and grabbed the boy's arm, and then released him even as Danny felt fear rising in his throat.

"Don't fucking touch me, you got it?"

Danny backed up and almost fell out of the end of the culvert.

Duke shook his head. "Whoa, hey, I'm sorry. You just startled me." He closed his eyes and whispered something unintelligible through clenched teeth. When he opened his eyes again they were unfocused, confused.

"You really need a doctor. I can't help you enough."

"No." He shook his head and winced in renewed pain. "I can handle it."

"I think your arm might be infected."

He muttered some obscenities and sucked in a breath. "You really want to help me?"

Danny hesitated for a moment, making the leap in his mind. "Sure."

"Okay, then you've got to make a few promises." His voice was little more than a hoarse whisper.

Danny nodded.

"One, you tell no one I'm here. Got it?"

When Danny nodded again, Duke continued. "Make sure you don't change your routine too much. Don't spend more time out here than you normally would; don't bring a lot of food out here if that's not something you'd normally do. Changing your routine is one sure way to get attention. And I don't need attention right now. Okay?"

"Okay." There was a slight vibration in the ground, getting stronger. "Train coming."

"Yeah, I feel it." He reached for the boy's arm. "Come back in here where they can't see you."

"Why?"

"Because I don't want them to see you, okay? They see you, they'll want to know what you're doing out here."

That made sense. Danny nodded and pulled back inside the pipe as the train went by.

Chapter 4

Sally sat in the tent, watching a freight train crawl past, studying the graffiti on the boxcars. She looked up as a very young man wearing an FBI windbreaker over a Kevlar vest approached. He looked like he was about eighteen, even though she knew he had to be older. He was dead serious, wearing wrap-around sunglasses, even in the tent.

"Deputy Barnard?"

She got up and offered a hand. "That's right, Sally Barnard."

He took her hand, with a grip like a dead fish. "Nate Brewster. FBI. I've been assigned to this task force." He smiled without showing his teeth. "I'm here to help."

She sat back down and narrowed her eyes. "Right."

"What would you like me to do?"

She would have sent him for coffee, but she had already sent Thomas. Then she remembered something she had thought of the night before.

"I've been thinking we should find out if there are any local mounted patrol groups, you know, search and rescue types, who would like to comb the state parks for us. Why don't you see if you can track that down?"

He paled. "Uh, I er, was hoping for something a little more directly involved."

"I'll bet you were."

Her cell phone chirped and she grabbed it, hoping it was something worthwhile. She waved a hand at the kid, willing him to disappear.

"Barnard."

"Deputy Barnard?"

"Yes, ma'am." The kid from the FBI was still standing there.

"This is Doctor Penelope Woodbury."

"Excuse me just a minute." To Nate she said, "This is important." She waited until he walked away. "Thank you for returning my call."

"No problem at all. What can I do for you? You said you needed some information on Kevin Markinson?"

"Yes, ma'am. He escaped from prison."

"I remember him. I got out his file, but he's not the kind of person you forget."

"Yes, ma'am." Sally tried to sound encouraging.

"First of all, he has an IQ of at least one-fifty."

"Really?"

"Yes. He's smart. But he's got some problems. He has periods of sanity interspersed with moments of total delusion. At times he's convinced he's still a soldier; he has to work within a code of honor. That's what he called it."

"So he's delusional; he's nuts."

"No. He's got a pretty good case of PTSD. At the time I saw him, I felt he was suffering from severe depression. He ought to be on antidepressants." She paused. "But as far as his mental status, the state has some pretty high standards for insanity. He doesn't meet them."

Sally sighed. "Yeah, the prisons are full of guys who don't meet those standards."

"I spent quite a lot of time talking to him. He told me more than he told anybody else here. I used some techniques on him—not coercion—but I got him to open up. He told me he considers himself an honorable man, a decent man—not a cop killer."

"I've heard that before. I don't think I've ever met one of these guys who thinks he's guilty."

"At the same time, though, he's got a pretty good case of survivor's guilt."

"What does that mean?"

"How much detail do you want? He went through combat, lost a lot of comrades." She paused. "I also think there was an abusive home life when he was a child."

"Okay, get to the meat. Tell me what's relevant to this situation."

"He's methodical. He doesn't do things in a hurry. He'll have a careful plan. But when the plan falls apart and he has to think in a hurry, he'll fall back on his training."

"His sniper training?"

"Scout sniper training. He doesn't just know how to shoot; he knows how to disguise himself, how to blend in, and how to track. He probably knows how close you are. He's not going to give up."

"Is he going to go nuts when his plan goes bad?"

"I don't think so. He never has."

Sally shuffled her papers. "Well, thank you, doctor."

"Good luck."

Sally hung up the phone, thinking hard. She needed more info on him. She looked through the papers, searching for something she might have missed.

Craig walked in and set his computer down again. "So, do you think our guy is armed?"

"God, I hope not." She picked up a report, something she had missed earlier. "Wait a minute."

"What?"

"This is a report from another prison break, fourteen years ago." She stopped and studied the paperwork. "There's written testimony here on his behalf from a corrections officer. It says during the escape, Markinson actually defended this corrections officer. He got in between him and the other prisoners, kept him safe." She blinked. "What's up with that?" She looked up at Craig, who shrugged.

"I haven't got a clue. He's the bad guy, but he turns on the other prisoners and helps a CO?"

Sally continued. "Six years ago, the time he got sent up before this escape, he was beat up by a rogue cop. He didn't defend himself, just took it. Sued the city and won, too."

"Your point?"

"This man does not want to hurt authority figures. He knows his place. We can use that." She looked again at the paperwork with the black marker all over it.

Craig asked, "Have you asked Bob to look into the CIA connection?"

She shook her head. "I'll give him a call."

When her husband answered the phone, she got right to the point, explaining what she needed.

"I'll see what I can find out. I've got a friend I can call at Langley."

"You really think they're going to tell you anything? I mean, seriously, you should see this file. It's more black than text."

"Well, he is a friend."

Sally snorted. "Yeah, right. The spooks never talk to anyone."

"I'm talking to you."

She laughed. "You're different."

"I'll let you know."

"Thanks."

"Love you."

"Me, too."

She looked up as Brewster walked towards her again. "What can I do for you, Mr. Brewster?"

"Can I get a laptop with an internet connection?"

"Are you serious?"

"Yes, ma'am. That way I can do some research, find this mounted SAR team you want."

"Talk to Craig Wallace."

He nodded and she watched him walk away, swaggering like he owned the place.

After the train went by, Danny looked at Duke again. His eyes were closed, his ragged breathing deep and at least somewhat regular.

Pulling out a sandwich, he began to eat, watching Duke as he slept. He wasn't sure what to do with this guy. That's a gunshot wound, he told himself. Even though he had never seen one in a person before, he knew a gunshot wound when he saw one. *So how did the man get shot? Why was he here?* Danny wondered if he should call the police. But he had just agreed not to tell anyone.

He knew gunshot wounds were a reportable injury, meaning any doctor treating one had to call the police. But of course, he was not a doctor, just a kid in over his head. It almost surprised him to admit that. He was definitely in over his head here, a dangerous spot to be in.

He put it out of his mind and read for a couple of hours, listening to the gurgle of the stream. Once or twice he heard a helicopter overhead, flying low. Duke woke with a start when the helicopter came by again, close enough to disturb the birds.

"Chopper. Get out of here, got to get to the LZ." The man's eyes were unfocused, wild. He looked past Danny, started to work his way towards the opening of the pipe on his knees and one good arm. His breathing was rapid now, and a line of fine spit hung from the corner of his mouth. "Goddamn gooks." He ducked as the helicopter noise became louder.

The unfocused eyes scanned Danny now, and the man muttered, "Come on soldier, move your ass. You don't want to miss your ride."

Danny didn't think the man was fully awake; he certainly wasn't aware. He could hurt himself. Was this like a sleepwalking episode? Danny remembered something about not disturbing a sleepwalker, but he felt that if he didn't do something, the man was going to get in serious trouble.

Duke grabbed at him. "I'm not leaving you here. Move it. Do I make myself clear?"

"Hey!" Danny shouted, pulling away.

Duke's eyes snapped into focus. "What the...? " He sat up, and then sagged back against the side of the pipe. "You're still here."

"Yeah."

The man was breathing hard. He dragged the back of his hand across his mouth.

"You okay?"

Duke focused on Danny for a moment. The boy was surprised by the look in the man's eyes. His face was full of fear, the eyes especially. That worried Danny. The look only lasted for a few seconds, then the man's face clouded over and the hard look returned.

"I'm fine, kid." Nearly a growl. Danny thought the guy was trying to convince himself. Duke lit another cigarette and studied the pack for a moment. "I guess I'll have to start rationing these." He stared out at the stream. "Have you heard that helicopter a lot?"

"Couple of times." Danny put down his book.

Duke shot him a glare, no sign of the fear at all. "You haven't seen any strange people around your house, in town or anything like that have you?"

"No."

"Nobody asking questions? Nobody looking for someone?"

"Not that I know of." Danny looked at Duke. "You seem awfully worried for someone who isn't running from anything. Almost as though you don't want to be found." He was pushing, testing again, hoping for a simple explanation. Looking for the fear once more, wanting to know if this man was afraid of the search, or if it was something else.

The man sighed. "Yeah, I guess so. Let's just say it would be very inconvenient for me to be found." His shoulders drooped.

Silence. *Again,* Danny thought, *no sign of the fear that was there in those eyes before. It isn't the search the man is afraid of. Something else then. Something in his mind maybe.* He didn't want to face what he now knew had to be true, that this man had to be the escaped convict everyone was looking for. If he didn't think about it, maybe it wouldn't be true.

Duke floored him with a question. "What are you going to do when you grow up?"

Danny blinked and turned away. "I don't know. I like to read about detective work, so I thought I might like to go into the FBI or be a police officer or something. I'm just not sure I could really shoot at people. Reading about it is one thing, but I don't know if that's something I could do for real." He shrugged.

"I don't think they really shoot at people very often."

"Yeah, maybe not."

"I was in the Marines, and on the whole it was pretty boring. They really wanted us to shoot at people, but unless there's a war on you don't do much shooting."

"Were you in a war?"

"Yeah."

"What, the Gulf War?"

"No."

The boy had to think for a minute. "What then?"

"Vietnam."

Danny brought his gaze back around to look at the man again, wanting to see his eyes. "Did you shoot anybody?" He realized as soon as it came out of his mouth that it was a stupid thing to ask.

The man looked away and took a long drag on the cigarette. When he spoke again, his voice was quiet. "I don't like to talk about it."

He went silent, and Danny thought that was the end of it.

"I shot a lot of people. That's what I was trained to do. I was pretty good at what they taught me." He paused and swallowed hard, the cigarette forgotten in his fingers, ash falling in little flecks on the blankets.

For a second Danny thought he saw the fear again, deep in those eyes, visible through cracks in the ice.

Duke took a long breath, ending in a sudden gasp. He closed his eyes for a second, letting the breath out through his nose. He opened his eyes again, searching for something. "It was a long time ago." His gaze came to rest, focused on something outside the pipe. Something a thousand yards off. Something nobody else could see.

Danny looked away, not wanting to see the look in the man's eyes. He had never seen eyes so vacant, so cold. Yet at the same time, there was something else, something deeper, hidden behind the ice.

Chapter 5

Sally was in the temporary office at the county complex when her cell phone chirped again.

"Yeah?"

"Hey."

"Hey, Bob. Whatcha got?"

"I actually heard back from my friend Roger."

"The one in Virginia?"

"Yeah. He'll deny it if any of this gets back to him."

Sally rolled her eyes. "What else is new?"

"Markinson is, or was, I guess, a real pro. He worked all over the world in the seventies and early eighties. My friend was disappointed when Markinson went down for killing the cop. He says Markinson didn't do it. It wasn't his style; he wouldn't take that kind of chance. He says Markinson was set up."

Sally laughed out loud. "That's creative."

"This guy's sharp. He was Markinson's handler."

She sat up. "His handler?"

"Yeah."

"So, he knows what he's talking about. Can I talk to him?"

"He doesn't exist. You do understand, right? He only talked to me because he's known me for a long time."

"Yeah. I get it." She paused. "It doesn't make any difference if Markinson is innocent. It doesn't matter. The man is a fugitive. If he wants to prove his innocence, let him do it in court. I still have to bring him in."

"Of course, that's your job. No, it doesn't matter, just in how he's thinking, that's where it matters. Anyway, I picked my friend's brain for a bit. He was concerned about the potential in this situation. He says Markinson doesn't do well under stress."

"What does that mean?"

"He didn't think he'd go nuts, but he said it could be touchy. He'll revert back to his training. He'll try to fight his way out if he feels he has to. Or, he might just wait it out, if he stays cool. He'll bide his time and sneak up on you. He's good at that, at least according to Roger. Markinson can move through the jungle without you knowing he's there."

"This doesn't sound good."

"Just be aware of what he's going to do if you push. Be ready for him to take a mile if you give him an inch."

"Right."

"He does have training on how to evade capture."

"I really wanted to hear that. You get anything else?"

"Did I mention he's double-jointed?"

"What?"

"He can slip cuffs."

"Good grief. Next you'll be telling me he can pick locks with his toenails."

"He can pick locks, but probably not with his toenails."

"Thanks. Can he hotwire cars, too? Fly a helicopter? Maybe he knows how to build a tank out of spare parts from a junkyard."

"Okay, now you're just being silly. The guy was a CIA assassin, Sally, not a spy."

She laughed. "I'll talk to you later, okay?"

"Love ya."

"Right."

As soon as she hung up, the deputy sheriff approached. "Deputy Barnard?"

She stood up. "Yes, sir?"

"I have a friend who lives near here. Um, she was married to a deputy who worked with me. She has a few concerns, and I thought maybe you could talk to her. Sort of reassure her."

She frowned. "I guess so. Give me her number." After the deputy walked away, Sally called, introduced herself, and listened.

"Yes." She cleared her throat. "My name is Ann Rutledge. I just wanted to know if your fugitive is in our area, and if so, how much of a threat he is."

"Ms. Rutledge, I'm not going to say you have nothing to worry about, but as far as I can tell, Mr. Markinson has no interest in harming civilians and is unlikely to bother anybody." She hoped she sounded more confident than she felt as she went on to explain how smart her fugitive was, and how he could be miles from here. "Nothing to worry about, ma'am."

She thanked her and hung up while Sally stared out the door at a bulletin board covered in fugitive flyers.

Danny spent the walk home thinking. Maybe he should just call an ambulance. Maybe Duke would thank him in the end. But then again, if he really was homeless and down on his luck, he wouldn't be able to afford an ambulance or a doctor. Of course, he was avoiding the real issue, the fact that this man was probably an escaped murderer. He knew he was deluding himself with any doubt about that.

He figured he could look up some first aid in one of his books, and help the guy out a little anyway. Rest was the most important thing, he was sure. The man would do better after a rest. He put the other worry out of his mind—that rest wasn't going to help him. Obviously this guy's problems were deeper than the physical one. There was something going on in the man's mind. Danny didn't have a name for it, but he knew where he had seen it before.

When he got back to his house he sat on the steps, staring out at the woods, and listening to the sound of yet another chopper. Chopper. Why did he choose that word? He'd never called a helicopter a chopper in his life.

His mother drove in.

"You ready to go grocery shopping?"

He didn't feel like going, but remembering Duke's admonition to stick to his routine, he agreed. "Sure, Mom."

As he walked over to get into the minivan, a state police cruiser rolled down the driveway. Two troopers got out and approached. Danny felt a twist of fear in his stomach without really knowing why. He didn't want to admit to himself that he was afraid, nervous about the secret he was keeping. He had to will his feet to stay still, to fight the urge to run. He was looking at the two young men with their crew cuts and their sunglasses and thinking they were the enemy. It surprised him. He'd never thought like that before. Cops were good, the policeman is your friend; if you're ever lost, find a policeman.

"Hello, ma'am," said the first man. "We're doing a house-to-house check to find out if you've seen anything unusual."

"Like what?"

You mean other than the helicopters all over the place? thought Danny. He bit his tongue to keep from saying it aloud.

"Well, ma'am, we're looking for an escaped convict. We don't want to worry you, but he could be dangerous." He held out a poster with a picture and description.

"Yes," she said, "I've heard about this guy, read about him in the paper. But we certainly haven't seen him around here. We're sort of set back off the road; I don't think he'd come in here."

"I'm sure you're right, ma'am. Just keep your eyes open, if you don't mind. There's an 800 number on the poster so you can report anything suspicious."

"Okay, we'll call if we see him."

"Thank you." He headed back towards his car. The other trooper had been walking around the house, looking at things around the yard, and into the house through the windows. As the first officer was finishing up with them, he came back to the cruiser and got in without a word. Just before they drove off, the first man rolled down his window and said, "By the way, does your land go back to the railroad tracks?"

Danny's mother nodded.

"We're going to be searching along the tracks, so if you hear a lot of commotion, like dogs and stuff, it's okay." They drove away.

"Wow," she said as they pulled out of sight. "Do you think he's around here?"

Danny felt an odd thrill in his stomach, replacing the twist of fear for a moment. "I don't know. It's kind of exciting. A real escaped convict in our neighborhood."

"Danny! It's not exciting; it's frightening. They said he could be dangerous. Maybe you should stick close to home until they catch him."

"Come on, Mom, he's probably long gone. You said yourself he wouldn't come in here. Besides, he's not going to hurt a kid. What threat could I be to someone like that?"

She got into the minivan. "I don't know. I suppose he could kidnap you." She paused. "What if he's a child molester?"

Danny shuddered and glanced at the poster. "It doesn't say anything here about him ever kidnapping anybody or molesting any kids. It says he was in jail for escape and for shooting a police officer, who was probably trying to take him back to jail. It's not as if he's a crazed serial killer. Besides, I'm sure he's miles from here. We're not even that close to the prison." His own suspicions were getting stronger even as he tried to talk his mother out of hers. The photo on the poster looked an awful lot like the man in the drainage pipe. It was an old picture, but the eyes gave it away. He decided he would read the newspaper article about the escapee when they got back to the house. That would satisfy his curiosity, and make him feel better. He hoped.

Danny followed his mom through the grocery store. She helped him pick out simple dinners to cook while he was home. Cans of beef stew, boxes of macaroni and cheese, frozen dinners. It was enough food for a week, even though she was only going away for a weekend. He wished she wouldn't talk about it so loudly, as though this was the first time he'd ever been alone.

"Here, honey. You can cook this by yourself, right?" She was holding a box of frozen lasagna.

"I can take care of myself," he said, rolling his eyes. "It's only for the weekend."

She took six boxes out of the freezer and put them in the cart.

He caught a glimpse of a heavyset youngster with torn clothes, standing behind an even heavier woman in an overstretched housedress. He did a double take. It was Eddie. The woman must be his mother. He wasn't sure he had ever seen Eddie with his mother, or if he had ever seen her at all. It surprised him to see them here, shopping like ordinary people, and he tried to push his mom the other way, hoping Eddie had not been in earshot when his mother talked about the weekend.

"Isn't that boy in school with you?" His mother craned her neck to look back as Danny tried to grab her attention with some ice cream.

"He's older than me. He's a jerk, too; can we just go?"

Eddie sneered at him, and Danny felt a twinge of fear in the pit of his stomach.

"No, I should at least say hello to his mother," Danny's mom hissed. "You never know who will turn out to be a customer." She started across the aisle, her right hand extended, turning on the charm. "Hello, Patricia, how are you?"

The woman turned, and Danny saw a flash of annoyance cross her face. "Oh, hi, uh …"

"Ann, Ann Rutledge. We met at open house at school last fall, remember?"

"Oh, yes." The woman glanced down at her cart, filled mostly with six packs of beer, frozen dinners on top. "How nice to see you again."

Danny picked up the chill in her voice, and hoped his mother did, too.

"Well," his mother was saying. "We should go. We have a lot to do." She turned away from the others and focused on Danny again. "Is this enough for the weekend?"

"Yeah, Mom. Can we go?"

Danny glanced back at Eddie to gauge his reaction, only to see him grinning from ear to ear now. He felt that twist of fear in his stomach again and let his shoulders droop as he followed his mother towards the checkout.

In the car on the way home Danny decided to approach a subject he had never really thought about before. It had something to do with the man in the pipe—his eyes, his expression, and at the same time, something to do with his father. He realized, as he thought about it, the look of fear on Duke's face was similar to one he'd seen on his dad's face at times. Before.

"Mom?"

"Yeah?" She switched off the music, a Disney cassette she had bought when Danny was about eight. She seemed to think he still liked it, and he didn't have the heart to tell her otherwise.

"What was wrong with Dad?"

She sighed. "What do you mean?"

"It's like he remembered things he didn't want to remember." *And it made him kill himself.* Danny couldn't say that out loud. Couldn't bring himself to remind his mother again.

"That happens," his mother said. "It happens to lots of people who have gone through that sort of thing."

Danny didn't want to bring up the episode that had resulted in his father killing himself. His dad had been a deputy sheriff and had quit as a result of a shooting. After that he'd barely been able to function. He'd jump at loud noises; he drank too much. He remembered his parents fighting all the time, and his mother begging his father to get help.

It was still a raw subject and he didn't want to go into detail with her. But he realized his mother might have just given him the key to Duke's behavior. *Lots of people who have gone through things like that.*

"It's stress. It was hard on him when things were not going as well as he would have liked. Your dad didn't handle stress very well after what happened."

Danny pushed aside the thoughts of his father for just a minute. Stress. Like being injured, in hiding, and going without food for nearly two days. Danny understood.

"They came up with a name for it, back in the seventies, I think. Posttraumatic stress disorder. They needed something to call it, especially after so many veterans were showing up with these symptoms."

Veterans. That caught Danny's attention. "But Dad wasn't in a war."

"It was a bad situation, Danny. This PTSD can affect people who were never in a war. People who go through bad things get it, too. Car accidents, even things like having your house burn down can cause flashbacks and the fear that it will happen again." She paused. "Your dad couldn't handle it."

They had reached home now.

"Does that help?" she asked as she got out of the van.

"Yes. Thanks, Mom."

She headed for the house. "I wish we could have done more for your father. I wish we could have made things right for him."

Danny wondered if Duke would be alright. If he was in the same danger. If the stress would overwhelm him. It sealed his decision. He hadn't been able to help his father. But this man... he could help.

When they got inside, the phone was ringing. Danny's mom grabbed it, balancing a bag of groceries on her knee and motioning for Danny to take it.

"Hello?"

Danny walked out of the kitchen to get some more bags.

She glanced at him as he brought in another armload of groceries. "Just put those on the counter, honey." Then she spoke into the phone again. "Yes ma'am, I understand."

Pause. Danny could barely hear the voice on the other end of the phone.

"For all we know this guy could be a hundred miles from here. And Danny isn't stupid. He wouldn't open the door to anybody he doesn't know." She looked over at Danny, biting her lower lip.

"He'll be fine. I can get Reggie to check in on him, too."

A deputy sheriff. That's who Reggie was. Danny turned and looked out into the back yard.

"Well, of course, he's probably in the city by now."

Danny glanced back at his mother as she hung up the phone.

She smiled. "No bloodhounds in the yard?"

He shook his head.

"I was just telling Mrs. Warner how smart you are, how you wouldn't let yourself get into a situation with this guy, even if the guy was around here, which I'm sure he's not. She's not available this weekend."

"Is he really a bad guy?"

"You saw the posters."

Danny nodded.

"Oh. I talked to somebody on the fugitive search team earlier. She said the guy is not nuts, whatever that means. He's smart."

Smart, thought Danny. The kind of guy who would enjoy reading thick books for pleasure. The kind of guy who would think it was funny Danny was reading a book about a fugitive. The kind of guy who would suggest *Crime and Punishment* for a follow-up.

He looked at the clock. Not enough time to go back out to the pipe tonight. He felt restless, but he didn't want to attract any unwanted attention, so while his mother fixed dinner, Danny wandered into the living room and picked up the previous day's newspaper. The headlines were about Monica Lewinsky, but the bottom of the fold had the story he was looking for.

"At about twelve forty-five this morning Kevin Markinson, a convicted felon, escaped from the Hudson medium security state prison. He is forty-five years old, six-four, and approximately one hundred sixty pounds, with long blond hair, blue eyes, and a mustache. Authorities believe he was injured during his escape.

"This is Markinson's third escape. He was convicted of murder in the death of a police officer during a previous escape. A corrections officer was wounded during another. He has made three previous attempts to escape.

"Markinson is a decorated Vietnam veteran, and is married with two children. His family is located in New York City, and authorities believe he may try to head there. He has a history of violence, and allegedly has connections to organized crime. Anyone who thinks they may have seen this man is urged to call the US Marshal's office or the FBI. He should be considered extremely dangerous."

The accompanying photograph was grainy and old. Danny stared into space for a moment, taking it all in. The physical description fit, right down to the injured and bleeding part. And the photograph scared him. That was a little too close for coincidence. He picked up the phone book and looked in the front for the phone number of the US Marshal's office. He thought about calling, and then decided against it. He would wait and see.

"Danny, you've been distracted all during dinner. What are you thinking about now?" His mother furrowed her brow as she spoke.

"Nothing important." Then he heard the television. He hadn't even noticed it before, but the evening news was on. That was unusual for his house. His parents had never watched television during meals; the set was in the other room. But Danny's mother had pushed her chair back from the kitchen table and was watching through the doorway while chewing on dinner, chewing being the operative word. Mom had cooked tuna casserole, and for some reason the macaroni was like rubber.

"The manhunt continues for the second day for Kevin Markinson, an escapee from the Hudson state prison. Federal Marshals are saying tonight they have some strong leads, and expect to have him in custody soon."

Danny's mother looked at him. "They haven't caught that guy yet. Are you worried about that?"

"That's silly," replied Danny. "Why would I be?" Inwardly he continued to wonder if there was any possibility that his new friend in the hideout was Kevin Markinson, escaped prisoner. Who was he kidding? He was hoping there might be a possibility the man wasn't Kevin Markinson. It didn't change his mind though. He was still determined to help the man, although he wasn't sure he should do too much for an escaped convict. Wasn't there a law against that? He shook his head. "Who is this guy anyway?"

"There was a story about him in the paper yesterday."

"Yeah, I read it."

"He killed a police officer in a shootout."

"Yeah." Danny thought about it for a moment, remembering a discussion about shooting people. "That's the same guy those state troopers were out looking for, right?"

"Right. I told you I talked to a deputy marshal on the fugitive task force today. You know he escaped not too far from here."

"Yes."

"That doesn't bother you?" asked his mother, putting down her fork.

"Should it?" Danny paused, trying to think of something to alleviate her fears. "I mean, come on, you think he's going to bother me? That's like some sort of book or movie. It'd never happen in real life." He tried a laugh, but it didn't come out quite right. He cleared his throat and got up from the table, taking his dirty dishes to the sink. He stood and stared out the window. *Tell her, tell her now.* But then he'd have to explain bringing the man the food, and bandaging his arm. He'd have to justify the help he'd already provided. People would think he was stupid or something. Maybe he was stupid, trying to fool himself into believing the man in the pipe and the man on the television weren't the same person.

She carried her bags out to the minivan and then stood on the back steps with him, slapping mosquitoes.

"Well, I guess you'll be okay. I've told Mrs. Warner I'm going away. She's going to stop in and check on you, and you can call her if you need anything. Dad's old friend Deputy Crandall is going to check on you as well, although he's busy, so he'll probably just call. I'll call, too. There's plenty of food in the house. I've written down the number of where I'll be for the weekend. I'll be back Sunday night." His mother paused. "Do you want me to wait until tomorrow to leave so you're only alone for one night?"

"No. I'll be fine." He was beginning to wish she would just hurry up and go.

"You won't talk to anybody you don't know or let anybody in the house, right?"

Danny rolled his eyes. "Come on, Mom, do I look stupid?" He'd avoided lying anyway. He'd already made up his mind. If the cops were searching the tracks, it was only a matter of time before they found Duke. He couldn't leave him there. He needed his mother to go.

"Well, all right." His mother leaned over and gave him a stifling hug. "I love you. You be careful, okay?"

"Come on, Mom." He wiggled out of her arms and backed into the screen door. "I love you, too. Don't you want to get going?"

"Okay."

Danny watched her get in the car, smiling and waving as she turned around and drove out of the driveway. He glanced up at a helicopter, wondering if they knew something he didn't.

Chapter 6

Sally was sitting in the same folding chair in the tent, staring at a topographical map spread out on the table in front of her, hoping for something, anything that would lead her to this fugitive before he did something stupid. She had scoured the records from the prison, gone over her notes from talking to the psychiatrist, and still didn't feel like she had a grasp of his psyche. She wasn't convinced yet that the man was a threat to the general population, but there were an awful lot of people out there between him and home. An awful lot of people who could get in his way. You never knew when somebody would try something stupid; try to be a hero. She could only imagine the results if some citizen tried to hold Markinson at gunpoint.

She turned her head at the chirping of a phone. Thomas answered it. She waited, hopeful.

"We've got a hit, about twenty miles from the prison." Thomas put the phone down. "Dog picked up a good scent; a blood trail again, followed it along the tracks for a while, and then lost it. The rabbit went into some water."

Sally sighed. "Show me on the map."

Thomas put his finger on the map. "South of the prison. He's heading the way we thought he would. He's like a homing pigeon."

"They're certainly easier to catch when they're this predictable. He wants to go where he thinks he's safe, somewhere where he knows the territory, where he can get help. He's probably not real happy where he is now." She paused, studying the map. "It wasn't part of his plan to be trekking through swamps. Especially not with an injury."

"Well, he's a city boy, right? He's not going to be hard to find in this kind of country."

"He is a city boy, yes, but he spent time in a jungle. I think he knows how to survive in this kind of country." She looked at the large green expanse on the map representing the state park. He could hide in there for days, but not without food or medical help. Bleeding the way he was, they might find him dead, which was okay with her. At least that way nobody else would get hurt.

Nate appeared out of nowhere. "I've got a mounted search and rescue unit."

"You do?" Sally was surprised. He wasn't supposed to find anything. It was just supposed to be busy work.

"Do you want me to have them search the parks?"

"Sure, Nate. Go ahead and arrange it. Just make sure they keep their distance if they spot him." She watched him walk away.

"Who the hell is that?" asked Thomas.

"He's our token FBI agent."

"He looks like he's about twelve."

"Yeah."

"He been wearing that vest the whole time?"

"Yeah. I guess he expects Markinson to jump out of the bushes and shoot him."

After his mother left, Danny locked the house and headed out with a flashlight to get Duke. It wasn't quite dark yet, and he knew the man would be there. Where else would he be? He'd said he was going to wait until dark.

He heard the beating of yet another helicopter, and wondered if they were looking for the escaped convict. Duh, he thought, of course that's what they're doing.

Danny climbed up into the pipe and said, "Hi," regretting it almost the instant he said it. Not very creative, was it?

The man looked up, but not as if he was startled. Except for the first time, the time the man had whacked his head jumping up, Danny had never seen the man startled. He seemed to be in a constant state of awareness, like he knew what was going on around him all the time. "Hey." Duke licked his lips. "Did you bring food?"

"Uh. No."

"Oh." The man frowned. "Nearly dark. I've got to get moving."

Danny swallowed, working up the nerve, and then asked, "How would you like to stay with me in my house for a couple of days?"

Duke narrowed his eyes. "Listen, kid, that's real nice of you, but you're not making any sense. What about your parents?"

"My mother is away for the weekend. We would have the house to ourselves. You'll be a lot stronger Sunday night than you are now."

The man shook his head. "Didn't it occur to you I could steal everything in your house, and then slit your throat while you sleep? Your parents didn't teach you not to let strangers into the house?"

"If you wanted to do that you would have suggested going to my house when I first met you. Or you would have killed me then. I don't think you're a killer." That was a lie. Danny knew the man was a killer. Maybe. Sort of.

Duke just stared at him for a moment. "Have you ever met a killer?"

"No."

"Then how would you know?" Those icy-blue eyes were locked on now, glaring.

Silence. Danny let it hang in the air for a moment, and then cleared his throat, gathering his courage, offering his reasons. "State police came to our house today."

"Yeah?"

"They're going to be searching the tracks."

"Really."

"Dogs."

"No kidding." Duke looked out the far end of the pipe. He brushed a mosquito off his arm. "When do your parents leave?"

"It's just my mom. And she already left."

The man swallowed and looked back at the boy. "Okay."

"So, you ready?"

"Yeah." He picked up his cigarettes, tucking them into his pocket, set his jaw, and got down out of the pipe, scooting over to the edge and dropping onto the bank. He staggered and almost fell.

Danny stood still, not offering any help, resisting the urge to put out his hand, unsure of what to do. He raised his flashlight and started to turn it on.

"No light. They'll see that," Duke barked. It was a different kind of voice, a voice Danny hadn't heard before. The voice of a man who was used to giving orders, and having them obeyed. He looked up at the sky. "We need to stay in the trees, away from the tracks." The man spoke as though every word required tremendous effort. "We should walk in the stream first. Lose the scent, throw the dogs off." He shuddered, as if the very concept of dogs scared him.

They crossed the stream after walking in it for a distance and then headed through the woods towards the house, two sets of shoes squishing on the pine needles.

The trip back to the house was slow, and neither of them spoke. When they got there, Danny unlocked the door and Duke sat down on the back steps, taking out a cigarette. Danny sat with him, just upwind to avoid the smoke.

"You know those will kill you." He thought it was stupid the moment he said it. He wanted to take it back and kick himself for saying it. He was beginning to feel as if he couldn't say anything right any more.

The man turned his head and blew smoke out his nose. "I don't expect to live long enough to die of cancer."

Danny hoped that didn't mean some sort of last stand here in the house. He cleared his throat and looked away. "How are you feeling?" he asked after the man had taken a few more puffs.

"Eh." He shrugged. "I've been better." He popped another antacid into his mouth as he ground the cigarette out under his boot, and then picked it up. "And I've been worse."

Danny watched for a moment as the man stretched out his left leg—his bad leg—and leaned back with his eyes closed. He had questions he wanted to ask, but he wasn't sure he could. Instead he sat in silence and watched for a few minutes.

"You hungry?"

The man jumped. "Huh?"

"Are you hungry?" Slight pause between each word to emphasize them. He had to resist the urge to use exaggerated hand motions to explain.

"A little."

"I've got some leftover tuna casserole. I could heat it up for you." He dragged the toe of his sneaker across the ground. "My mom's not the best cook, but it's edible."

"Okay."

Danny got up and went into the house. In a few minutes, as he was taking the food out of the microwave, the man came in, ducking his head through the doorway. Danny realized he hadn't seen Duke in any kind of light before, just in the dark pipe. He really looked bad now. His face was pale and covered with fine wrinkles that reminded Danny of his grandmother. His nose definitely looked like it had been broken, probably more than once. The jaw line was lumpy too; that must have been broken as well. His hands and wrists were thin, almost delicate, with incredibly long fingers. He was tall, taller even than the boy had thought. Well over six feet, nearly six and a half feet, but at the same time he was impossibly thin. Danny wasn't sure he had ever seen anyone so tall who was also that skinny.

The man's eyes wandered over the room, taking it all in.

As he sat to eat, Danny tried to watch him without really staring; trying to hide the fact he was interested. Duke occasionally met his glance, and Danny would look away, almost ashamed to be caught looking at him.

Duke didn't eat much, mostly just picked at the food. Danny assumed it was the taste. "I'm sorry; my mom isn't the best cook in the world."

The man looked at him. "Huh?"

"The food. I'm sorry if it doesn't taste good. My mom tries real hard, but…" He shrugged his shoulders.

Duke looked down at the food on his plate, poked it with his fork, and took a mouthful. "Tastes okay to me," he said.

"Do you want something to drink?" Danny asked.

"Got milk?"

Danny fixed him a glass of milk. "Can I get you anything else?"

"I need a vitamin."

"What do you mean?"

"A multi-vitamin tablet."

"Oh. I think we have some." Danny rummaged through the cupboard and came up with a large bottle of pills, which he handed off to Duke.

"You got any ibuprofen?"

Danny looked at the other bottles. "I think we have acetaminophen."

"I can't take that. Bad for my liver." He got to his feet, looked at the medications, grabbed a bottle of generic ibuprofen, and poured four out onto the counter.

"Do you want any dessert?"

The man shook his head as he swallowed the pills. "I'm all set. Can I use your phone?"

"Sure." Danny pointed out the phone in the den, and then went back into the kitchen. He couldn't quite hear the conversation; he felt guilty for trying.

"Nice gun collection you've got," Duke said as he walked back into the room.

Danny looked up from the dishwasher, where he was loading the dinner dishes. It took him a minute to place the comment, and then he remembered his dad's gun cabinet in the den. "Yeah, my dad liked to hunt."

Duke twirled one of the kitchen chairs around and sat down, stretching his left leg out. "You ever go with him?"

"Sometimes. I didn't shoot though, when we were hunting." He shrugged his shoulders and turned back to the dishes. "I'm just not interested in killing things. My dad thought I was chicken or something."

"Too many people in the world like to kill things." He paused. "Your dad likes to hunt?"

Danny cleared his throat. "Liked to hunt. He's dead."

"Oh." He looked back at the den. "So why do you still have the guns?"

Danny shrugged. "I don't know. My mom hasn't thrown any of his stuff away; we still have all of it."

"How long has it been?"

"Six months."

The man nodded.

Danny paused for a moment, then asked, "How about you? What do you think about killing things? Like for sport."

"What kind of question is that?" He paused. "You know, I really don't know. I guess I never really thought about it much." He rubbed his chin, thinking it over. "I don't like killing. I used to go hunting, when I was a kid, with my uncle, but I can't do it anymore. I don't think I could go out in the woods and shoot some defenseless animal." He turned away. "When I was in the Marines, there were a few guys, nuts, who liked to kill. Weird guys. They didn't usually last long."

"What was it like?"

"What, the Marines?"

"Killing people."

The man cleared his throat. His eyes met the boy's for just a moment, and Danny saw more humanity in them than he had seen before, just a glimpse of the soul through the cracks in the ice. The man shifted his gaze to stare out through the doorway and on out the front window on the far side of the living room with such intensity Danny looked that way as well. There was nothing there. He looked back at him as the man spoke, struggling to hear as his voice dropped to a near whisper.

"It's never easy. Even if you're in danger yourself. I can still see the faces, especially their eyes. That's what you never get used to, the eyes."

Danny swallowed hard. Duke continued to stare out into the darkness, looking at something only he could see.

Then he shifted his gaze back to the boy, his eyes the old blue-gray ice, his voice back to normal. "Listen, if it's all right with you, I think I'll get some extra sleep. I could use some rest on a real bed." He raised one side of his mouth in a feeble half-grin, exposing a couple of tall, yellowish teeth.

"Sure, it's not that early anyway."

"I just have to make one more phone call, if that's okay." He grabbed the kitchen phone and punched in some numbers.

Danny stood in the doorway, awkward.

"Justin, this is Kevin. Sorry I missed you. I'll call back tomorrow." He hung up the phone. "Voice mail."

Danny nodded and led the way to the guestroom, pointed out the adjoining bathroom. "Do you want a toothbrush or anything?"

"That'd be nice. And a razor. I want to shower and shave. I might wait until morning though. I'm beat."

Danny found him a new toothbrush, and got out some towels, then headed for the living room. He wanted to check out the paper, see if there was anything else on the escaped prisoner.

The current paper had nothing in it. It was all Monica Lewinsky this time. Danny was surprised the story had dropped out of the news so quickly. He reread the other story, studying the picture for a long time. It had to be an old picture. It was a mug shot, and the man looked a lot younger than he did now. Danny had to sort it through in his mind; the man didn't look younger in the picture, because he had never seen the man. The man sleeping in the guest bedroom was not the same man as the photograph, right?

He considered picking up the phone and bringing the whole thing to an end, but he ran up against the same roadblock. He didn't want to do that now, because there would be a million questions. Who treated the murderer's wound? Who helped him hide from the searchers? How did he end up here? He sighed and headed upstairs.

Sally sat down next to Craig in the small office at the county complex in Poughkeepsie. "I guess that tap on her phone paid off."

"Well, we kind of figured he'd call his wife at some point."

"And I thought he was smarter than that."

Craig shrugged and played the tape for her.

"Hello?" A woman's voice. Markinson's wife.

"Hey."

"Where are you? No, wait; don't answer. I don't want to know. What did you do? Are you okay?"

"I'll live, just really tired. Don't know if I'll make it home anytime soon. Love you."

There was a click, then a dial tone.

Sally shook her head. "That's all we have?"

Craig nodded. "He wasn't on the line long enough for a good trace. He knows what he's doing. But let me enhance the background noises. He's not in a city. You can hear frogs in the background."

"Frogs?" said Thomas. "What kind of frogs?"

Sally held her hand up for a moment, listening to the tape, the rhythmic sound that had been barely audible now clear. "Those sound like bullfrogs. You hear them in the country, near water." She turned towards Thomas. "He's still out in the bush."

"But he's using a phone," said Thomas. "Either somebody's helping him or he's broken into somebody's house."

"Yeah," said Craig. "There's not a lot of pay phones in the woods."

"He sounds worn out," said Liz.

Sally nodded. "We need to keep him that way. Let him think the only way he's going to get any rest is to give up."

Kevin struggled to sleep. His whole body ached, and every time he closed his eyes, the pictures came back. He opened his eyes again, and longed for a drink. One drink, just enough to make it go away. Stress, that's what it was. They always came back when he was stressed out. Really tired, or hurt, or just in trouble. Sometimes he had a hard time sorting out what was really happening around him because the stupid pictures in his head were so real. In the past ten years he hadn't been this bad off. He had been beaten to a pulp a few years ago, and he'd certainly had trouble then, but even that hadn't brought on flashbacks like he was having now. He tried to fight off the pictures, tried to keep his mind on the present, but it wasn't working. The past intruded on his brain, forcing its way into his mind, filling his senses, overwhelming him.

The first thing the new guys did was take off their packs, and flop down on the ground, usually leaning against a tree. Kevin made it his personal mission to keep them from doing it. Walk into a strange place, you don't know what's what. The enemy had them figured out; knew the routine. Kevin had seen it happen twice now, the landmines planted at the base of the trees, and the soldiers—the new guys. Never his friends; you don't make friends with the new guys. He remembered it like it had just happened. His friend, the one guy he allowed himself to get close to, with his comment—"Bits and pieces of moose and squirrel." That was what it was like. You had to laugh. So you wouldn't cry.

Chapter 7

The marshals drove back out to the motel in silence. As Sally headed to her room she paused. "Any of you guys want to run in the morning?"

"I'll go," said Liz.

"Great. Six sound good?"

Liz groaned. "Fine."

Sally was stretching the next morning when Liz joined her.

"You think the guys are going to run with us?"

Sally shook her head. "Craig'll run, but he ran yesterday. I only do this three days a week, but he runs every other day, like clockwork."

"Doesn't that work out to three days a week?"

"Sort of, but I run on Saturday, Monday and Wednesday. It fits into my schedule better." She started down the road at a steady jog. "Thomas swims; I guess he doesn't run at all."

"You mind talking while you run?"

"Doesn't bother me. I don't run very fast."

"Where do you think this guy is? Markinson?"

"Don't know. If I did know, I'd have him."

"You think he's lying down, or is he still moving?"

"He's not still moving at this point, unless he found wheels. He's lost a lot of blood. Guy's an alcoholic; he's a bleeder. I wouldn't be surprised if he's still bleeding."

"You think he bled out and we just haven't found him?"

Sally slowed to a walk, wrinkling her nose. "I don't think so. Never even occurred to me. I think I'd know if he was dead." She picked up the jog again.

"How?"

"I don't know, just a feeling, that's all."

"How long you been doing this?"

"What, running?"

"No, the fugitive thing."

"I've been in the Marshal's service for fifteen years. Didn't get to do this until I had about six years in. Served a lot of papers. You, you were lucky. I picked you out of a pile of applicants and bypassed all that time."

"I appreciate that."

"I want good people working around me." Sally swung across the road and headed back towards the motel.

Danny fixed a couple of plates of frozen waffles, and went to check on Duke. The man sat up as Danny opened the door. "You want some breakfast?"

"Breakfast?"

"Yeah, I fixed some waffles."

The man blinked and looked around, as though he couldn't quite remember where he was. "Okay, sure. I'll be right there."

Danny headed back out to the kitchen. Duke came out in a few minutes. He had taken off the bloody shirt, cleaned up some of the dried blood on his arm. He was shoeless as well as shirtless, his bare feet slapping on the vinyl floor.

It was hard not to stare. The man's stomach had a long scar across it, probably from a knife. There was a small round scar on the right side of his chest Danny was sure was a bullet hole. The lower left side of his neck bore a similar scar. On his right biceps there was a tattoo of a snake coiled around a dagger, on the left biceps, below the wound, was a figure Danny recognized as the Grim Reaper. There was a plain dagger tattooed on his concave stomach, of which only the blade was visible. A fourth tattoo on his right forearm said "Semper Fi". His arms and chest were not puny, although his ribs showed. He looked like he could stand to gain at least thirty pounds.

He was holding his cigarettes and matches, and he looked from the food on the table to the back door. He cleared his throat. "I'm just going to have a smoke. I'll be right back."

Danny nodded. When the man came back in, he smelled of cigarettes, and Danny sneezed. The phone rang. "Hello?"

"Hey, Danny. This is Deputy Sheriff Crandall. Friend of your dad." He cleared his throat. "Was a friend… uh… how you doing?"

"I'm doing fine, sir."

"Listen, Dan, you know this escaped prisoner, the one everybody's looking for?"

"Yes, sir."

"We're closing in on this guy; he may be somewhere near you. Would you mind staying close to home today?"

Closing in? was his initial thought. He didn't voice it. He fought off the pain in his stomach. "Sure, Sheriff Crandall. No problem." He hoped his voice sounded a lot better than he felt.

"You haven't seen anything, have you?"

He looked over at Duke. "No, sir."

"Well, okay then. You take it easy. Bye now."

"Goodbye, sir." He hung up and stood there staring at the phone, his stomach doing flips.

"Who was that?"

"Sheriff."

"What?"

"Friend of my father." Danny noticed, before Duke sat down, that his pants were more than a bit dirty.

"You want me to wash your clothes for you today?"

"Huh?" Duke paused with his fork halfway to his mouth and tilted his head towards the boy, looking at him and bringing his right ear closer.

It occurred to Danny the man was hard of hearing. He raised the volume a little. "I can wash your clothes, maybe you can take a shower, get cleaned up. It'll make you feel better."

Duke inserted the piece of waffle into his mouth and chewed for a minute. "Sure."

"Can I get you anything else?"

"Coffee?"

Danny hesitated, looking over at the coffee maker. "Do you know how to make it?"

Duke frowned. "I always buy it."

Danny opened the freezer, sure his dad used to work some magic with beans and a grinder. He took out a red foil bag. "I think these are the beans."

Duke held out a hand. "Just give me a couple, that'll do."

"Are you sure?"

"Yeah."

Danny watched as Duke popped two coffee beans into his mouth and chewed, then shuddered as he washed them down with orange juice.

Duke shook his head. "Do you have the instructions that came with the grinder or the coffee maker?"

"I might be able to find them."

"That'd be good."

Sally looked from face to face at the members of her team. "Okay, so he called his wife last night."

"Is that where he's headed?" asked Thomas.

"Probably." This came from Craig.

"But he's smart; why would he head there if he knows we're watching?" Thomas got to his feet and stretched, fingertips touching the drop ceiling.

"His plan is messed up. He's going on instinct. His wife means safety, comfort. That's what he needs." Elizabeth looked at Sally.

"Right. Liz, do we have anyone watching Markinson's wife?"

Liz consulted her notes. "Yep. Locals are doing shifts. Since Thursday morning."

"Sounds good."

While Duke was sleeping, the doorbell rang. Danny walked over, looked through the sidelight, and let Mrs. Wagner in.

"How are you doing, Danny?" she asked. She was about sixty-five. Her hair was just starting to gray. She was soft all over, about five foot three, almost the perfect grandmother. Her flowered dress hung off her body, as though she had recently lost weight.

"I'm fine, Mrs. Wagner."

"Your mom was really worried about you. She was hoping I could stay with you, but with Mr. Wagner… well… you know." Her pale blue eyes were focused on a point somewhere to the right and above Danny's head.

Mr. Wagner was a little older than Mrs. Wagner was. He'd fought in World War II, and had been fine for a while. But lately he had something going on in his brain, and he seemed to always believe the Germans were after him. He refused to go outside the house, and spent most of his time in the basement, trying to crack the coded messages he heard on the radio.

"Yeah, I know. It's okay. I'm fine, really."

"Your mom is especially worried, because of that escaped prisoner." She paused. "I guess it took a lot for her to leave you. She must really have a lot of confidence in you."

Danny was surprised. He didn't think his mom had any confidence in him at all. At least not since Dad had been gone. "I'm fine, Mrs. Wagner. You probably ought to get back to Mr. Wagner."

He waved at her as she drove away.

Sally's phone rang just as she picked it up to try calling the deputy sheriff again.

"Yeah?"

"This is Deputy Crandall. We found your man."

She almost dropped the phone. "You what?"

"He was crawling around in a Dumpster outside a convenience store in Red Hook."

"Brooklyn?"

"No, not Brooklyn. This is a town."

"Where is it?"

"Couple of towns north of your search area. You want to ride over with me? They're bringing him in now."

"I'm on my way."

"They're running the prints. Haven't got them back yet, but we're pretty sure he's your guy."

"Is he hurt?"

"Not seriously. Everything else matches up good."

Her stomach began sinking. Why the hell would they drag her out here if they weren't sure?

She knew the minute she saw the man he wasn't Markinson. He was sitting in a cell in the basement of the police station, but even in the dim light she could tell this man was too old, closer to sixty than fifty. He was wearing an army field coat and green pants, and his long hair was more gray than anything else. He turned watery blue eyes to her as she approached.

"That's not him."

"How can you be sure?"

She glared at the deputy, and then turned back to the man in the cell. "Stand up."

The man obliged, getting to his feet and swaying slightly.

"Oh."

"He's only about six feet tall." She glared at Crandall again. "Master of disguise or not, he can't make himself shorter."

"Do you think I can get something to eat?" the man asked, approaching the front of the cell.

Sally wrinkled her nose. He smelled of rum. "Make sure they feed him before they kick him loose, right?"

"Yes, ma'am."

She was halfway out the door when she heard the young cop announce the prints were indeed not Markinson's. She shook her head and bit her tongue, fuming.

When Duke got up he showered and shaved. Danny met him at the door of the bathroom and said, "I couldn't do much with the shirt. Do you want to borrow one of my dad's? He was shorter than you, but probably weighed more. It should fit." He held out a blue tee shirt with a pocket on the front, and then reeled back at the sight of the man's shoulder without a bandage on it, even though he'd seen it before. It looked worse now, like it had been through a meat grinder, with raw flesh and fresh blood. There was just the hint of the white of bone at the base of the wound. The boy felt bile rising in his throat. He wondered how the man could stand it.

The man seemed to realize what the boy was staring at. "Probably ought to wrap this mess back up again," he said, looking at his shoulder. Danny led the way into the bathroom, and applied gauze and tape to the injury, fighting the urge to vomit.

"You're getting good at this," Duke said. "Maybe you ought to be a doctor."

Danny wondered if doctors felt this way every time they looked at blood. He wasn't sure he could handle that feeling in the back of his throat all the time.

The man took the shirt and put it on, tugging it slowly over his left arm first, then sliding it over his head. It was a bit loose, but short. He shrugged. "It'll do." He grabbed his pack of cigarettes and headed for the back door.

"Hey, you want some lunch?"

The man grunted a reply. Danny stuck his head out the door. "What?"

"Whatever."

Danny cooked the food, choosing boxed frozen manicotti. The man picked through the microwave dinner, only eating about a third of it, and it was small to begin with. He was reading the instructions from the coffee grinder while he ate.

"You don't eat much, do you?" asked Danny.

"Huh?"

"Aren't you hungry?"

"Not very often." Duke looked at him. "My stomach hurts. I eat because I know I have to."

"Do you know why your stomach hurts?"

"Ulcers."

"Isn't there anything you can take for that?"

"Sure. Just hard to come by right now. Gone through a whole roll of antacids in the last day and a half. I've got a lot on my mind right now." He stood up. "I'd eat chocolate. You got any chocolate?"

Danny had eaten his three Snickers bars already. He didn't think there was any more chocolate in the house. His mother refused to keep any on hand because she claimed he'd be eating it every five minutes. He rummaged around in the cupboards. "Just some chocolate chips." He grabbed the bag, which was sitting next to a half-empty bottle of gin.

"That'll do." Duke downed a handful of chips. "Was your dad a gin drinker?"

"Yeah."

"Not real serious about it, if he leaves the bottle half full."

Danny frowned. That didn't really make sense.

The man showed his little half-grin, and then headed for the back door, cigarettes and matches in hand again. He paused to look back at the boy. "It runs in families, you know." His eyes were soft, but serious. "I'm a Jack Daniel's man myself, doing the twelve-step thing."

Danny nodded. There didn't seem to be anything to say. He thought the twelve-step thing might be AA, but he didn't want to ask.

After cleaning up the lunch dishes Danny walked down the driveway to get the newspaper. Duke waited at the house, smoking yet another Camel, while Danny grabbed the paper out of the tube. Duke held out his hand for it, and flipped through it, looking for a certain story, Danny was sure of it. The story he was looking for was on the second page now, with a different picture. Danny had already looked at it. A newer picture. It looked like it had been taken with some sort of surveillance camera. Danny picked up rocks and chucked them into the bushes as the man read, deliberately trying to avoid noticing what the man was looking at.

"I need to make a phone call."

"Sure."

Chapter 8

When they went back into the house, Duke walked into the den, picked up the phone, and punched in the numbers. He waited a few seconds, and then said, "Yeah, Justin. It's Kevin. I'll try again later." He slammed the receiver down and turned on the television. He flipped through the channels, shutting it off within a few minutes, apparently annoyed with the sports. He thumbed through the paper again, and then must have realized there was no news.

"How's your shoulder?" Danny leaned against the side of the doorway as he asked.

"What?" The man turned around to look at him.

Danny raised his voice. "How's your shoulder, your arm?"

"Sore. How else would it be?" He shook his head. "You don't have to shout."

"You feeling any better?"

"Yeah, I guess. Just a little edgy." He got up, walked around the room, looking at the pictures on the wall. He focused on one with a smiling man holding up the front end of a large deer lying stretched out in front of him. "That your dad there, with the dead animal?"

"Yeah."

"You look like him."

Danny didn't think he looked like his dad, but he studied the picture anyway, and thought maybe he could see a resemblance. "Do you have a family, any kids?"

"Why should you care?" The man glared at him, and then sat back down, staring out the far window.

"I don't know. I just figured we could talk." Danny looked away, wishing he hadn't started the conversation.

"Okay. Yeah. I have a wife and two kids. They're about your age, both boys. I haven't seen them in a while." He stared out the window, looking at something beyond the horizon. "I've been married for twenty-three years." His voice went quiet. "Let's see, that would make Michael twelve and Andy fifteen. About your age, right?"

"I'm thirteen."

"Oh, shoot. This is August isn't it?"

"Yeah."

"Andy's birthday is in August. He either just turned fifteen or he's about to. I think it's the seventeenth. Missed another birthday."

"Today is the fourth. What are you going to give him for his birthday?"

"What? Today is the fourth?" The man looked confused.

"Your son, what are you going to give him for his birthday?"

"I didn't think about it. It's been six years since I've even seen him." He sighed. "Some father I am."

"Are you going home?" Danny paused. "Home to see your kids?"

"That was part of the plan. I kind of screwed it up, though." The man paused for a minute. "You're about the same age; what do you want for your birthday?"

Danny shrugged. "I don't know. Money is always good."

"That's what I usually give him. Ever since he got too big to play with fire trucks. I guess I was hoping for something more creative."

"My dad gave me a rifle last year."

"Really?"

"Yeah. A twenty-two. He just didn't want to admit I don't want to shoot Bambi."

"Have you fired it?"

"Sure. I'm pretty good at paper targets."

Duke frowned. "I don't think my wife would approve of my giving the kid a gun. Besides, they live in the city."

"That must be rough. Living in a city. I love it out here, even though I'm not a real outdoors type."

"I never lived anywhere else but the city. The noises out here are a bit much."

"So what did you want for your fifteenth birthday?"

"Whoa. That was a long time ago." He turned and looked at Danny, then stared out the window again. "I was a ball player. Basketball though, not baseball. Everybody played baseball back then, but I was tall. I liked basketball." He paused. "You ever see the '64 Celtics? That's what I wanted to do. I wanted to play on a team like that." His voice developed something, a sort of far-off sound. "I don't know about my fifteenth birthday, but I know for my sixteenth I wanted a new pair of sneakers. My family didn't have a lot of money. My old man was a disabled veteran working a low-paying job, doing security on the docks. Too many kids and too much booze added up to a pretty piss-poor existence." He stopped for a second.

Danny held his breath. He wanted to hear more.

"I got a sweater. A fucking sweater." He shook his head and stared at the boy for a second. "I'm sorry, excuse my French." His eyes shifted again. "She knew I needed the sneakers and she bought a stupid sweater." He laughed, or at least made a sound that would pass for a laugh. "I guess I know what not to get my boy, ay?"

Danny let the silence settle for a few minutes, then swallowed hard and went right for the jugular. "You know there's an escaped convict somewhere around here. I read about it in the paper. And my mom and I got stopped by two state cops on our way to shopping."

The man took the change of subject in stride. "And?"

"The picture wasn't very good, but it kind of looked like you."

"Why are you doing this? Do you really want to know?" He stood up and paced the room, limping. His voice developed an edge, a hint of something under the surface. The quiet man who had gotten a sweater for his sixteenth birthday disappeared. "You know everything changes once you know the truth. If you don't know, you're safe. Once you know, well…" He paused, and turned to look at the boy. "Can we leave it at that?"

"But—"

"Leave it!" He was shouting now. "What do you think this is? One of your silly books? You think everything will turn out all right just because you want it to? Happily ever after?"

Danny backed away, starting to feel real fear, and wondering if he had bitten off more than he could chew.

"You know how those books always end, don't you? The bad guy dies." Duke must have recognized the boy's reaction, because he turned to walk out of the room, approaching Danny's position by the door with an awkward shuffle and a bowed head. "Oh, shit. Look, I'm sorry; I'll go."

"No, that's okay. Really, you've got one more night you can stay here. Stay. Please. Then you can hit the road again." Danny turned on his heel and walked through the kitchen and out the back door, leaving the man standing alone in the den. Duke came out a few minutes later, and lit a cigarette. Danny scooted away, sneezing. The man walked over to the garage and gestured towards the basketball net.

"Do you have a ball?" The scary guy was gone again, just as fast as he had appeared.

"Yeah, but I'm no good." Danny said as he walked over, opened the big overhead door and went into the garage. He came out with a basketball, and began half-heartedly shooting at the net. It mostly missed. "See what I mean?"

Duke let his cigarette dangle on his lower lip, and grabbed the ball on the rebound. He began shooting one handed, hooking his left thumb in a belt loop. "Take your time, line up the shot, don't rush, and practice, practice, practice." He fired off a succession of shots, all of which went into the net. "I used to be pretty good. Look, keep the ball on your fingertips, like this. Try it."

Danny took the ball and began shooting again.

The man shook his head, "No, no. Take your time; don't shove the ball. Use your fingers to push the ball towards the net; give it a little spin. And don't aim for the net. Aim for the square on the backboard."

Danny tried again, and actually made a shot. "All right!"

"Good job." He smiled as he spoke, that same sort of half-smile with one corner of his mouth, nothing in the eyes.

"I've never really bothered with sports, 'cause I'm just not good at it."

"I think being good at something has more to do with practice and persistence than natural talent. You've got to work at it." He cleared his throat. "It helps to have a good teacher, too."

Danny nodded and took another shot. This one bounced off the rim. "So who taught you to play this well?"

The man hesitated, letting the ball bounce away. He looked past the boy, with that faraway look in his eyes again. "I had an older brother. He helped me focus; kept me reaching, and taught me all this stuff." He raised his right arm, waved it to encompass the net, the ball, the whole general game.

Danny frowned and went after the ball. "So what happened to him?"

"Who?" He swiveled his head back to look at the boy.

"Your brother."

"He died. A cop killed him."

"Like in a shootout or something?" *Stupid.* Why the hell did he say such stupid things?

The man shot him a look of such venom Danny backed up a step, swallowing hard. Then the features almost seemed to melt, the anger washed away, and the man spoke in little more than a whisper.

"No. He was participating in a peaceful anti-war protest. This was in 1968, on my sixteenth birthday. When they were arresting him, they threw him back on the sidewalk so hard it caused something to rupture in his head, and he died instantly."

Danny let the ball slide out of his hands. "I'm so sorry."

Duke gave him the half-grin, lifting one corner of his mouth and letting it droop again, along with his shoulders. He seemed to age right before Danny's eyes. All of a sudden the young man with the talent for basketball was gone, and the bitter old man was back. "Without him there to keep me on track, I got a little messed up."

"What about your parents, your father?"

The hatred flared in the eyes again and the head snapped up. "My father was an shi… well, he wasn't a nice guy. He drank too much. I told you already, didn't I?"

Danny nodded.

The man sat down and took a long drag on his cigarette, closed his eyes, and leaned back again.

The phone rang inside the house, and Danny ran past Duke into the kitchen.

"Hello?"

"Danny?"

"Hi, Mom."

"How are you?"

"Fine."

"You see anything going on down there?"

Danny looked out the window. "No."

"Reggie Crandall check up on you?"

"Yes."

"Good."

"You having a good time?"

"Yes, I am. Well, I'll check in again later, okay?"

"Yeah. Thanks, Mom." He hung up the phone and stood looking out the window for a moment, watching a faint line of smoke rising towards the tops of the pine trees.

Duke looked up as he came back out.

"My mom. Checking on me."

"What?"

"That was my mom, on the phone."

"Oh."

"I told her I was fine."

"Are you?"

Danny hesitated for a moment. "Yeah."

"Good."

"He wasn't on the line long enough to get a trace, but he's still in New York state. He's got to be in a wet area, somewhere close to the train tracks, somewhere close to where they found the scent." Sally looked at Thomas, testing him. They were all sitting in the little office at the county jail, surrounded by maps and empty doughnut boxes. What was it with cops and doughnuts? Give her a nice piece of fruit anytime, rather than the greasy old fat pills.

"Pretty big territory," he said with a shrug, leaning back in the folding chair, lifting the front legs off the ground. "He's obviously found a place to lie down. We know that from the phone call." He turned towards the map, dropping the front legs of the chair back to the floor. "We look for an area that fits, someplace within… say, fifteen miles of where the dog lost the scent. He couldn't have walked much farther, not bleeding like he was. Someplace wet, someplace with relatively few houses, because we know this rabbit is smart. Plus he's hurt, which would attract too much attention in a city. Besides, the frogs mean rural."

"How do we know he didn't get a ride somewhere along the rail line? He could be anywhere," Craig said.

"Well, I have to tell you, I would prefer to be looking for him in the city. I hate bugs and muck and swamps. But I think Thomas is right. He's got good instincts." Sally nodded. "Get some detailed maps. Let's see what we can find."

As they spread out the maps on the table, Elizabeth brought some sandwiches over. "You hungry?" she asked Sally.

"Yeah, thanks."

"Anything there for me?" asked Thomas.

Liz tossed him a sandwich.

"So, Sally, how's your husband?" Thomas asked.

"He's okay. I think he likes retirement."

"I didn't know you were that old," teased Thomas. He knew her husband was a few years older than she was, and had easily put in the twenty years required for retirement.

"Yeah, I am getting old. Too old to be doing this stuff." She sighed and took a bite of her sandwich. "I'd like to get going and find this creep so we can all go home to our families."

Liz dusted some crumbs off her blue jeans. "So what do we know about this guy, considering he's never attracted a lot of attention?"

"Aside from the basics—his background, his family—not a lot. Hold on a minute." Sally set her sandwich down and started rummaging through the piles of stuff on the table. She came up with her notebook and flipped through it.

"We can't really predict what the guy will do, can we?" Thomas sounded skeptical.

Sally looked up. "I don't think we can guarantee anything, but we can get a good idea." She pointed to the page she was looking at. "For instance, it would be highly unusual for this guy to take hostages. He's not likely to fight if cornered. He's very institutionalized; he's spent enough time in prison he's actually fairly civilized. That psychiatrist thinks he's more the type to bide his time and wait for an opportunity, rather than trying to bull his way out of a situation. He's not a kid." She paused, looking over the top of her reading glasses. "He's actually pretty close to my age."

Thomas snickered. "Old, then."

Sally frowned and went back to the notes. "He will most likely try to arm himself. He'll feel more comfortable with a weapon, but other than the one cop he shot he has never shown a tendency to use a weapon on law enforcement."

"One's enough, don't you think?" snorted Thomas.

"Well, that is the reason we've been asked to help out with this one." She sighed. "I don't want you guys to get complacent, either. He is dangerous. He's a pro. He's just not nuts."

Danny settled in the den to play a computer game, glancing at the man lying on the couch, just staring at the ceiling.

"This what you do all the time?"

Danny looked back at him. "No, I don't usually spend much time playing games. I read a lot."

"Don't you have any friends?"

"Not many." Danny thought about that answer for a moment. "Not really any, I guess." He turned back to the computer, pushing his glasses back up.

"Nobody you hang out with, or play with or whatever?"

"I'm a little old to play."

"You're playing now."

"I guess I like to be alone."

"Do you really like to be alone or is that just how you end up all the time?"

Danny turned away from the game again to glower at the man.

The man was still staring at the ceiling. "Now me, I like being alone. I'm not much of a talker, and people always want to talk."

Danny frowned. "You're talking now."

"Just trying to be polite."

Danny turned back to Railroad Tycoon. His train had crashed. "Rats."

"So, why don't you have any friends?"

"I don't know. I guess it's because people are always picking on me."

"Everybody?"

An image of Jessie flashed into his brain. "Well, no."

"So that gives you some people to be friends with."

"Why are you so interested in my social life?"

"I was just wondering how you could spend the whole weekend alone without anybody noticing. I didn't want to be surprised by one of your friends walking in, looking for you."

Danny nodded. He understood. "You don't need to worry about it."

The man closed his eyes.

Danny started to turn back to his game, and then a thought occurred to him. "Duke?"

He opened his eyes and looked over. "Yeah?"

"Have you thought about a disguise?" He paused. "You know, for when you leave."

"How many of those detective stories have you read?" the man responded.

"Seriously, my mom used to color her hair. If you had short brown hair, and with your mustache shaved off, you'd look different. If you wanted to, that is." He looked back at the computer screen, not seeing the game.

"You're a smart kid." He got to his feet with a groan. "Let's see what you've got. Just in case I wanted to, you understand."

They started upstairs to look in the medicine chest and Duke glanced at the family pictures, portraits of a young boy, obviously Danny, family portraits, always smiling. Then he froze on the stairs, pointing at a photo of a young man in a police uniform, holding some sort of certificate.

"Who's this?"

Danny glanced at the picture. "My dad."

Danny saw something flash across the man's face. "Your father is a fu... uh, a cop?"

"He was."

"So what happened?"

Danny was looking down at the stairs, moving the toe of his sneaker back and forth. "He accidentally shot someone. A kid—about fifteen years old—who had a gun. It wasn't a real gun, but my dad thought it was. The kid was waving the gun around, and had been holding a little kid hostage. My dad shot him. Killed him. Then they found out it was just a pellet gun. My dad quit. Resigned the next day. He spent the next six months drinking, until he shot himself."

"I'm sorry, man. That must be tough. I'm sorry I brought it up."

Danny sighed and changed the subject. "Let's go see what we have upstairs in my mom's medicine chest."

"So you want to be a fed, to make up for your dad's mistake, or are you trying to prove something?" Duke asked.

Danny stopped. "I never thought about it that way." He shook his head and continued on up.

Sally noticed the news truck parked outside the county jail when they arrived back at the office that afternoon.

"What's with the press?" Thomas muttered.

"Don't know."

They passed the news crew setting up in the sheriff's office. He called out as they went by. "Hey. Deputy Barnard."

Sally saw the look cross the reporter's face.

Thomas grinned as Sally turned back towards Crandall. "Yes, sir?"

"Michelle, this is Deputy United States Marshal Sally Barnard. She's with the Southern District of New York; they sent her up here to help us out with this fugitive. I'm sure she'd love to talk to you."

Sally glared at Crandall, who gave her a big smile.

"Deputy Barnard? Would you mind saying a few words about the fugitive?"

Sally sighed. She hated talking to the press. This had possibilities, though. If her quarry had access to a television, he might see what she had to say. Maybe she could make him nervous; flush him out. "Sure, Michelle, was it?"

"Michelle Aguiar." She stuck out her hand.

Sally shook the reporter's hand. "I can spare a few minutes."

Danny helped him cut and color his hair, pulling out the electric clippers his mom used on his dad's hair.

"This was a great idea," Duke said. "I wouldn't have thought of it." He headed downstairs, after scooping up the cut hair into the empty box. He ducked into the living room, with Danny following. "What did you do with that shirt I was wearing?"

"I threw it in the trash," Danny replied.

"Would you mind getting it?" He dropped the box of hair on the floor next to the fireplace.

Danny heard the back screen door slam as he headed for the trash can in the basement. When Danny came back with the shirt, the man was setting a pile of leaves and dry sticks on the hearth.

"You wanna get me some newspapers, please?"

Danny walked over to the pile of papers beside his mother's chair and grabbed one off the bottom.

Duke crumpled the papers and put them in the fireplace, after checking to make sure the damper was open. He then pulled out his matches and got the papers going, adding bits of pine needles and sticks. Once the fire was going, he threw the hair, the box, and the shirt onto the flames.

"Why are you doing that?" asked Danny.

"It's called destroying evidence." The man gave the boy a hard stare, a what-are-you-going-to-do-about-it kind of stare.

Danny looked away. "Evidence of what?" he wanted to say, but he didn't. He was starting to understand. Maybe this was a game. Maybe they were both playing a game, circling around the truth, neither of them wanting to admit how much the other knew.

"It's for your protection, you know. The less you know, the less trouble you'll be in when it's all over."

"Trouble?" Danny repeated.

"There'll be trouble; I can guarantee it." The man got to his feet, and then headed for the den as the flames died down. "I want to try to catch the news. You doing dinner?"

Danny nodded, and followed, turning towards the kitchen, his head reeling.

Duke parked himself in front of the television and watched the local news.

When he heard the story, Danny came to the doorway of the den, dinner forgotten.

"Deputy Sally Barnard, of the United States Marshal's Service, today announced an intensified search for escaped cop-killer Kevin Markinson." A picture of Markinson appeared on the screen. An old picture, from about six years ago by the date. Long, blond hair, mustache, and icy blue-gray eyes. Mouth set in a hard frown. Wearing an orange jumpsuit and holding one of those board things, with a number on it, and "Wanted by NYSP." Then the picture changed to a small red-haired woman with a badge, standing at a podium, pointing to a map. The caption said DUSM Sally Barnard. "We're setting up more roadblocks, tightening the net. We believe Markinson is in a rural area, away from any centers of population. With the helicopters, dogs, and our house-to-house search, we should have this guy in a matter of hours."

The picture of Markinson appeared on the screen again, and the announcer continued. "The authorities have emphasized that this man is extremely dangerous. If you see him, do not attempt to approach him. Just call the US Marshal's office or the State Police."

The picture changed then to a young woman holding a microphone, standing outside an English Tudor style house. "This is Ellen Joslin reporting from the exclusive Queens neighborhood where Kevin Markinson's wife, Cindy, lives with their two children."

The man frowned, leaning forward, staring hard at the set.

The woman on the television continued to talk as she approached the front door. "Mrs. Markinson has agreed to talk with us about her husband." The door opened and a black-haired woman who looked to be in her late forties stepped out, shutting the door behind her. "Mrs. Markinson, what can you tell us about your husband? Does this escape surprise you?"

"Frankly, it does," she replied in a soft voice.

"God dammit," Duke muttered, rubbing his chin with his right hand.

Duke turned his head to see Danny standing there, watching the television. He stood up, grabbing the side of the chair as he wobbled for a moment. He shut off the television just as his wife was pleading for him to give himself up, to avoid getting hurt.

"House-to-house search." Danny said.

"Yeah."

"Roadblocks."

"Uh-huh."

"What are you going to do?"

"I'm going to eat dinner. How about you?"

Dinner started out quiet. Duke chewed his food slowly, staring at the instructions for the coffee maker now.

Danny looked at his plate, not really wanting to eat at all. "If you were me," he asked, "what would you do?"

"Not a fair question."

"Why?"

"Because I'm not you, and you're not me." Duke set the instructions aside and looked at his food, pushing it around with his fork. "Different values. Different experiences." He took another bite.

"What do you think I should do?"

"If it were entirely up to me, I'd like you to pretend you never saw me. But that isn't going to fit into your value system." He paused, chewing more food. "Of course, a lot of what you've already done doesn't fit into your value system." He stared at Danny.

Danny nodded, looking down, and resisting the urge to squirm under that stare. "If anybody had asked me on Wednesday if I'd be breaking the law by Friday, I would have laughed at them."

"Bothering your conscience?"

"I don't know. I had a hard time sleeping last night, and I wasn't even as sure as I am now." He looked at the man. "It is you, isn't it?"

"I told you before, you don't want to know. Just don't ask. It won't bother your conscience as much if you don't know for sure." The man got to his feet. "You can go a long way on lingering doubt."

Danny looked up at him. "Do you see a way out?"

He paused before answering, as if listening to the sound of bloodhounds baying. "Not right at this moment. Not for either of us." He took his cigarettes out of his pocket and headed for the back door.

Chapter 9

Sally was sitting in a hard wooden chair in the sheriff's office at the county jail. She looked up as Reggie Crandall walked in, taking off his hat.

"Busy week," she said.

"Yeah, never seen anything like it," he replied, shaking his head.

"So these guys just walked away. I guess they didn't think first. More cops around here than you can shake a stick at."

The deputy shrugged. "If they had any brains they wouldn't be in jail in the first place," he said, hanging his hat on a wooden coat tree in the corner.

"Those two of them?" she asked, nodding towards two scruffy looking young men in muddy clothes being shepherded past the doorway.

"Yeah. Didn't take long to pick them up." He paused. "I want to ask them some questions; maybe we can track down the other three with some help from these two."

She got to her feet. "Let me know if they say anything about my rabbit." She shook Crandall's hand and started out the door as he picked up the telephone.

Duke was sitting in the den again, just staring into space. Danny walked in, started to sit down on the floor opposite the chair, and then jumped up again as the phone rang. He picked it up, looking at the man across the room.

"Hello?"

"Danny, this is Deputy Sheriff Crandall again."

"Hi."

"How are you doing?"

Danny hesitated for a second before he responded. "I'm okay, Deputy Crandall."

"Nothing going on there I need to know about?"

Danny saw the look cross Duke's face, as it registered that it was law enforcement on the other end of the line. He thought of just telling the sheriff to come on out here, that he was worried about noises or whatever. Even as the thought ran through his mind, he wondered why. He looked into the eyes of the man on the other side of the room—a man he was now convinced really was a killer, an escaped felon, and probably a danger to him—yet he couldn't do it. He didn't feel any actual fear, not for himself anyway. But he almost felt fear for the quarry, the hunted man sitting in his den.

"No, sir. Nothing at all; it's been quiet."

"Things are wild here. I'm probably not going to get a chance to get out there tonight."

"It's okay. Really. You don't need to come out here." Danny saw Duke's face turn white.

"Well, all right then. You take care. I'll check in with you tomorrow, and don't be afraid to give me a call if you need anything."

"Yes, sir."

"Good night."

"Bye."

Danny set the phone down and walked back around the huge oak desk.

"Had your chance there, didn't you?" Duke asked.

Danny nodded.

"Why didn't you tell him?"

"I don't know." He really didn't know. What he did know was that he wanted to understand this feeling, to know more about the man, to understand him. "Did you do it?"

He swung his eyes in the boy's direction without moving his head, focusing on the boy's face. "What?"

"What they said you did."

"Which part?"

"Any of it. All of it. Did you kill that cop?"

Duke closed his eyes for a moment. "No."

"So why do they say you did?"

"I was convicted of it, didn't have much of a defense."

"So if you didn't do it, what happened?"

He opened his eyes and looked at Danny. "I walked away from a work-release job. My wife had just had a baby. They'd told me about it, but they wouldn't give me a furlough; wouldn't let me go see her."

"Why were you in jail?" Danny interrupted. If he was going to get the story, he wanted the whole story.

The man blinked. "I violated my parole."

"Why were you on parole?"

"I did nine months of a one-year sentence for possession of a handgun without a license. They kicked me loose and I left town. Went to New Hampshire. That's where I met my wife." He paused. "Where was I?"

"You walked away from a work-release job."

"Oh, yeah. Okay. A young kid, maybe seventeen years old, picked me up. In a stolen car, for chrissake. All I wanted to do was see my kid, see my wife. I would have gone back." He took a deep breath through his nose, felt his pocket for his cigarettes.

"A cop pulled us over. I don't think he was looking for me; it could have been the car that tipped him off. Or the stupid kid running a red light. He pulled us over, and the kid pulled a gun. Fucking huge revolver, a Dirty Harry gun." Duke sighed. "I didn't want to see anybody get hurt, or to see a cop get shot. I mean come on; I walked away from a minimum security gig. It wasn't like I was going to go down for life. I grabbed the gun, trying to get it away from the stupid kid, and the cop shot at him. The bullet hit me instead."

Danny sat, staring.

The man swallowed hard and continued. "Of course, Carlos—the kid—got the gun away from me then, shot the cop, and took off. My prints were on the gun. The cop was dead. I was in no shape to run off. What could I do?"

"Is that where you got the scar on your neck?"

"Huh?" He reached up and touched the left side of his neck. "Oh, no. Not that one. This shot I took in the chest. Talk about getting the wind knocked out of you." He smiled that little half-smile again, and then looked away. "If I ever find that little bastard …"

Danny was shocked. The story was incredible. But it meant, to him at least, that this man was not what the cops said he was. If he didn't kill that cop, then why was he in jail in the first place? Which meant his escape wasn't really bad, right? He knew he was rationalizing now. "So you broke out for revenge?"

"Not really." The man shrugged. "But I'd love to get Carlos back here, get him to confess, and get a new trial. I want to be exonerated. Then, I'd love to kill him."

"So you're going to get right and then kill him? You'll go back to jail for a murder you did commit instead of one you didn't?"

"What are you, Jiminy Cricket?"

Danny was on a roll now. "Well, think about it. You went to jail for something you didn't do, right? So, if you can get that guy to confess, you could have a normal life, right? No more jail. No more running."

Duke looked at him. "A normal life. What the hell is a normal life?"

"You could actually live with your family."

The man looked away, his face clouding. Danny wondered if Duke was really capable of living an ordinary life, or if the man simply thought there was no way he could.

Duke shook his head. "No way it's ever going to happen. It's been fifteen years now; the kid disappeared. I'm going to spend the rest of my miserable life in jail or on the run."

"What about your lawyer? Doesn't he have any private investigators working for him, people who could look for the real killer?"

Duke snorted. "Not a real high priority, I guess."

"You've put so much energy into running. If you'd put half as much into finding this creep, you'd probably be free by now." Danny surprised himself with that speech. He had no idea where it had come from. What right did he have to accuse this man of anything? Worse, what if he made the man angry?

The man looked at the boy, meeting his gaze with a steady stare. "We tried. We couldn't find him. End of story." He cleared his throat, felt his pocket for his cigarettes, and got to his feet.

Danny didn't follow him this time.

They had burgers for dinner, in the tent. Sally was starting to get frustrated. She sat and stared out at the woods beyond the tracks. She would have preferred to be out there, chasing this guy herself. Instead she was here, sitting on her hands and waiting for word. It was getting on towards dusk now, and the mosquitoes were out in full force. They'd have to pack it in for the night soon.

"We got something," Thomas said.

"What?" Sally felt a quick twist of excitement as she turned her head to look at him. He shut off the phone.

"Search team on the railroad tracks found a real strong scent, along with some blankets and stuff, in a culvert under the tracks."

"Let's go; I want to see this."

They went as far as possible by helicopter, and hiked in the rest of the way. Sally and Thomas scrambled down the slope towards a group gathered around the opening of a large pipe under the tracks.

"I hope you guys haven't touched anything," she said as she approached the culvert.

"No, ma'am; we were waiting for you," said the handler of a huge drooling bloodhound.

She looked down. "Cigarette butts. Get those, Thomas. We need to check for prints and DNA."

"DNA?" Crandall snorted. "You know how long that takes? You'll be lucky to get anything back on the prints in less than a week."

Sally glared at Crandall, and then motioned to Thomas, who pulled out a plastic bag, a pair of tweezers, and bent to pick up the butts. "Unfiltered."

"He smokes Camels." She looked into the pipe, waiting for a moment to allow her eyes to adjust to the dim light. "If I had to guess, I'd say we've got somebody helping this guy." She climbed up into the culvert and bent down, examining the blankets. "Blood," she said. "It's got to be him." She pulled a pair of tweezers out of her pocket and picked up a scrap of white paper. "Wrapper from some kind of first aid supplies. Looks like gauze pads." She cursed under her breath. "This is going to make it harder." She picked up a sandwich bag with crumbs in it. "Looks like he's eaten, as well. He'll go a lot farther with food and first aid." She shook her head.

"The trail is dead from here. He must have walked in the water again," the dog's handler said, pointing at the stream.

"He could have gone through the swamp, right?" said Thomas.

Sally nodded. "But one way or the other, we're getting closer."

Crandall scratched his head. "If he went into that swamp, you can forget about him. He'll drown. You'd have to be an expert to get through there."

Sally looked at him. "He's pretty good in swamps. I don't think he's going to drown. We keep looking." She turned to Liz. "I want to go with a hard perimeter now. Maybe a four-mile radius around this area. He couldn't have gone much farther than that. Set up roadblocks. Nobody in or out without a search."

Liz nodded. "You want to evacuate civilians?"

Sally glanced at the deputy, who looked like he was going to be sick. "No, I don't think we need to. Crandall, what do you have for roadblocks on your escapees?"

"Just the main roads in the area where they were working. Not this far north."

"Do we have enough manpower for another house-to-house?"

"Not at this point."

She tightened her lips in a hard frown. "Why the hell does everything have to happen at once?"

"We've got two helicopters from the state," the deputy offered.

"Have them run a pattern inside my perimeter."

"Yes, ma'am."

"Keep them up as long as possible. Do they have those special heat-seeking cameras?"

"I think we've got one of those."

"Good. We are so close to this guy. I don't want to lose him." She tried not to think of the other possibility—that he might have already gotten a car and was already gone.

Chapter 10

Danny was having a hard time staying awake, even though it was only eight o'clock. "Are you going to try to take off tomorrow?" asked Danny with a yawn.

"What?"

"You going to run tomorrow?"

"Yeah, I guess," Duke responded. Also yawning.

"You'll need money. And a gun."

"I'll do something."

"I've got some money. And I know where my dad kept the keys to the gun cabinet." Danny shrugged. "I can help you out."

"You shouldn't." The man fished out his cigarettes and counted them. "You're talking about aiding and abetting a fugitive. That's a felony."

"Who's going to know?"

"Be serious. You think I'm not going to get caught?" He examined the cigarettes, took one out, and rolled it back and forth between his thumb and forefinger. "I'm not going to walk away from this. You should recognize that at this point."

"What about my dad's car?"

"What about the roadblocks?" Duke responded. A helicopter flew overhead, really low, rattling the windows. "What about the fucking helicopters?" He leaned forward, putting his head in his hands.

Danny got up and went upstairs to his room as Duke headed out to smoke. Danny opened his bank, took out two ten-dollar bills, and trotted back down the stairs. He headed out the back door. The man was sitting in his usual spot, on the steps.

"Here," said the boy, holding out the money.

"I can't take your money, kid." Spoken without looking at him.

"You'll pay me back."

"You could get into big trouble."

"Why? I don't know who you are. Maybe I don't read newspapers," replied Danny.

"What do you want to help me for?" asked Duke, still not looking at him, examining the cigarette instead, rolling it back and forth in his fingers, dropping ashes on his pants.

"I don't know." He shrugged. He put the money on the step, and then walked back into the house and into the den. He crossed the room to the large oak desk, opened a drawer, reached in as far as he could, and took out a small metal box, opening it and removing a key. He looked up as Duke entered the room. Danny set the key on the desk and said, "Lock it up when you're done."

The man shook his head. "I don't want a gun."

"Okay, do what you want."

"You getting a kick out of this?" asked Duke. "Is this a game?"

Danny shrugged, staring at the floor.

"Do you have any idea what you're doing? Haven't you been paying attention?" He picked up the newspaper, folded it open to the page with the picture of the escapee and said, "Look, don't you see the resemblance?"

"I don't believe it." Danny told the lie without emotion. It had become easy to lie. Sometime during the last couple of days it had become a habit.

Duke leaned forward, focusing on Danny's face. "What the hell do you mean you don't believe it? You don't think this is just a little too much coincidence?" He started pacing again. "I didn't want this, didn't want your fu… uh, your help, do you understand?" He paused to take a deep breath through clenched teeth. "I didn't even want to be here. This is insane. You're trying to give me a gun, a car. You're out of your mind. Don't you see what you're doing?"

"I don't believe you did it. I don't believe you're a murderer." He paused. "You told me you didn't do it."

"But—"

"You could take me with you. I could be your hostage, get you through the roadblocks."

Duke stared at him. "No way. I don't do hostages. Kidnapping is a federal offense. Kidnapping is something they never let go of; you can't walk away from that. Like killing a cop." He backed up a couple of steps. "Don't you see what any of this would do to you? You think you could possibly get a job as a fed after this? It may already be too late, if I can't figure a way to get out of this."

"I'm only thirteen."

"You think that makes a difference? You're starting down the wrong path. What am I saying, starting? You're already on the way. You can't help me. I never should have let you help me in the first place."

"So you'll figure a way out. Isn't that what you do?"

"What if there is no way out?"

Danny couldn't answer. Visions of the man holed up in this house with the cops outside ran through his head again.

Danny went to bed early, with his head spinning. He had no idea what to do. He had been tempted to pick up the phone, call the police, and get it all over with. But at this point, he felt like he was in so deep himself that he couldn't call because he would get into trouble.

Still, as he lay in bed with his brain running in circles, it occurred to him there might be something he could do. Not to help catch the man, he was beyond that; he wasn't going to give him up, but help him to escape. He hadn't thought about the tool he had available, more valuable than money or guns. He could get information. He sat bolt upright in bed and looked at the clock. Nine-thirty. Not too late for a nervous little boy to call his father's friend at the sheriff's office. He jumped out of bed, pulled on his jeans, and trotted down to the den.

When he burst through the door, the man leapt to his feet and skittered sideways like a nervous horse.

"I have an idea," Danny said.

Duke flopped back down on the couch. "Give me a fucking heart attack, why don't you?"

Danny picked up the phone and dialed the home number Deputy Sheriff Crandall had given him.

The man narrowed his eyes, frowning.

"Sheriff Crandall?"

"Yes."

"This is Danny Rutledge."

"How are you doing?"

"I was just a little nervous."

"You don't have anything to worry about."

"Yes, sir."

"Do you want me to send someone to pick you up, bring you down to my office for the night?"

"No, I'll be all right here. No, you don't need to send anyone. I was just wondering what you were doing about finding this fugitive." Danny glanced over at Duke, who was still staring at him.

"We found a culvert under some railroad tracks. Looks like somebody helped the guy."

"Railroad tracks near here?" Danny's stomach clenched.

"Right, maybe a mile from your house. You need to stay inside, okay?"

"Oh, yes sir. I'll be sure and stay in the house."

"Are you sure you don't need anything?"

"No, I don't need anything. Right. Thanks, Deputy Crandall."

He hung up the phone and stared at it for a moment. He wondered how he could have been so naïve. How could he have ever thought he could just bring this man here and nobody would ever know? He glanced over at Duke, who was looking at him, waiting.

Danny swallowed. "They're in the neighborhood. They found the culvert."

"Shit. Should have policed it up. They've probably got prints now, certainly blood evidence. God dammit." He got to his feet and stared out the window.

"So what do you think? Do you want to take the car and go?"

"I don't know."

"You should go now. You should run now, while it's dark, while they're still thinking about it."

"It's too late." The man's voice was quiet and flat, as though what energy he'd had was gone for good.

"So what are you going to do?"

"I don't know."

"What can I do?"

"Go get some sleep."

Danny blinked. "How can I?"

"Why shouldn't you?"

"They'll kill you, won't they?"

"Don't be ridiculous. I'm not armed. I know how to deal with cops." The last word sounded as though he was spitting out something that tasted bad. "Go on now, off to bed with you." Like some kind of benevolent babysitter.

Danny turned and left the room, feeling even more useless than he had before.

Kevin sat in front of the television for half the night. He couldn't sleep. The news announced the escape of five county inmates. Oh, bloody hell. That was just perfect.

They were probably going to bring in the fucking National Guard at this point. On top of the fucking US Marshals and the fucking FBI. His language, he told himself, was deteriorating. He wanted to beat his head against the bleeping wall. That didn't sound any better. He sat bleary-eyed through Saturday Night Live, which he didn't think was as funny as it used to be. Back in the seventies it was great. Then again, he remembered being drunk most every time he watched it back then. Oh, well. He finally fell asleep on the couch, with the television on.

Danny tossed and turned. He could swear he heard sirens, all night long. What he did hear—at what appeared to be two in the morning—was the doorbell. He leapt out of bed, suddenly awake, every nerve in his body on edge. He pulled on a pair of jeans and ran down the stairs. Duke wasn't in the guestroom. Danny nearly panicked, wondering where the man was. The doorbell rang again, and Danny ran down the hall, almost colliding with Duke coming out of the den.

"You hear that?"

"Somebody's at the door." Danny felt the now familiar twist of fear.

"Go see who it is."

"Suppose it's cops?"

"Cops don't ring the bell at two in the morning. Cops would just bust the door down."

Danny started to go to the door, and then came back to the den. "You should go." He looked at the man, who was busy loading a shotgun. Danny nodded and tried a half-grin, unconsciously imitating the man.

"Did you see who it is?"

"Not yet." Danny backed out of the room and turned towards the living room.

Duke tucked the shotgun into the crook of his right arm and headed for the back door. He hesitated long enough to turn towards the boy for just a second. "Thanks."

Danny nodded.

Chapter 11

Danny walked to the front door, turned on the outside light, looked through the side window, and was surprised to see Eddie standing on the steps. He could see a Toyota pickup truck, but couldn't tell how many people were in it. The moon was bright behind the scattered clouds, but it didn't provide that much illumination. Eddie rang the doorbell one more time.

"What do you want?" Danny called, without opening the door.

"Can I use your phone?" asked Eddie. "My buddies are having car trouble."

Danny thought it over. He knew this kid, didn't like him, but didn't really have any reason not to trust him. Still, his instinct told him to be careful. He looked out the sidelight again. No sign of anyone else near the door. "No."

"What?" Eddie sounded surprised.

"No. I'll call somebody for you. Tell me who you want me to call."

Just then, there was a loud thump and the door shuddered. Danny backed up, fear coursing through his body. The doorframe gave way and a guy who looked to be about twenty shoved his way in, with a gun in his hand. Eddie was right behind him.

"Hi, kid," said the man. "You alone?"

"Yeah, uh, but my mom will be home any minute." Danny's voice trembled. He looked towards Eddie, trying to figure out what the boy was doing, trying to figure out what was going on, but the teen refused to meet his eyes.

"Yeah, right, in the middle of the night."

Another guy, slightly older, walked in. "Hey, Paully. Al's going to cut the phone line." He looked around. "Nice place."

"Yeah, Jack, your little cousin did good." Paully grinned and ruffled Eddie's hair.

Kevin slipped out the back door, leaving it open in case he needed to get back through it in a hurry. He still carried the shotgun in the crook of his right arm, pointed towards the ground. His brain was starting to shut down, thoughts flying through his head so fast he couldn't sort them out. *Go now. Run now, while you still can. Hold off the cops with the shotgun.* His vision was starting to go, narrowing to that tunnel he knew so well.

He stopped on the back steps, listening, falling into sniper mode. There was a change in the noises, the fucking jungle noises. It had been hard to hear them, but now he couldn't hear them at all. What did that mean? Somebody was close by, moving, and not being careful about it. He crept towards the sound of footsteps, and nearly ran head on into a heavyset young man coming around the corner of the house, dressed like a commando and holding a hunting knife in his hand.

Kevin leveled the shotgun at the kid, ignoring the stab of pain in his shoulder as he held the gun with both hands. "Hey pal, whatchya doing? Where's your fucking green beret?"

The kid looked like he wanted to faint. He started to run, backpedaling and nearly tripping over his own feet.

"Freeze! I know how to use this, and don't think I won't. I cut my teeth shooting punks like you." The kid stopped. "Drop the knife on the ground."

He obeyed. "Who the hell are you?" he asked.

"A friend of the family," replied Kevin, picking up the knife. "Who the hell are you?" *Obviously not a cop.* He dropped the knife in a pocket.

The young man shrugged, didn't reply.

"Well, let's go meet your pals." Kevin again cradled the shotgun in the crook of his right arm. He closed his eyes for a second, feeling dizzy, fighting the tunnel vision, and then steeled himself, motioning the kid towards the back door. The dead leaves in the yard started dancing and he glanced up at a helicopter circling overhead, casting its spotlight back and forth. He was surprised he hadn't heard it, and resisted the urge to drop to his belly and shoot at it.

As they entered the house, Jack called from the dining room, "Hi, Al. Did you get the phone line?"

"Uh… not exactly," replied Al.

"What do you mean?" asked Jack, and then his eyes widened.

"Hey, guys. Did I miss the party?" asked Kevin, stepping into the living room. "Let's get rid of the guns, kids."

Paully grabbed Danny, pulling the kid in front of himself and holding his gun to the boy's head. Jack was backing away from Kevin.

"What the fuck are you doing, Paully?" yelled Eddie.

"Shut up," snarled Paully. "And you, cowboy. Drop your gun or the kid dies."

"Mine's bigger than yours." Kevin leveled the shotgun with both hands.

"I'll kill this kid." Paully's voice quavered as he poked Danny with the weapon.

"You don't want to do that. You want to spend the rest of your life in prison?" Kevin inched forward as he spoke. "Let the kid go." He kept moving, one step at a time. "You shoot him, you're dead. I won't wait for them to send you to jail. Judge, jury, and executioner right here."

"Stop. One more step, and I swear I'll kill this kid."

Kevin stopped, focusing his attention on the kid and the man holding him, everything else gone. Danny was trembling, with tears in his eyes. "Tough guy, aren't you? Picking on a little kid like this. You want a hostage? Take me." He set the shotgun on the floor and spread his hands, keeping them well away from his body. "Let the kid go. I'll make a much better hostage. No whining. I guarantee it."

Paully pushed Danny away and pointed the gun at the older man. He held it in one hand, stretched out straight and tilted sideways, gangsta style. "Back off or I'll shoot you; I mean it." His hands were shaking.

"Danny, get over there, by the kitchen." Kevin shifted his attention away from the man with the gun for one moment, watching the boy, who looked like he could barely walk. Then he refocused on the idiot in front of him, staring down the barrel of a little semi-auto. "Go ahead, scumbag. Think you can hit me at that distance? You know, right now you're looking at home invasion, assault—simple stuff. You shoot me and you're looking at life in prison for murder." He started creeping forward. "You ever been in a state prison? They'll like you—young and pretty." He made kissing noises. "Where do you think they'll send you? Auburn? Maybe Attica? Sing Sing?" He was nearly within reach now, towering over the younger man. "Lots and lots of guys. All of them bigger and tougher than you." He paused. "Then again, don't they have the death penalty in this state now?" He glared at the kid. "Wanna fry?" He reached towards the gun shaking in the young man's hand.

Paully pulled the trigger.

The tiny auto kicked hard despite its size. The bullet went over Duke's shoulder and just to the right of his head, burying itself in the plaster of the living room wall.

"Jesus Christ," Duke muttered as he ducked.

Danny gasped and grabbed the doorframe to keep from dropping to the floor. He wanted to cry. Thirteen years old and he just wanted to fall on the floor and bawl his eyes out. His ears were ringing from the gunshot and he could barely make out what Duke was saying.

"You're pushing your luck, creep," Duke said, straightening up. Danny could see the man's face was white, but the anger was still there in the set of his jaw.

"I told you to back the fuck off!" Paully was screaming now.

"Hey Danny, go in the kitchen and call the cops," Duke said, his gaze never wavering, still holding Paully in that icy stare.

"No! Nobody moves or I'll shoot."

"What? Again? You going to hit something this time?" He reached towards Paully once more. "Come on, man; give me the gun."

Paully looked towards the others for help, and then back at Duke. "You guys. Jack. Al. Help me out."

"No way, man," Jack responded. "You're on your own with this. I'm not gonna do hard time for kidnapping and murder."

Eddie was shaking his head, looking as though he had only just realized what was going on.

"Maybe we can walk away from it," said Al, looking from the front door to the back, as if deciding which way to run.

"Yeah, sure. You guys take me as a hostage; you'll walk away." Duke narrowed his eyes. "Cops will never shoot a hostage, and they won't risk hurting me by trying to hurt you." He smiled. "Come on, guys. Leave the kids here. Let's go."

"But Duke…" Danny started. He wanted to remind the man about the roadblocks, the helicopters, and the dogs.

"You shut up," Duke snarled at him, keeping his eyes on Paully.

Danny backed up, closer to the kitchen and the phone.

"You know, this may be a good idea." Paully looked like his brain was cooking. "Give me the keys to the car in the garage, kid."

Danny looked at Duke, waiting to see if it was okay with him. The man smiled without meeting his eyes. "Sure Danny, get the keys. In the kitchen, right? Next to the back door."

Danny understood. He moved towards the door. He didn't want to leave Duke with these guys, but he knew the man was giving him an out. Telling him to go. Sending him for help.

"Al, go with him," Paully commanded. He put his hand up to his head, as though it hurt to think. Lowering the gun a bit, he said, "Can we get something to eat?"

"Two o'clock in the fucking morning and you're thinking about food?" retorted Duke. "Let's just get in the car and go."

"Jack, you go outside and cut the phone line. Cut it this time; don't come back with another cowboy." Paully was almost shaking now.

Al looked like he was thinking hard. "Hey, Paully, this guy's got my knife."

"What are you talking about?" asked Paully.

Duke glared at Al, who was standing in the doorway of the kitchen, dividing his gaze between Danny and Paully.

"He took my knife off me when he surprised me outside."

"Al, get the motherfucker's knife." Paully grinned. "What were you going to do? Stick me when I relaxed a little?"

"Something like that," Duke replied, as Al removed a large serrated knife with a big black handle from his back pants pocket.

Paully stepped up to him and smashed him in the face with the gun. The older man staggered back a step, but didn't fall.

"You gonna be a hero, right? Don't even think about it, asshole."

Danny yelped and started towards Duke, but Al grabbed him and held him back.

"Easy there, kid. Take it easy." Al's voice was shaking, as though he needed to try to calm himself down at the same time.

Every fiber in Danny's body wanted to fight these guys. He wanted to kick and scream; do something. Anything. He considered biting the man who was holding him, but the more he squirmed, the harder it was to reach the guy's arm. He glared at Eddie, who looked like he wanted to melt. The teenager was still standing in the same place he'd been when Paully had first grabbed Danny. That seemed like hours ago now. His jaw was slack. The only sign of life he showed was when he occasionally blinked.

By two-thirty they were all in the kitchen except Al, who was tossing the den in search of the key for the ammo cabinet. He'd already broken the glass to get to the guns. Danny was standing by the microwave, watching a plate of food go around and around. His brain was in neutral; he almost felt like he was in shock. Jack was standing by the back door, smoking a cigarette, dropping ashes all over the linoleum. Eddie was sitting across the table from Duke. The older man was sitting next to Paully, who was still waving the gun around. Duke had a large red mark high on his cheek, by his eye. It was already starting to swell up. Danny had tried to get some ice for it, but Paully refused to allow it.

Danny was surprised by Duke's reaction to the situation. He had thought the man would easily overpower the three creeps; tie them up or something. Anything but what he was doing. He was sitting and appeared to be staring into space as if he couldn't think of what to do. Almost the same reaction Eddie seemed to be having. But this escaped murderer ought to be tougher than this, right? He should be able to overcome this crowd of misfits with one hand tied behind his back. So why wasn't he doing it? When was he going to make his move?

"Hey kid," Paully said to Danny, who jumped.

"What?"

"Can you make us some coffee?"

"I don't know how."

"You don't know how to make coffee?"

"I can do it," Duke muttered.

Paully narrowed his eyes and stared at the older man. "As long as you don't try anything."

"What the hell am I going to do, grind your nose?"

"Smartass."

"Sticks and stones."

"Just make the fucking coffee, old man."

"Yes, sir." Duke hauled himself to his feet.

Paully spoke to Danny. "Kid, can you get me something to eat?"

"Sure." Danny opened the freezer and handed the coffee beans to Duke, and then whispered, "What are we going to do?"

"Wait it out."

"So who are you?" Paully asked, chewing on a piece of fried chicken, one of those tiny unidentifiable pieces that come in a TV dinner.

Kevin wasn't going to answer; he didn't even bother looking at the man sitting beside him. "Who do you think I am?"

"Don't know. Maybe you're a friend of the kid. Come here to have a little homo rendezvous with him while his parents are out of town."

Jack snorted.

"Fuck you."

"Whoa," Paully said. "Big man." He picked up another piece of chicken, chewing like a cow working a cud. "You know who we are?"

This question he would answer. "Yep."

"You're so smart, tough guy, who are we?"

"All three of you walked away from the county jail. Your name is Paul Sandisfield. You were in for simple assault. Jack Otis was in for possession of marijuana. Alan Beckett was in for damaging public property. I can only assume he was cutting the heads off parking meters or something equally brilliant. You escaped yesterday afternoon; ran off from a work detail with two other guys. What you idiots didn't know is that you walked away right into the biggest manhunt this county has ever seen."

Paully put down his chicken. "How the hell do you know so much? You a cop?"

Kevin snorted. "I watched the news last night. You guys are all over it."

"Shit, Paully. How are we gonna get out of this?" whined Jack.

"Let's take a break, okay? We stay here for a couple of hours. Lay low and take it easy."

"There're helicopters out there," said Jack.

"I know, but they're not here yet," replied Paully.

Kevin listened to the exchange, making his plans. Make himself a target; give them something to pick on besides the kid. Easy. He'd done it before, through most of his childhood. He let his thoughts drift, absentmindedly rubbing the break in his nose, remembering a small apartment, a father with big fists, and the siblings he needed to protect.

He woke with a start. He'd heard something, a cry maybe, from the living room. He got to his feet and walked out there. There were two cops standing in the doorway, hats in their hands. His mother was crying. His first thought was that something had happened to his father. Something bad, he hoped.

"Ma. What's the matter?"

"Hank." She reached towards him. "It's Hank." She broke down in tears.

"What, Ma? What about Hank?"

One of the policemen cleared his throat, and then spoke. "He was with a group of anti-war protesters. They were resisting arrest. He fell against the sidewalk, and somehow—I don't know—he's dead."

Kevin felt his entire body go cold, right to his soul. "Some cop beat him up?"

"No, really. He was fine one minute; they thought he just had a concussion, and then he had a seizure or something. He died."

"Some cop killed my brother." The brother who had made him a great basketball player, helped him keep the other kids alive when their father raged. The brother he loved more than his mother, more than his other siblings, more than himself even. He wanted to lash out, to avenge his brother's blood, but he turned away from the door, walked back into the kitchen, and sat down again. The chair felt surprisingly warm, as though it was remembering what he was like before he knew. Before he went all cold inside.

Now he could hear his father. Oh great, he was coming home, probably drunk. He sat at the table, not moving, as his parents talked to the police. He listened to the police leave. He heard his father walk into the kitchen, stopping at the refrigerator. The man set something on the table, and then sat down. Kevin looked up. It was a six pack of Pabst

Blue Ribbon. What was this, some kind of peace offering? He took one and drank it in a hurry, hating the taste. His father did the same, tipping the can up and pouring the liquid down his throat. Kevin took another and drank two more in a space of twenty minutes. His father belched and got out another six pack. Kevin slowed down, but kept drinking.

He didn't bother running the next morning. He woke up with a pounding head and a dry mouth, and threw up in the toilet. He walked back into his room and looked at his little brother asleep in bed. He wondered if he even knew yet. Kevin walked out into the kitchen. His sister Jean was starting breakfast. She looked at him.

"What happened to you?"

He looked at her. She didn't know. Maybe it hadn't even happened.

"Are you okay, Kevin?"

He walked over to her and gave her a hug. Then he walked back to the table and sat down.

"There's something wrong, isn't there? That's why Mom isn't up, right? Did something happen to Mom? Did Dad kill her?"

He felt cold still, and he shivered. He almost felt like crying, and that led to shame, which led to embarrassment, and finally back to the cold anger. He shook his head. "Hank's dead."

Jean dropped the pan she had been holding. It clattered to the floor.

Chapter 12

A noise startled him and he looked out the kitchen window, his mind back in the present. He listened to the helicopter as it circled like an angry hornet. "They'll be here soon enough." *Come on guys, get mad at me. Pick on me.* Kevin felt his face throb. *Hit me again; I dare you.*

"Who?" Jack whipped his head around to stare out the window.

"Cops."

"Why? What makes you think that?" asked Jack.

"They're looking for someone, and they won't quit till they find him."

"Yeah, they're looking for us," said Paully.

"You really think all this is for you?"

"It's not?" Jack stepped closer to the table, towards the older man.

"You motherfuckers don't qualify for all this. If you hadn't screwed up your timing, they probably wouldn't even bother coming after you." He glanced at Danny, who was edging towards the door while he kept the shitheads occupied.

"So who are they looking for?"

"You'll find out eventually." He felt something warm running down his left arm, and glanced at it. Blood. *Oh, shit.*

"You know your arm is bleeding?" asked Jack.

"It does that."

"Who the hell are you?" asked Jack, cocking his head sideways like some kind of parrot.

"Your worst nightmare."

Paully snorted. "Yeah, right. What are you going to do, bleed on us? We've got the guns."

"Yeah, but we've got the brains." *Come on, Paully. That ought to at least qualify for a smack upside the head.* Instead, to his disappointment, it qualified for a pistol whipping. To the shoulder. He had a hard time staying conscious through the pain. *Don't pass out; don't pass out. They'll hurt the kid. Don't do it.* He fought the fuzzy brain and the ringing in his ears, trying to keep his senses.

"You'll keep your fucking mouth shut now." Paully smirked.

Kevin had to agree. He fought the urge to throw up. His head was starting to hurt, and his vision was narrowing again. He let his head drop to the table. The sound of the helicopters echoed in his brain. He knew where this was going, knew where his mind was taking him, whether or not he wanted to go. He let it go, not really having any choice.

Danny was standing by the door, still hoping for a chance to duck and run. The phone was dead; no way to call for help. The key would be to run for it, dodging bullets, and try to get help somehow. He knew there was help out there. He could hear the dogs. Hear the helicopters. They'd be here soon. The search he had been afraid of, the state police and the marshals he'd been dreading, would be here soon. He'd have to run to them, ask them to come back to the house, while trying to figure out a way to keep them from recognizing and arresting Duke.

He was still calling the man by the nickname; still refusing to acknowledge the fact this man in his kitchen was a cop killer. He winced with empathy as he saw Paully hit the man in the arm, knowing somehow how much that would hurt. He saw Duke lose the battle with consciousness, and hoped the man would be out for a while. He knew what Duke was doing—taunting the others—drawing their fire so Danny could be free to run. It hadn't worked so far, and Danny was ashamed he hadn't yet been able to live up to his end of the bargain.

"Hey, kid." Paully startled Danny with a loud request. "Get me some more food."

Danny rummaged through the freezer, searching for something to feed them. He was thankful now for his mother's enthusiastic overstocking of the pantry.

"What do you know about this guy?" Paully asked as Danny stuck a boxed frozen meal into the microwave.

Danny shrugged.

"What's he doing here?"

"He's just keeping me company."

"Who is he?" Jack chimed in.

"Just a friend."

"What's his name?"

"I always call him Duke." Danny watched as the man opened his eyes.

"What the hell kind of name is that? It sounds like a dog's name. So where'd he come from?"

Danny shrugged.

"You always let strangers into the house?" Paully laughed. "Well, maybe you do. You let us in."

When Kevin dragged himself back to reality they were talking about him. He lifted his head, looking around. He couldn't have been out very long, because everybody was still in the same place.

"What do you think? Is he a fed or something?" Jack asked.

"No idea. Why don't you search him, see if he has any ID?" Paully responded.

Jack looked at him. Kevin was looking back at him, with an icy-hard stare.

"You got any ID?" Jack asked.

"Nope." Not even a name, rank, and serial number. Give them nothing.

"He says he doesn't have any ID, Paully."

Paully didn't seem to want to search him, either. That actually cheered him up a little. They were afraid of him, even though they had all the weapons.

"Why don't you guys get some sleep?" Kevin said. His brain was still fuzzy. Still working at about half-speed.

"Shut the fuck up," growled Paully.

"You kiss your mother with that mouth?"

Paully raised his gun again, started to bring it down to hit him.

"Don't," Danny said, his voice trembling.

Shit, that changed the focus of their attention back to the kid. Kevin shot him a quick glance.

"Why the hell not?" responded Paully, stopping in mid-swing.

"He's hurt."

"Maybe I should hit you instead." The man stood up, and crossed the room towards the boy. "Or something else." Paully produced a wicked grin.

"Leave him alone," Kevin said.

Paully put a hand on Danny's shoulder, slid closer to him. Danny trembled.

"Who's going to stop me?" Paully asked, rubbing his crotch.

"Touch the kid and I'll kill you. Doesn't matter how or when, I will kill you." Kevin's voice was getting weaker.

Paully hesitated, backed up a step. "How are you going to do that?"

"I'll hunt you down and take you out. Don't think I won't. You'll be dead before you hear the shot."

"You really think you're capable of killing someone?" Paully said with a snort. "You don't look like you can tie your own shoes."

Danny drew in a sharp breath.

Kevin stretched out his right arm, trying to draw attention to the tattoo on his forearm. "I've killed a few people. I don't think you can tell me that I'm not capable of doing it again."

"What the hell are you talking about?" said Jack.

"I was right. He is a fucking cop." Paully walked back across the room and held the barrel of the tiny automatic against the man's head.

"Pull the trigger, Paully. Pull the fucking trigger." Kevin let his voice develop an edge.

Paully's hand shook.

"Come on, motherfucker. You man enough? Kill me; kill me now. Before I kill you. Before I chew you up and spit you out like the slimy piece of shit you are." He got right in the kid's face, up out of his chair, screaming at him. Then he grabbed the gun by the barrel, trying to get it away from him.

"Let go of it, asshole." Jack fired the shotgun into the ceiling.

"Holy shit!" Al yelled, covering his head and ducking.

Eddie actually yelped.

Kevin ducked and dropped his arm back to his side. Paully switched the gun to his left hand and punched Kevin hard in the mouth. He sagged backwards, grabbing for the table with his left arm, which brought renewed pain.

"Don't you guys know anything?" Danny shouted. "Look at his arm. That's a Marine tattoo."

"So?" Paully looked at the boy, backed up a step, out of the man's reach, while shaking his right hand.

A note of desperation came into the boy's voice. "Does the word Vietnam mean anything to you?"

Paully stared at Kevin. "You're that old?"

"Is that a compliment?" Kevin responded through clenched teeth. He looked straight at the younger man. "You should have killed me when you had the chance. You're dead. You're just still walking around. But you are so dead." He grabbed the chair, set it back upright, and settled into it, with a glance up at the huge hole in the ceiling.

Paully laughed as he lowered the gun, ignoring the threat. "I've seen movies about that war. It was cool. All jungles and firefights and shit."

"Yeah, cool." Kevin sneered. "You learn all your history from movies?"

"'I love the smell of Napalm in the morning.'" Paully paused for a moment, conjuring up images he had seen on some big screen. "Everybody got stoned all the time, and went around shooting kids and old people."

"Not me."

"So, what did you do?" asked Jack.

Kevin closed his eyes, took a deep breath through his nose. He wanted a cigarette. Fuck the cigarette; he wanted a drink.

"Leave him alone," Danny pleaded.

Kevin opened his eyes again, rolling them to look at Paully. "If I'm going to be telling stories, do you mind if I have a cup of coffee?" He would have preferred a shot of whiskey, but what could he do? It briefly crossed his mind to ask the kid to bring him the bottle of gin, but he fought off the urge.

"Yeah, sure, kid. Get him a cup of coffee." Paully looked like he had a sudden revelation. "I could use a drink myself. You got any beer in the fridge, kid?"

Kevin met the boy's eyes for a moment, his face set in a firm frown, the left cheek twitching a little.

Danny shook his head. "No."

"No beer? What kind of house is this?"

This is the kind of house where the men drink hard liquor, Kevin thought. He hoped the boy wouldn't offer the gin, hoped as well nobody would go looking through the cupboards. He didn't want to think about what would happen if they added alcohol to the mix in here.

Danny filled a stoneware mug with coffee and carried it over to Duke. The man took a sip, and then took a deep breath.

"So, what did you do?" Jack asked, pouring himself a mug of coffee.

"Joined the Marines when I was seventeen."

Danny felt his jaw drop. Seventeen. Only four years older than he was. How could someone that young go out and kill people?

Paully walked over to the fridge and began to root through it. He finally pulled out a carton of orange juice and lifted it to his lips, took several gulps, burped and put it back. Then he picked up a mug and poured a cup of coffee.

Jack continued the questioning. "So, what did you do? Sit in a trench and shoot at gooks?"

"I was a sniper."

"No shit."

Duke shot him a glance.

Danny noticed as he scanned the faces in the room that there was a different feeling here now. Not quite respect, but closer to it.

"So, you killed people," whispered Eddie, the first time he had spoken in what seemed like hours.

"I tallied fifty-five confirmed kills." He paused. "Lots of political hits. I can hit a target between the eyes from a thousand yards. Torso shots up to nearly fifteen hundred yards." Another pause. "Could, I could do that, then."

Danny picked up on it, despite the correction. The man said can, not could. He said he can hit a target from a thousand yards. Ties to organized crime, the newspaper said. Danny glanced towards Paully, wondering if he had heard it too.

Duke took a deep breath. "It was a long time ago. I didn't kill any civilians." Another pause. "Didn't kill any kids or old people, either."

"Fuckin' A." This from Paully.

Danny watched the man pull himself together.

"I know how many I killed; I know who I killed. Never flew over in a chopper and sprayed a bunch of people with a machine gun. I picked them off, one by one, from a distance. Lots of them were officers."

Eddie spoke up now. "You must be very brave, right?"

Duke gave him a hard stare.

"I mean, if you did all that stuff, killing people and all."

"You don't have to be brave to kill people," Duke said in a voice just above a whisper.

"But you're a hero," Jack persisted.

"No."

"You did brave things," Eddie insisted. "All that war shit."

He shook his head. "I did what I had to do. I'm not really very brave. I wanted to live, that's all."

"You get any medals?" asked Eddie.

"Two Purple Hearts and a Bronze Star." The man's voice was a whisper now, his head sagging toward the table.

Danny gulped. They didn't hand out medals to cowards. This man who worked so hard to deny being brave, who insisted he wasn't a hero, must be one.

"What'd they give you the Bronze Star for?" asked Jack.

Duke licked his lips and swallowed. He shook his head. Danny could swear he saw a glint of a tear in those cold eyes. Couldn't be, though.

"So are you screwed up in the head?" Paully asked. He looked around the room, reading the questions on the others' faces. "Well, a lot of those guys are, you know."

Danny bit his lip.

"Yeah. I am. You should be afraid. Very afraid." Duke snorted, a half-grin appearing on his face as he lifted his head in new defiance.

Danny waited, steeling himself for the blow he expected Paully to deliver. He anticipated the pain, knowing how much it would hurt even if it didn't come to him. It didn't come at all.

Instead, Al walked in and tossed a small key onto the table.

"Is that what I think it is?" Paully asked.

"Ammo cabinet," replied Al. He then tossed the badge from the desk onto the table.

"What the hell is that?"

"My dad used to be a cop," Danny blurted out. "That's an old badge of his."

"Is that true, Eddie?"

Eddie shrugged. "I don't know."

Danny stared at Eddie, shocked at the bald-faced lie. "You do too know. My dad came out and talked to your dad one time, told him to straighten up. He worked for the sheriff."

Eddie stuck out his lower lip in defiance. "Did not."

"I think it probably belongs to our friend here." Paully looked at Duke.

Duke looked away. "I am not a cop," he said in an almost inaudible voice.

Paully looked over at Danny.

Duke spoke again, louder now. "All right, whatever. I am a cop and you're all under arrest."

Paully laughed, a maniacal laugh that seemed to worry Duke. He'd apparently heard that sort of thing before.

"You're losing your grip, aren't you?" he asked.

Paully swung the gun this time, connecting with Duke's face once more. "I've had enough of you, smart-ass."

Danny started to come across the room, but Duke eyed him as he rubbed his jaw. The man shook his head, and the boy stayed by the door.

"Jack, you watch these two. I want to look at the guns." Paully got up, grabbed the key off the table, and headed into the den, accompanied by Al and Eddie.

Jack got to his feet, the shotgun shaking in his hands.

Danny looked at Duke, who was looking at him. He looked bad. His lip and arm were bleeding and one eye was swollen shut.

The man closed the other eye for a long moment, taking a deep breath through his nose, gathering himself. Then he opened his one good eye and shifted his gaze to the young man with the gun. "How long you been doing this kind of stuff, Jack?"

"What?" Jack almost jumped out of his skin as he swung the shotgun back towards Duke.

"You taken a lot of hostages before?"

Jack looked confused. "Do I look like I've done this before?"

"Frankly, no. I don't know what the hell you're doing with Paully. He's the one to watch. It was him that talked you into running, wasn't it?"

"Yeah."

"You should have served your time, Jack. You know you're looking at felony charges now. You won't do that kind of time in the county lockup."

"You talk like a cop. Are you sure you're not one?"

"Would it make a difference?"

"I don't know."

Duke lowered his voice. "You turn on them; it will go easier for you. You and me, we could take them, call the cops, and walk away alive."

"You must be a cop." Jack looked at the boy. "Is he a cop?"

Danny shrugged. "I don't know."

Jack looked at Duke again. "If you are a cop, Paully will probably kill you."

"You mean quicker than what he's doing now?"

"Yeah. I mean like he'll probably just shoot you in the head."

"I'd prefer that to the death-by-degrees thing he's got going." He looked towards Danny. "Is it okay if the kid gets some ice for my face now?"

"I don't know. If Paully comes back in here, he'll get mad at me."

"Well, we can't have that now, can we?" He looked out the window now; the sun was just starting to turn things gray. "Did you guys steal that truck?"

"Yeah."

"Well, that ought to lead the cops here. You idiots parked in the middle of the driveway, right where the helicopter can read the fucking license plate."

"Should we move it? Put it in the garage?" Jack sounded nervous.

"It's a little late now."

"Have you done this before?"

"What, hostages? Do I look stupid?"

"You just sound like you know what you're doing."

"Yeah," came a voice from the doorway. It was Paully. "That makes you either a cop or a con." He was holding a deer rifle with a scope mounted on it. He handed a pistol to Jack, who stuck it in his waistband. He leveled the rifle at Duke. "So which is it, motherfucker? You a cop or a con?"

"Shoot me. Go ahead. I don't give a flying fuck." Kevin dropped his head onto the table.

"Yeah, maybe I will. With this. This is your kind of gun, right? What do you think would happen if I held this against your head and pulled the trigger?" Paully laughed again.

That brought some very unpleasant pictures into Kevin's head. He kept his eyes closed and his head down. It would be better not to see it coming. He was so tired he had almost reached the point where he didn't care. He could see where this was going, this whole mess. It was going to end in a fucking firefight with the cops. He was going to die in this stupid fucking house in the middle of nowhere. This whole stupid run had gone wrong from the beginning. He'd paid that idiot corrections officer enough to walk out the gate; he was supposed to have handled the tower screws, too. Getting shot was not part of the plan. And this mess wasn't part of the plan, either. He never should have come here, allowed the kid to bring him here, or help him. These fucking assholes were going to kill him, or the cops would. The four-letter words were starting in his brain again. His face hurt. His arm hurt. He just wanted to go home.

"Why don't you go fuck your mother some more," he whispered to Paully.

Paully turned the rifle around and slammed the butt into Kevin's head, bringing him the release he needed.

Chapter 13

Danny stood by the counter, shivering, and staring at Duke, who was passed out cold, his head resting on the table. There was blood everywhere—dripping from his arm, his mouth, the cut on his cheek.

Paully walked over towards him again and Danny wanted to throw up. "Your friend can't help you now, can he?"

Danny glanced over at Eddie, who deliberately turned away.

Paully put a hand on Danny's shoulder. It felt like it was burning him. Danny shrugged it off, moving away.

"Where you going, little boy? Think you can get away from me? You give it to him, don't you? You can give it to me."

"Leave him alone, Paully," said Jack.

"What are you, my mother?"

"What'd you want to pick on a kid for?"

"Maybe I should pick on *you*." Paully crossed the room and got into Jack's face, leaning into him. Jack retreated, his back to the wall.

Danny heard sirens. First panic, then relief flooded every pore of his body.

"What's that?" asked Al, pushing past to look out the window towards the driveway. "Fuckin' A. State police."

"About time," said Duke, lifting his head. "Are we having fun yet?" He looked out the living room window. Danny followed his gaze. A mixture of state and local cops were standing behind their cruisers, with guns pointed towards the house in the early dawn. The three creeps were all staring in that direction.

"Go, Danny," Duke whispered.

"But, Duke…" Danny started to protest under his breath. How could he leave this man, the man who had risked his life to keep him safe? The glare from Duke was enough to send him towards the back door at full speed.

"Hey!" shouted Paully. "Who's watching the kid?"

"Obviously not you." Kevin got to his feet and headed towards Paully, swaying, his ears ringing. *Keep their attention; don't let them go after the kid.*

Jack grabbed Danny halfway out the door. "I don't think so."

Paully raised the rifle, pointing it at Kevin, who stopped. Paully then looked at Eddie. "I have an idea." He paused, shaking his head. "Fuck this. We should have just driven off when we had the chance." He walked over to Jack and grabbed the boy away from him, and then headed into the living room, pulling Danny along behind him.

Eddie, Al, Paully, and Danny all went into the living room, leaving Jack to watch Kevin in the kitchen.

Kevin moved to the doorway, watching as Paully grabbed Eddie and pointed him towards the front door. "You go out there," Paully said, "and tell them we've got two hostages. Tell them to let us go."

"Okay, Paully." Eddie opened the door, raised his hands over his head and marched out into the front yard. "Don't shoot!"

Kevin watched as the teenager ran out to the cars, and the cops took him around to the far side of the barricade. He continued to watch as Eddie talked to them, waving his arms, and pointing at the house.

Paully walked over to the open window, kicked out the screen, and then threw the rifle down on the sill. He stretched out on the floor, pulling the butt of the rifle into his right shoulder.

"Al, you take the boy over to the doorway. Keep the door open, and hold the kid in front of you with the gun on his head. Make sure the cops can see the gun."

"Paully, I don't know about this."

"Shut up!" Paully shouted. "You want to go to prison? You want to go to fucking Attica?"

Danny didn't resist as Al dragged him over to the front door. He had no idea how this was going to end. He couldn't see Paully going down easily. He had visions in his mind of the cops shooting tear gas into the room, a fire starting, and the whole house burning down. His mother would love that.

Tears welled up in his eyes as Al pressed the cold barrel of a large revolver into his temple.

"It's okay, kid," Al whispered. "I won't hurt you."

"I'm scared."

"So am I, kid. So am I."

Danny jumped as Paully fired the rifle out the window. The noise made his ears ring.

"Fuck me!" shouted Paully. "Come and get it, pigs!" He worked the bolt and fired another round.

Danny saw a police officer fall. He could feel his legs finally starting to give out. He sagged, and Al slipped an arm under his armpits, holding him up.

"Hang in there, kid, just a little longer."

Sally answered her cell phone, squinting at the clock. "Barnard." Who the hell would be calling her at 5:00 in the morning?

"Deputy Barnard, I've got a hostage situation inside your perimeter. I wanted to let you know that I'm redirecting my manpower to that, and away from the search for your fugitive."

"A hostage situation? Inside our perimeter?"

"Yeah. Close to that pipe under the railroad tracks."

She sighed. "Not my man?" *He wouldn't do that; it couldn't be him.* She tried hard to convince herself.

"I don't think so; they think it's the three from the county break. They're holding a kid and a man."

"Do you need our help?"

"No, ma'am. We're calling in the state SWAT team. This just means I'm pulling some of the manpower that was helping out on your search."

She frowned. Something the deputy sheriff had said struck a chord. "A man and a kid? Near the tracks?" She thought for a moment, considering the stuff she'd found in the pipe, the stuff that looked like it belonged to a kid. "Are your men still out there on it?"

"Yes, ma'am."

"Can you just keep me apprised? If it's inside my perimeter, there's always a chance my fugitive is involved."

"Sure."

She hung up the phone. No sense going back to sleep. She punched in the numbers of her team, one at a time.

Kevin eyed Jack, who was still holding the shotgun.

"Hey, Jack."

The young man swung around, leveling the shotgun at him.

Kevin raised his hands. "Hey, whoa there. I'm not a threat, okay?"

Jack jumped as the sound of another shot came from the living room. "What do you want?"

"I want what you want. I want to walk away from here in one piece, or at least in as many pieces as I am now." He chuckled, using every bit of strength he had to try to relax the young man.

Jack frowned. "Just sit tight and we'll all get out of here."

"No, we won't. Those cops aren't going to let us walk. Especially not with Paully in there shooting at them."

"Really?"

"Tell me. Did Paully mess with the kid while I was out? Did he hurt the boy?"

Jack thought for a moment. "Nah, he just scared the kid. Paully's a pretty scary kind of guy."

"You scared of him?"

"Fuck, yes."

"You give me that gun, I'll take Paully out."

"I can't." Another volley of shots from the living room drew Jack's attention.

Kevin sank back into the chair. He needed a plan. *Think.* If Jack wasn't going to cooperate, he would have to go. He turned his head at the sound of more sirens. Marvelous. Had Paully actually hit someone?

Kevin slid off the chair, crouching next to it. He ignored the pain in his shoulder, and the blood soaking his shirt. Jack was looking into the living room, walking that way, glancing sideways towards Kevin as he went. When his focus was towards the others, Kevin jumped. He wrapped his right arm around Jack's neck; using every ounce of strength he had left to immobilize him. He took the shotgun with his left hand, ignoring the screaming pain in his biceps. Jack fought back, but Kevin was taller and had a lot more knowledge of fight techniques. He swung around and slammed the butt of the gun against the young man's head. "Sorry, buddy," he whispered, as the young man slumped to the floor. He dropped to the floor himself as he heard another shot from the other room, but realized Paully was still shooting out the window towards the police. Not at him.

He swallowed hard as he sat up, tasting blood in his mouth, and still fighting the pain in his arm. Positioning his left arm tight across his chest, Kevin twined his fingers in the fabric of the shirt for support. He glanced at his shoulder and swore under his breath as he fought his way to his feet, trying to decide what to do. The last thing he needed was to get shot by these guys or the cops. *Give it up and go out the back way?* The house was surrounded, but at least they wouldn't think it was him shooting at them. He sure as hell didn't need an assault charge tacked on to his sentence. Or attempted murder. *But what about the kid?* What about the kid? The cops would make sure he didn't get hurt. Piece of cake; go right out the back door. He started heading that way and then stopped, letting his head hang for a moment. *Not without the boy.*

Okay, play it the same way he had before. Get them to kick the kid loose. Offer himself as the hostage; play their game. He took the handgun off Jack, emptied the bullets, and picked up the shotgun. He opened the back door and looked around, looking for the cops he figured were there. He couldn't see them, but he knew they were there. He didn't want to hang out in the doorway for too long, or a sniper would pick him off. He shuddered. *God, that was a scary thought.* He didn't want to be here, doing this shit. What the hell happened? He'd never been this stupid in his life. He never let himself get so soft, or cared about anyone like this before, except maybe his wife and his own kids. But why did he care about this kid? Why couldn't he just walk away?

He pushed Jack's inert body out onto the steps. Let his friends think he had abandoned them. He then walked towards the living room, thinking hard. How to get the boy away from them without getting him hurt? He tucked the gun into his waistband, in the small of his back, and pulled the shirt over it.

Wait a minute. He stopped, went into the den, and got another handgun out of the gun cabinet. He put in his back pocket without loading it. He didn't want anybody using it on him. Then he went into the kitchen and grabbed a steak knife out of a butcher block. This he inserted into his left boot. He took a deep breath, leveled the shotgun, and limped into the dining room. He could see it now—the whole scene—in his head.

He would go out there, outside, after he made sure the kid was safe. Then he'd get the cops to shoot him. He had no intention of going back to prison. He had no chance of making a run from here, with cops all over the place. There was no telling how soon the feds would arrive. He knew they would; they were in the fucking neighborhood, for chrissake. He wondered if that lady marshal would show up. Maybe she'd blow his head off. Somebody would.

Al was standing by the open front door, holding Danny with one hand and the revolver with the other. Paully was at a window, holding the deer rifle. This was going to be easier than he thought.

Duke crossed the room in two quick strides and pressed the barrel of the shotgun against Paully's head. "Drop it."

Paully rolled and swung the gun around. "Shoot the kid, Al! Shoot the fucking kid!" He pointed the rifle at Duke and Danny screamed.

"No!"

Duke pulled the trigger. Danny felt like someone had hit him in the head with a brick, and everything went black.

When he opened his eyes again, Duke was aiming the shotgun at Al. Holding it up, level, tucked into his shoulder, and looking down the barrel. Dead serious. Of course, Al was still holding him up, so the shotgun was aimed at him, too.

Al pressed the handgun tighter against Danny's head. "I'll kill this kid."

"Sure, go ahead. Shoot your ticket out of here." Duke smiled, the same little half-grin Danny had seen so many times before. "I've got no connection to that kid."

Danny stared into the man's eyes, cold as the bluish ice on a hockey rink. No anger, no nothing. Just that cold, unblinking stare. The man was covered in blood; some his own, some undoubtedly Paully's. And what had happened to Jack? The same thing as Paully? No, he hadn't heard a shot from in there. He tried to crane his neck and see around the corner, to figure out what had happened.

Al swallowed. He tried again, weaker this time. "I'll shoot him. I will."

Duke sighed. "Okay, pal. Time to give it up. It's been fun. Really it has, but don't you want to get out of here before they start throwing tear gas?"

Al persisted. "Put down the shotgun. If you shoot me, the kid will die."

"Okay, then. We've played this game before. I'll put the shotgun down, you'll let the kid go, and I'll be your hostage. The jury will go a lot easier on you with me for a hostage than a kid. And who knows, maybe you'll get away with it. You won't have to worry about taking care of the kid. Be a lot easier to dump my body in the river, wouldn't it?"

Duke put the shotgun on the floor and pushed it away with his foot.

"Yeah, and you'll pull out another gun and shoot me."

"You're smarter than I am. Oh, well." Duke took another gun out of his pocket and put it on the floor, too.

Al looked at him. Then he pushed Danny towards the steps, where he staggered and nearly fell. "I'm letting the kid go, but I've got one more hostage in here!"

Danny hesitated, looking towards Duke. He didn't want to leave him.

"Walk out there with your hands in the air, you understand? Walk slow, keeping your hands away from your body. Don't run. And tell them who I am, Danny."

"What?" asked the boy, confused. How could he possibly tell the police who Duke was?

Al looked hard at the man.

"Go on, Danny, before he changes his mind. Get out of here, and be sure and tell the cops my name."

Danny staggered down the concrete steps of his front walk and stumbled towards the police cars, with his hands up, just like Duke had told him. "Don't shoot."

"It's okay, kid; nobody here is going to shoot you." A dark haired female police officer motioned him over her way. "Are you okay?"

Danny nodded, and then bent over and vomited until it felt like his stomach was turning itself inside out.

The woman stood beside him, patting him on the back. "It's okay." When he straightened up, she spoke again. "Why don't you come and sit down? Daniel, is it?"

"No, uh, I mean, yeah, that's my name. Danny Rutledge. But I don't want to sit down. I need to watch. I need to see what's going on." Danny made his way towards the vehicles closest to the house.

"Are there more hostages in there?" asked a burly guy in a SWAT uniform.

Danny nodded. "Yes, one more hostage." He remembered Duke's insistence he tell the police his name. He wasn't sure he was ready to do that. He still couldn't see why; couldn't understand what the man was thinking.

The SWAT team leader turned to Danny. "What went on in there?"

"It's a long story. But they're down to one hostage. Just my..." He hesitated. He had been about to say friend, but he remembered something Duke had told him—something about aiding and abetting. "The two guys that are left, one of them is a young guy. I think his name is Al something; he escaped from the county jail last night."

"That makes two of them. Are you sure there isn't another one in there? A guy named Paully?"

"He's dead." Danny shuddered as he recalled the shotgun blast, the blood and guts splattered all over Duke, and the mess all over his mother's precious white carpet. What was he thinking? *Who cares about the carpet?*

"Do you know who the other guy is?"

Danny hesitated.

" Two people coming out, lieutenant." One of the other cops leaned over towards the man talking to Danny.

"Excuse me for just a minute, would you, son? Stay back, okay?" The lieutenant moved away. "I don't want anyone shooting, you understand me? I see one man with his finger on the trigger, it's a demotion." He looked at each of the other officers as he spoke.

Danny watched as Al shoved the gun against the right side of Duke's head and grabbed his arm. The two of them walked down the front steps. Duke was staggering a little, forcing Al to almost hold him up. That looked good, thought Danny. That made it look like Duke was a real hostage. An innocent man.

"I'll kill him, if you don't back off!" Al shouted, his voice shaking.

The sun was higher in the sky now, coming out from behind the clouds for a second. Al hesitated, holding his hand up to his eyes to shield them.

Chapter 14

When they arrived at the county complex, Sally hurried down the hall to the sheriff's office and entered without knocking. Crandall looked like he had been up all night. He was just setting the phone down.

"Have you been over to this hostage thing?"

"No. I was thinking about it, but I've got an awful lot going on, between that and your thing. Can't do everything myself."

"Would I be in the way if I headed over there?"

"Yeah." He met her eyes, and she knew he was happy to have found a reason to pull rank on her.

"Okay. You know anything about it?"

The deputy leaned back in his chair, rubbing at the stubble on his chin. "It's a kid I know. Son of a former deputy. Kid is about thirteen. His mother left him alone this weekend; I've been checking up on him. I guess my three county fugitives broke into his house and now they're holding him hostage."

"I'm sorry to hear that. You said there was a man being held as well."

"Yeah, I can't figure that out."

"You know there was some evidence in that culvert of a kid using it."

"Not this kid. He wouldn't help your fugitive."

"How far is the culvert from this kid's house?"

"Mile or so."

"You don't think there's any possibility that this kid helped my fugitive?"

"I've been talking to the kid on the phone all weekend. He hasn't said anything unusual."

"If he was helping a fugitive, do you think he'd tell you?"

Crandall frowned. "Even if the kid did help him, your man wouldn't let himself get taken down by these three clowns. Didn't you tell me he's ex-CIA? It can't be Markinson."

"So where is he, then?"

"Maybe he slipped through somehow. Maybe he's hiding somewhere. How the hell do I know?"

"Anybody on the scene have a visual of the two hostages yet?"

Crandall shook his head.

"Have you talked to the kid's mother?"

"Yeah, just got off the phone with her. She's on her way here." He shook his head again. "This is nuts."

"Do you want to know who I am now, Al?" Kevin asked.

"What?" The younger man turned his head.

"My name is Kevin Michael Markinson. This whole party was for me. The helicopters, the dogs, the fucking National Guard. Do you understand?" He looked into Al's eyes, giving him the stare. "I escaped from a medium security state pen Thursday morning, for the third time. I was down on a murder rap. I was convicted of killing a cop."

Al looked like he was going to faint. "Fuckin' A."

"Those cops would love to shoot me themselves. They're certainly not going to hesitate to let you do it." Kevin smiled. It hurt. He could feel blood dripping from his lower lip.

"God damn."

"Yeah. Cool, isn't it?"

"What the hell do I do now?"

"Well, the way I look at it, you can put the fucking gun down, or you can get shot. I recommend the former, from personal experience."

Al looked like he was going to be sick. He looked around, staring at the cars, the cops. He lowered the revolver.

"Hold your fire," the lieutenant said under his breath.

Al threw the gun on the ground and raised his hands as he walked towards the police. The other man was left standing alone, swaying, and looking like a good breeze would knock him over. The rain that had been threatening all weekend finally started, with big drops hitting the ground, raising little puffs of dust.

Danny felt as if everything was moving in slow motion.

Duke stood his ground, waiting, and blinking the raindrops out of his eyes. The cops were waiting too, watching him. Most of them were still holding their guns across the hoods of the cruisers. Jack was sitting up in the back of an ambulance, his head bandaged. Al was leaning against the hood of another car, legs spread, in the process of being searched. Yet another ambulance was just leaving the driveway, red lights and siren on.

"Are you all right, sir?" the big lieutenant shouted. Speaking softly, he said to his men, "Stay here; wait for him."

"What's going on, Mike?"

"I don't know." He looked over at the boy. "I just have a feeling about this; that's all."

Danny realized he had to tell them. He had to protect the officers, just in case. He turned to the man next to him. "His name is Markinson, Kevin Markinson."

"Shit," said the lieutenant. "This man is a fugitive, guys. Big time. Watch it." To Danny he said, "Does he have a gun?"

"I don't think so."

The lieutenant directed his next command to Duke. "Time to give it up, Markinson. Let me see you down on the ground, arms away from your body, face down, palms up. You got that?"

The man turned his head, slowly, as though he was moving through jello. He took a couple of steps towards the army of cops and Danny felt the tension rise. Somebody racked the pump on a shotgun, the sound echoing in the silence.

Danny was watching Duke, wondering what was going on in his head. *Did the man want to go back to jail or not? Why didn't he just give up? He'd set it up that way, hadn't he? That was why he wanted them to know who he was, right?* But Danny began to realize, as he watched the man reach for something behind his back, that there might be another plan in his head. This man claimed to be a coward, but he was actually brave. He had done what he could to keep himself alive; and he didn't want to go back to jail. It looked like he might have something else in mind.

The rain was falling harder.

"On the ground, Markinson!"

When he saw the man reaching, saw his hand going behind his back, Danny darted around the back of a small SUV and ran towards Duke. He had figured it out now, figured out what the guy was planning, and he wasn't going to let it happen. He wasn't going to watch Duke go down in a rain of fire. He wasn't going to let him die.

"Hold your fire!" the lieutenant shouted.

"No, Duke, no!" Danny heard himself shouting, as if he was in a dream, or in another world. The words echoed in his brain.

Duke looked at him. Danny could see the confused look in his eyes; the cracks in that ice were wide open now. The man looked vulnerable, unsure of himself, not even aware of what he was doing. He looked at the gun, as if wondering why he had it. He chucked it off to the side and raised his hands. Or tried to. As he lifted his arms his legs buckled and he sagged to the ground.

Danny tried to catch him. He reached for the man, felt the dead weight, and couldn't hold him. He turned towards the police. "Can't you see he's hurt?"

In a matter of seconds there were three police officers on Duke, one with a gun jammed into the base of his skull.

"Don't you move, asshole."

Duke closed his eyes and tried to turn his head so his mouth was out of the dirt.

"I'm so sorry," Danny said, even as the dark haired woman cop put an arm around his shoulder, pulling him away. "I'm so sorry." He wanted to cry now. He'd held it off for so long. He'd been through so much, and the relief was so great, it was like a wave hitting him. It was pouring now; the rain coming in huge drops with no space between them, and he turned his face up and let it wash over him.

Chapter 15

The big SWAT guy waved at the EMTs now. They brought a stretcher, trotting over the puddles. The cop pushed Danny away.

"Somebody take this kid out of here." He leaned over the man as the EMTs worked. "What's your name?"

Kevin mouthed the words.

"Speak up, I can't hear you."

"Kevin Michael Markinson." He paused. "Staff sergeant, United States Marine Corps. Serial number... uh," his voice trailed off.

"Sure, buddy. Sure you are." He turned to another member of the team. "You heard that, right?" He turned back to the wounded man. "Kevin Markinson, you're under arrest for felony escape. You have the right to remain silent. Anything you say can and will be used against you in a court of law. You have the right to an attorney. If you cannot afford an attorney, one will be appointed for you."

"He didn't do anything!" Danny tried to run to where the officer was standing, but the female officer held him back. "He kept me safe. You can't arrest him for that." Danny watched as Duke was strapped down, and then loaded into the ambulance. He could see fresh blood oozing down the man's arm, running off into the wet dirt. His face was white, and his breathing was shallow. But the worst was the look on his face. His eyes were open above the plastic oxygen mask, but it was as though any spark of life he'd had was gone. Even from here he could see that. The man's face was a mass of bruises, but there was more. The ice was gone from his eyes. They had that unfocused sort of look from before—that time in the pipe when the man had been having a flashback or whatever it was that had been going on. The time he was not there. It was like he was here now, physically, but he wasn't here. His brain was somewhere else.

Danny found himself wishing he could start the day over. Why had those three creeps chosen his house? Why had Duke come in? Why hadn't the man just run? He knew though; the man couldn't have run, knowing Danny was in danger. It was a weird conclusion. It made him wonder what was going on. Kevin Markinson the cop killer wouldn't have done that. Wouldn't have sacrificed his freedom for a kid, would he?

"I don't want to stay here alone," Danny said to the entourage in general, not really focusing on any of the cops. He was shivering in the early morning air; shivering not just from the cold and the rain, but from the whole thing. He wanted to cry. He kept trying to swallow the lump in his throat, but it just wouldn't go.

"Okay, you can come with us," said one of the police officers, the dark-haired woman with the name Santiago on her name tag. "Maybe we can call your parents from the hospital." She tried a tentative smile, and Danny was sure she was going to offer him a lollipop next. After helping Danny into the back of a Ford Bronco, Santiago radioed in. The boy listened.

"Can you patch me through to County?"

"Ten-five."

"County dispatch."

"This is unit twelve. Can you get me to Deputy Sheriff Crandall?"

"How are we going to handle the hospital?" her partner, Buckley, asked. "The SWAT team isn't coming with us, right?"

Santiago held up a hand. "Deputy Crandall? We have the boy and we're transporting three fugitives to the hospital." She raised her eyebrows and looked towards her partner. "Kevin Markinson. Yeah. We've got two others, as well. One of the county fugitives is dead. No. Uh, Jack Otis and Alan Beckett. You'll contact the Marshal's service, right?" She listened for a moment. "You've already called them? At the hospital, right. Thanks." She put the radio mic away.

"Okay. You stay with Markinson, while I keep an eye on the kid. The sheriff already called his mother. He'll meet us there with her. He's going to send the Marshals to take possession of Markinson, too."

Kevin Markinson, cop killer, was gone, at least mentally. He was conscious again, with help from the oxygen mask on his face. But he let his mind slip. No sense wasting energy on an impossible situation. No more gun, but he still had the knife in his shoe. *Wait for a chance.* He wondered why he was being given a chance. He should have died back there; those cops should have killed him.

When the car stopped at the hospital, Santiago helped Danny out and they headed towards the ambulance entrance.

Buckley followed the stretcher into the building.

Danny was watching, with tears welling in his eyes. Santiago took his arm. "Come on, let's go wait for your mom."

Danny looked back at Duke as they wheeled him away. "Is he going to be okay?"

"Yeah, he's probably just weak from losing all that blood. Looks like somebody was using him as a punching bag. What went on in that house?"

Danny didn't think she actually expected an answer. He wasn't sure he could have given her one. He followed her as she headed over to talk to Buckley.

Danny watched through the open door as a young doctor bent over Duke. Buckley was sitting in a chair outside the treatment room, looking bored, but he got to his feet as Santiago approached.

Danny drifted away from them as they chatted, staring into the room. The gray-haired nurse started taking Duke's vital signs, while the doctor cut away the bloody shirt and the soaked gauze.

"Blood pressure eighty over forty," the nurse announced.

The doctor looked up. "What happened to him, anyway?"

Santiago poked Buckley and he cleared his throat. "He was shot."

"This is old, though."

"Yeah, he was shot Thursday morning."

"Looks like he was beat up pretty good, too." The doctor touched the bruise on Markinson's temple, and then shone a penlight into the man's eyes.

"Yeah, I guess." Buckley shrugged.

"He was beat up this morning," Danny put in.

The doctor looked over. "What's with the kid?"

"We were just leaving." Santiago pulled on him, as Danny tried to get one last look at Duke.

Kevin pulled his hand away as the nurse tried to draw some blood from his arm.

"What's his name, officer?" asked the doctor.

"Kevin Markinson."

"Oh, yeah? The guy who's been all over the news? Mr. Markinson. Hey, look at me."

"Sergeant, you idiot. I'm a fucking sergeant." Kevin opened his eyes and turned them towards the voice. Where the hell was he? Didn't look like the hospital at Da Nang, although it did look like a war zone. It seemed as if the place was packed.

"Look, we're trying to help you, but you've got to cooperate. We need to draw some blood." He turned to the nurse. "Get a type on him; he's going to need a unit of whole blood." He paused as he examined the wound. "I want an X-ray, ASAP. We'll probably need a CAT scan, too." He spoke to Kevin again. "We're going to need to clean this up, okay?"

"Yes, sir," Kevin muttered, and then closed his eyes. He felt the cold of the fluids dripping into his veins. He didn't want to slip away, as tempting as it was. The voices were getting fuzzy. He relaxed a little, letting the blackness come, but trying to keep from going completely. He struggled to figure out where he was, trying to remember what had happened. The pain in his arm was familiar, but he didn't remember getting shot. Nothing was making sense. It looked like a civilian hospital.

"We need to get him upstairs for an X-ray, and we need you to fill out some paperwork for us," the nurse said to Buckley, as the doctor studied the man's arm.

"You think he's going to stay put?"

"He's out," she replied.

"Okay." Buckley turned away. "They'll bring him back here, right?"

"Sure," she said. "Maybe not right here, though. We've got a car accident coming in."

"Any news on the police officer they brought in earlier? Guy's name is Steve Worton?"

Kevin didn't hear the reply.

While Santiago pulled him towards the exit, Danny watched as a huge black man with ropes of long greasy hair pushed the gurney with Duke on it out of the treatment room.

Buckley turned away, and then stopped. "Oh, you know what, let me just cuff him to the gurney." He slapped a pair of cuffs on Kevin's right wrist and headed for the desk.

Chapter 16

Kevin stayed quiet, but gnawed on his lower lip until he tasted fresh blood. The pain kept him sharp. It was coming back to him now. He knew where he was, sort of. It looked like a civilian hospital because it was a civilian hospital. No telling where; he had no idea where he had even been for the last few days. Somewhere upstate, but it didn't really matter. As the orderly wheeled him into an elevator, Kevin realized the man was talking to him. He focused on the words, keeping the ringing in his head at bay.

"All over the news, aren't you?" the man said.

Kevin kept his eyes closed, keeping up the appearance of unconsciousness.

The man leaned over and talked into Kevin's ear. "Hey Duke, you go for it. Cut out when you get a chance."

Kevin opened his eyes and the big man winked at him. "Teddy?"

"Yeah, man."

"What the hell?" He tried to remember where he had seen this guy before. "Clinton?" Had they brought him all the way up to Dannemora?

"Yeah. I'm out. Doing this as part of my parole."

Kevin stared at the big man. "No way."

"Yeah. My old lady lives near here; they figured I'd be more settled with a job down this way."

"Really? So I'm not at the prison?"

"Nah, this is Saint Francis hospital. You want to go back to sleep now, 'kay?"

Crandall stepped into the office, hat on his head. "Deputy Barnard?"

Sally looked up. "Yeah?"

"We've got your man."

She got to her feet. "You have a positive ID this time?"

"Apparently he admitted it. They're taking him to a local hospital. You were right all along; he was with the boy. Guess my county escapees worked him over pretty good." He chuckled. "He wasn't as tough as you thought, ay?"

She frowned. "Why are they taking him to a local hospital? Why not take him up to the prison hospital?"

"That's a couple of hours away. He was hurt pretty bad. The state SWAT guy says he was barely conscious. He gave him his name and rank, like he was still in the Marines. I don't think he's going anywhere."

"God, he's delusional. Somebody watching him?"

"Yeah, one of the locals."

"You make sure they watch him close. He's not going to cooperate if he's out of his mind, you understand?" Crandall nodded and Sally looked over at her team. "Thomas. You're with me. You two finish up here and we'll meet you back at the office. Somebody call off Nate. I am so glad this is over." She grabbed her bag and hurried out after the deputy sheriff.

Kevin closed his eyes as the elevator doors opened and Teddy wheeled his patient towards X-ray. "Might be a bit of a wait. Things are crazy here today."

The technician poked her head out. "It's going to be at least twenty minutes before I get to him, okay?"

"Sure. Look, I'm gonna park him here in the hallway. I just want to get a cup of coffee. I'll be gone at least ten minutes myself." He lowered the rail on the side of the gurney, and started whistling as he walked off.

The painkillers were doing their job. Kevin opened his eyes and had a hard time focusing, but he recognized a chance when he saw one. He looked at the cuffs. There was an IV needle stuck in the back of the same hand. This was going to take some doing. He reached across his body with his left hand, peeled off the tape, pulled the IV needle out of his right hand, and then sat up, pulling against the cuffs. He gripped the side of the cart as waves of dizziness washed over him. Now the hard part.

Buckley hadn't tightened the bracelet down. Kevin concentrated for a moment, pulling his hand towards his body, and slipped his right thumb out of joint, letting his hand slide through the handcuff. He climbed off the gurney, surprised at how cold the floor felt. What happened to his fucking shoes? He looked down. At least he still had his pants. He pressed his hand against the gurney and popped the thumb back into joint, then yanked the oxygen mask off his face and held his left arm with his right as he wobbled down the hallway.

Danny followed Santiago, looking back again to see Buckley leaning over the desk.

"I need to use the bathroom."

Santiago looked around. "Hold on a minute." She walked back to the desk and then pointed in the general direction for Danny.

It was maybe ten minutes later, as he was coming out of the bathroom, that a petite red-haired woman with fire in her eyes stormed through the door with a younger man wearing a blue windbreaker on her heels. She showed a badge to the receptionist and was pointed towards Buckley, who was sitting by the empty treatment room, scribbling on some papers.

"I'm Deputy Sally Barnard, US Marshal's service. Are you Buckley?"

"Yes, ma'am." He stood up and offered his hand. She ignored it, looking past him at the curtained-off area.

Danny came to a stop, staring at the woman. He remembered seeing her on the television.

"Where's my prisoner?"

"They took him up to X-ray."

"Your partner with him?"

Buckley looked over towards Santiago. "Uh, no, he was out cold, and I had some paperwork to do, so I figured…" His voice trailed off.

Barnard turned. "Thomas—find X-ray. Call me when you get there. For your sake, Buckley, he had better be there. I can't believe this. You left him alone?" She paced for a minute, and then went to the desk again.

Santiago pulled at Danny's arm. "We should go back out to the waiting room."

He shook his head. "I just want to hear this."

Kevin looked down at his hand and realized it was bleeding. Obscenities ran through his brain. He located a supply closet, found some gauze and tape for his hand, and then took off his prison issue pants, slipping into a set of surgical scrubs, complete with hat, mask and booties. Working his arm through the sleeve took a bit of doing, and he nearly passed out when he got the shirt caught on the tape. He refused to give in to the blackness at the edge of his vision. He didn't want that now, didn't want to sit and rest for a minute.

Gritting his teeth, he pulled the mask down around his neck, figuring it was enough to throw people off. He didn't want to attract too much attention by walking around with it over his face. Remembering the money, he took the twenty dollars out of his pants and tucked it into the pocket of the shirt. He thought for a moment, grabbed a pair of latex gloves and slipped them on. Then he headed for the nearest elevator. After pushing the button, he folded his arms, trying to support the left one with the right without attracting too much attention. He turned his head and slouched as the door opened, wondering why he had been cursed with this height. A young man with curly brown hair got off, wearing a blue windbreaker with some sort of gold writing on it. Kevin looked at the man as he walked away, struggling to focus his vision, and realized the jacket said POLICE and US MARSHAL on the back. *Holy shit.* Kevin grimaced and stepped into the elevator, took a deep breath, and let it out in a sigh as he punched the button marked G, shaking his head.

Sally answered her cell phone. "Thomas? Tell me you found him."

"Sorry. He's gone."

"I expected that. Okay, I'll get security; you start scouting around up there." Closing the phone, she turned towards Buckley. "I hope you know how to sweep floors, buddy, because that's all you're going to be doing when I get through with you. He's gone."

She turned back to the receptionist. "I need to talk to whoever is in charge of security." She waited, her temper boiling while the woman dialed, and then took the phone.

"Hello, this is Sally Barnard, Deputy US Marshal. Who am I speaking to?"

"Robert Byrd, chief of security."

"Okay, Chief Byrd. I have a problem. We need to seal this building; I have an escaped prisoner."

"An escaped prisoner?"

"Yes, sir. He was being treated for a gunshot wound."

"You have a description?"

"Okay." She paused to take a breath, then called up the statistics from memory. "Six four, forty-five years old, one-sixty, long blond hair, mustache, blue eyes, Marine tattoos on his arms. His name's Kevin Markinson."

"The guy on the TV?"

"Yes."

"I can seal the building; post my guys at the doors."

"Okay, thanks." She hung up the phone and turned towards Buckley. "I don't believe this."

Buckley shrugged.

Santiago stepped closer to the desk. "Where's the prisoner?"

"That's a good question."

"He got away?"

Buckley nodded. To Barnard he said, "His hair's brown by the way, short and brown."

"Nice of you to let me know." Sally opened her phone again and punched in the numbers. "Thomas."

"Yes, ma'am."

"Local cop says our man has short brown hair now."

"Like he shaved it," said Buckley.

"Shaved. You got that?"

"Got it."

Kevin pushed himself off the wall as the elevator came to a stop, and stepped out, looking for an exit. It didn't take more than a few seconds to figure out he had been deposited right back in the middle of the emergency room area. It still looked crazy in here, with three patients in the hallway and people in scrubs running around. Scanning for a way out, he spotted yet another problem in the form of one more of those blue windbreakers with the gold letters on it. The red-haired woman marshal he'd seen on television was standing by the nurse's station, talking into her cell phone. She was between him and the exit. In addition, there were hospital security guards standing by the door, shifting from foot to foot, talking to each other. He hesitated, and then decided to just go for it.

He headed straight for the door, and excusing himself to the older of the two guards, walked through the first set of automatic sliding doors. Glancing back, he saw the marshal put the phone down. Her eyes met his for one second.

"Hey, you, wait just a minute there."

One more set of doors. He increased his pace. Chances were she didn't even recognize him. Not with his face looking like this, and his hair cut short.

"Uh, doctor?" This came from one of the guards. He ignored the man and kept going.

"Thomas, I think he just walked right by me." She dropped her cell phone and pulled her Glock. "Markinson!"

He turned his head, looked right at her. She was close enough that she could see the bruises on his face, see fresh blood on his lower lip. He turned away and kept walking.

"Stop him! Stop that man!" She ran towards the door, watching in disbelief as her fugitive walked right out the door and took off running stiff-legged through the parking lot. She had her gun up, but there were way too many civilians around to get off a shot. What the hell were all these people doing here on a Sunday morning?

He was tall, but he had a bum leg. She could catch him; she knew she could. Tucking the gun back in its holster, she ran after him. She gasped as he ran right in front of a car on its way out of the lot, heard the squeal of the brakes. In what seemed like less than a second, he yanked the driver's door open, pulled the woman out of the car, and jumped in. Sally got her weapon out again now, she was within ten yards, but with him in a vehicle she wasn't going to catch him. As the tires squealed in protest she considered emptying the clip into the back end of the hatchback. Then he was gone.

Green Honda Civic. New York plates. She walked towards the woman on the ground as she recited the number to herself.

"Are you all right?" Sally offered her a hand, and helped her to her feet. She grabbed for her cell phone. Gone. Dropped inside.

"I, uh, I think so. What was that?"

"Escaped prisoner, ma'am." Sally went back into the hospital, close to the boiling point.

He drove south for an hour or so and stopped at a shopping plaza. He sat in the parking lot, drumming his fingers on the steering wheel, because the store wasn't open yet. When they opened the doors, he dropped the keys into the glove compartment, tucked the woman's purse under the seat, and locked the door as he got out. He headed for Bradlees to find something else to wear. He pulled the rubber gloves off as he went into the store, selecting a cheap pair of canvas sneakers and gray sweat pants, leaving just enough money for a pack of Camels.

"Rough morning, doctor?" The cashier smiled at him as she took his money.

"Yeah." He was surprised by the sound of his own voice, the exhaustion and obvious pain. He cleared his throat. "Can I get some matches?"

He changed in the bathroom, leaving the scrub top on, and dumped the bottom half of the scrubs in the trash. It was nearly two when he stepped out of the store. An ancient, rusting Volkswagen Beetle pulled up to the curb. A bearded young man jumped out and ran into the store, leaving the engine running. Kevin walked over, opened the car door, and climbed in. As he adjusted the rear view mirror he saw two small faces reflected in it. Turning around he saw there were young children in the back seat.

He slammed the palm of his hand on the steering wheel. "Shit." He clenched the steering wheel and took a deep breath. "Okay, kids. Out of the car, wait for your daddy on the sidewalk." Kevin reached across and popped the passenger side door open.

The little one whimpered. The older one took his sister's hand and shoved the seat forward, pulling her out onto the sidewalk. The boy pushed the door shut, and Kevin shoved the VW into gear. He peeled out just as the man came out of the store.

He abandoned this car less than an hour later, in another parking lot, next to a pay phone. Once again he locked the keys in the vehicle. It felt like forever before a beige Cadillac pulled up, and Kevin was sure the cops were going to show up at any minute. He climbed into the back. "What took you so long? Do you ever check your messages?"

"Sorry, boss, I was going over security for a Stevie Nicks concert upstate, up in Woodstock. My wife beeped me there. How's it going?"

"I guess it could be worse. At least I finally got you. I need a place to crash."

"Let me make a call." Justin Stewart picked up a cell phone while waiting at a red light. He talked for a minute. "Okay boss, we've got an empty apartment. I'll take you there."

Kevin lit a cigarette, leaned back, and closed his eyes at last.

Chapter 17

The two deputy marshals were in the waiting room, Sally alternating between pacing and checking her cell phone to make sure she hadn't missed a call. "He's long gone by now," Thomas said, pointing out the obvious.

"We know where he's going, don't we?" she said. "He'll head for the city. We've got his wife's house under surveillance, taps on her phone and his lawyer's phone, and we're updating the police every shift. We ought to be able to find him." She looked at her phone again. "I guess we go back to the sheriff's office for now. No sense hanging around here any longer."

Danny was sitting alone now in the lobby of the hospital. The two local cops were engaged in furious conversation on the far side of the room. He found himself rooting for Duke; wishing he would make it. The man deserved to get home; deserved to see his wife and kids.

Danny watched his mother approach from the far side of the room and realized he'd never seen her look quite so white and shaky. His mom was actually trembling. Danny stood up, and she grabbed him in a bear hug.

"Are you okay?"

"Yeah, Mom. I'm fine."

"They didn't hurt you?"

"Nobody hurt me. Nobody even touched me." He pulled back, embarrassed to be seen hugging his mother in public. He noticed Deputy Sheriff Crandall standing behind her at this point. He swallowed hard, wondering if it was going to start now, if he was in trouble for helping Duke.

"Deputy Crandall says you had quite a group in the house this morning." Danny could see his mother was staring at him hard as she spoke, and her voice was tinged with fear.

"Yes."

"You let them in?"

"It's a long story."

"Are we free to go, Sheriff?"

Crandall nodded, and then cleared his throat. "I guess I should go see what's going on with this escape."

Kevin stepped aside as Justin opened the door, and then limped into the small apartment. It was clean and very simply furnished, yet it still managed to look comfortable. Off-white wall-to-wall carpet, beige sofa, galley kitchen. It smelled stale though, as if no one had been in the place for ages. He went into the narrow kitchen and opened the fridge. "Justin?"

"Yeah, boss?"

"Come here." He started taking out five six packs of Budweiser, piling them on the kitchen floor. "Who was here before me?"

"Been empty for a while, but you know, booze keeps well," replied Justin.

"Actually, Justin, any booze around me doesn't have to keep well. You know that. You can take it home with you, okay?" Kevin walked around the small kitchen, opening the cupboards. "Here, take these, too." He pulled out several bottles of various kinds of liquor. *No Jack Daniel's, thank God.*

"Do you need anything?" Justin asked.

"Yeah, I need some stuff from Cindy's house."

"They're probably watching her."

"I know. You think you can get there and back without a tail?"

"Sure." The younger man responded to the challenge with a grin.

"Can I borrow some cash, too?"

"How much do you need?" Justin pulled a roll of bills out of his pocket.

"A hundred." Kevin sat down with a pen and paper and wrote up a list of the things he needed—clothes, watch, shoes. He handed the list to Justin and hunted up a phone book. "Some of this stuff is in my safe. She knows the combination."

"I'll see you in a bit then, okay?" Justin said, as he handed Kevin five bills.

"Oh, hey, no. You don't need to do that today. It's Sunday, right? Tomorrow will be fine." Kevin looked up from the phone book. "You go home, or go do your security thing, or whatever."

"Thanks, boss."

"Thank you, Justin." He looked up again. "Can you call Cindy and let her know I'm okay?" He thought for a moment. "And would you bring me some bottled water? Tomorrow?"

"Sure. Here're the keys." Justin tossed the keys on the coffee table and started to head out.

"Justin?"

"Yeah, boss?"

"Chocolate. Bring me some chocolate, okay?"

Justin smiled. "Sure, boss. Get some sleep. You look like shit."

Kevin called a Chinese take-out restaurant and ordered some food. Then he put his feet up on the couch and smoked while he waited.

Sally sat in the hard wooden chair in the sheriff's office and stared at Crandall.

"They didn't know."

"What the hell do you mean they didn't know? The whole bloody county was swarming with cops looking for him and they didn't think he was worth keeping an eye on?"

"Look. I told you, Deputy Barnard, there were two local officers with him. One of them stayed with the boy; one of them was watching Markinson. The man was unconscious for God's sake. How could he just get up and walk away?"

"That's what he does." She got to her feet and started pacing. "He's escaped from custody no less than four times, Deputy. Your local officer couldn't even be bothered to stay with him." She really wanted to keep on with this, but couldn't see the point, so she sighed and shifted gears. "Can I talk to that prisoner now?"

"Yeah." Crandall led her down to the jail and into an interrogation room.

The kid cuffed to the chair looked to be about nineteen.

"Mr. Beckett?"

He lifted his head. "Yeah."

"I'm Deputy US Marshal Sally Barnard. How're you doing?"

He shrugged.

"You've had a busy day."

"I guess."

"Can I get you anything? Cup of coffee? Cigarette? Stick of gum?"

"No."

She sat down across the table from him. "I need to know what went on in that house."

Chapter 18

Thomas put the phone down, shaking his head. "I just got word from the state police that they found the stolen car. He left it in a parking lot, locked with the keys in it, and the woman's purse untouched." Thomas paused, leaning on Sally's desk. "There was an interesting report from the same shopping center."

She looked up from her notes. "What?"

"Somebody resembling our man stole a vehicle from right in front of a store. I don't know if it could have been him, though. There were two kids left in a running car. The thief had the kids get out before he drove off." Thomas shook his head. "The creep we're looking for probably would have taken the kids and dumped their bodies somewhere."

"Why do you say that?" asked Sally.

"He's a creep. He's just a killer."

"You don't know him at all, do you?"

"Do you?" Thomas asked, raising his eyebrows.

"I think I do. I've read everything I could find on him." She picked up the large loose-leaf notebook from her desk, and dropped it on his. "Take this home tonight and read it." She bent over and got into his face. "You might learn something." She turned to walk away. "By the way, I'll bet it was him that let those kids out. You forget what he did earlier today? He went back into that house, outnumbered, to save the boy." She paused. "He likes kids. Or something." She headed out of the room. "I'm going home, Thomas. Read that file."

Kevin ate as much of the pork lo mein out of the carton as he could. He hadn't eaten all day, but he wasn't hungry. It didn't matter. He ate anyway. He forced himself to drink a full glass of tap water, even though the taste of the chlorine made him want to vomit. Then he pulled off his shoes with his feet and walked around on the carpet, trying to make fists with his toes. He closed his eyes and moved slowly, doing his Tai Chi, stretching only his right arm, keeping the left folded tightly across his stomach, the fingers twisted in the shirt again.

Damn. He needed to relax. He finally wandered into the bedroom and flopped onto the bed on top of the blankets, fully clothed. He was feeling lousy. He knew it would be hard to sleep again. He almost wished he hadn't asked Justin to take the alcohol away. Every time he closed his eyes the pictures came back again, taunting him, filling his brain.

"Hey, sniper."

He opened one eye. It was dim in the tent. Daylight outside, but he'd been up all night, manning the tower, picking off sappers with an M-14 with a starlight scope. He looked at the kid talking to him, but didn't speak.

"You listening?"

He opened the other eye now. What the hell did this guy want? "What are you doing in here?" *This tent was a restricted area. Snipers got to live with the officers, mostly to avoid this sort of situation.*

"I snuck in."

"No shit. What do you want?"

The kid looked around. He was about eighteen. Didn't look like he had done a whole lot of time on the line; his uniform was still green, the creases still sharp. His blue eyes darted back and forth, and sweat stood out on his upper lip. His brown hair was short. "Look, I want you to do something for me."

So that was what this was about. Kevin had heard about this sort of thing, but he hadn't experienced it firsthand.

"I can pay you."

Kevin snorted.

"Really. I can get whatever you want—cash, drugs, booze. I have friends in the rear. Supply guys."

Kevin sat up, grabbed a crumpled pack of Camels from his wooden shelf, pulled one out, and lit it with his heavy silver Zippo.

"I just saw this guy, the drill sergeant from when I was in boot camp. He's a real jerk. I want you to kill him. You know, knock him off." The kid was whispering now.

Kevin raised an eyebrow. "You think I'm some kind of murderer? Worse than that, you think I'm a hired killer?" In one swift motion he had his K-bar at the kid's neck.

The kid turned pale.

"You think this is what I do? Cut people's throats? Kill anybody I feel like?" he hissed through the cigarette in his teeth. He stared at the kid, eyes boring into his soul. "You want somebody dead? You do it."

The kid shook his head and backed up.

"Why don't you go fuck yourself?" Kevin growled.

The kid straightened up and ran.

Kevin shook his head and lay back down. This place was getting to him.

He opened his eyes again, staring at the ceiling, thinking hard. How had he gone from the one to the other? From the disciplined, principled killer he had been in the war, to the hired killer he had convinced himself he wasn't? How had he slipped into it so easily? He started working for Vincent Marconi, and then for Roger. That was something different, wasn't it? Is that when it all changed? Then he stayed on with Charles Marconi when he took over for his father. *Never any question; just do it. It's just a job. Just business. What happened to your honor?*

Maybe it was time to get out. He closed his eyes again and fell asleep, without any more head movies.

Sally unlocked the door and walked into the house. "I'm home, Bob."

"Lost him, didn't you?" Bob came into the entry and gave her a hug. She gave him a quick kiss on the lips. He was older than she was, in his early fifties, just starting to lose some hair in a circle on the top of his head. He was still fit, but not as fit as he had been.

He was followed by the two large greyhounds, claws clicking on the clay tile as they entered the foyer. The bigger of the two, a brindle male, was whining.

She dropped the bag on the floor and sighed. "Hey, I didn't lose him. They called me too late." She rubbed the ears of the hounds, one with each hand. "You know the details?"

"No."

"You fix any dinner?"

"I ordered in. You hungry?"

"Yeah, let's eat and I'll tell you all about it."

She filled him in on the details as they ate pizza and drank Coors out of the bottle.

He interrupted her narrative. "Hostage? These three inmates took him hostage? Are they nuts?"

"Yeah, him and a kid. They had no idea who they were dealing with. I talked to one of them afterward; they were just totally clueless."

"Did he hurt them?"

"No." She paused. "Well, he killed one of them. Looks like self-defense. He killed the one who shot a cop during the standoff." She stopped again, thinking. Her fugitive had killed a cop killer before that guy could kill anybody else. "He could have done some real damage, but he didn't."

"He got the kid out, right?" Her husband pressed her back to the story.

"Yeah." She glanced at the dogs, watching as one big nose slid onto the table, getting closer to the pizza. "You lie down, Moose," she said, with an angry look at the bigger dog. "He had a chance to run. He was outside the house, but he went back in and tried to get them to take him instead of the kid. They beat him up and he just took it."

"That's him all right. Sounds like the guy Roger talked about."

She watched the dog lie down. "Markinson took a few lumps, but the kid was in great shape, just a little scared." She paused for a minute. "The kid wasn't scared of him, though. They told me the kid ran into the line of fire when Markinson pulled a gun on the cops."

"He pulled a gun on the cops? That's not like him."

She shrugged. "I wasn't there. I'm just going on second hand knowledge. I'd say he was having a bad day."

"Did the kid know who he was?"

"I think so."

Bob looked thoughtful for a moment.

"You have an idea?"

"Go on with your story. I need to think a little more on this."

She continued.

He interrupted again. "So one of the local LEOs left him alone?"

"Yeah. For five, maybe ten minutes."

"Markinson would have been gone in a lot less than that."

"I wouldn't even have taken him to a public hospital. They should've known better. I mean, come on, how long would it take to get him to the prison hospital? He wasn't even hurt that bad." She took a drink. "I still can't believe they left him."

"Somebody watching him would have just slowed him down, wouldn't have stopped him. He'd chew his own arm off to get away."

She gave a half-hearted laugh. "He does have brass balls; you've got to give him that. He walked right by me. I could have touched him. Didn't recognize him until he was halfway out the door."

"He changed his appearance. I warned you about that."

"He turned and looked right at me when I yelled at him. Like he was going to stop, you know?"

"That's the institutionalization. He's conditioned to respond to his name, to obey orders."

"Yeah, but he's not conditioned well enough. I told him to stop and he kept going."

"It's not your fault, you know."

"I know. I'm just trying to figure out what to do next."

Bob picked up a piece of pizza. "Is the county going to prosecute the kid?"

"For what?"

"Markinson was there before the other three. You found the stuff near the kid's house, right? Somebody treated Markinson's arm, right?"

She put down her beer. "Are you thinking what I think you're thinking?"

"You're smart; you figure it out. This guy made sure the kid didn't get hurt. He cared about the kid, didn't he?" Bob raised his eyebrows. "What do you think he'd do if the kid was going to go to jail?"

"The kid's too young. He'd have to be fourteen to be tried as an adult. And he'd chew his own arm off to get away."

"Yeah, but not the kid's arm. He had the opportunity to take the kid hostage and he didn't. He must have had a chance to walk away and leave the kid with the others. Yet he didn't. He has some kind of weird moral landscape, this guy." Bob paused. "And he doesn't have to know the kid's too young, right?"

Sally could feel Bob's eyes on her, watching as she got undressed. She caught his smile and made a face at him, picking up on the hidden meaning behind it.

"I've been on the road, Bob. I am not in the mood." She pulled a floppy tee shirt on over her head.

"I know. I just like to look at you." He patted her side of the mattress. "Come to bed."

She climbed in beside him, and turned on the television.

"The media seems fascinated by this story."

Bob grunted in reply.

"Why?"

He rolled over to look at her. "Why, what?"

"Why do they care about this guy?"

"He's white. He's got a family, two kids, a pretty wife. She lives in an upper-class neighborhood. He just escaped from custody without a shot fired. He has ties to the Mafia. It's all high ratings stuff. I wouldn't be surprised to see him on one of those prime-time news programs someday, protesting his innocence."

"God, Bob, the guy's a creep. He's just a hood, like any other hood."

Bob sighed and rolled over. "Can we go to sleep now?"

She clicked the remote and the television faded to black.

"Where do I look now, Bob?"

"What'd I tell you he cares about?"

"His family."

"I'd start there."

Chapter 19

Early on Monday morning, Sally marched up the stairs, looking for Thomas. He was sitting at his desk, drinking coffee from a paper cup while staring into his monitor. "You're with me today," she said, tapping him on the arm.

"Yes, ma'am. Where're we going?"

"Queens."

"Anywhere in particular?"

"Little private suburb called Forest Hills Gardens. You know it?"

"No. Why are we going out there? It's not in our district." He was trotting to keep up with her, as she practically ran down the stairs.

"Cindy Markinson lives out there with her two kids."

"We're going to see Markinson's family?" Thomas stopped. "I thought we didn't do that."

"We don't, as a general rule."

"So why are we now?" He was trotting after her again.

"Just looking at all the options." She threw her bag in the back of the Suburban. "Let me dig out the maps."

Sally noted the plain brown sedan parked across the street, the two guys in cheap suits watching the house. She nodded at them as Thomas pulled the SUV into the driveway of the English Tudor, blocking in a Volvo wagon. It looked as if Markinson's wife and kids were just on their way out. Sally jumped down out of the truck and started up the sidewalk, her badge in her hand. "Come on, Thomas."

The black-haired woman, her face going pale, turned to the two boys. "Get back in the house. Get in the house and stay out of the way."

Sally put on her best smile. "Mrs. Markinson?"

"Yes."

"I'm Deputy US Marshal Sally Barnard; this is my partner Deputy Neelon. May we come in?"

"Do you have a warrant?"

"No, ma'am. I was hoping we could just talk, friendly-like." Sally saw the expression on the woman's face go from hostility to curiosity.

Cindy shrugged and backed up, holding the door open. "I'm calling my lawyer."

"You don't really need to; we'll only be here a few minutes. I just wanted to ask a couple of questions."

Cindy turned and headed for the phone.

Sally walked in and began wandering around the living room, picking up pictures, studying knickknacks, trying to get a feel for this guy. There weren't a lot of pictures of him. The whole house was bland suburban nothingness, as though all the pictures came with the frames. No little homey touches. The place was a mess, clothes piled in chairs, papers scattered on the worn pile carpet, which was in need of vacuuming. The mess made it obvious that someone actually lived here, and two of them were teenagers, Aside from that, there was nothing to reflect the fugitive; nothing that said what he might be like. "This is a pretty ritzy neighborhood. Your husband's money pay for this place?"

Cindy hung up the phone. "Actually, it was the money he got for getting beat up. What is it you want?"

"Yeah, I heard about that. Very unprofessional. When was that? Six, seven years ago?" She hesitated, and then turned to look into Cindy's eyes. "Have you seen him?" The woman was a bit taller than she was, her black hair showing a few strands of gray in it. She was older than her husband, close to Sally's age, she remembered from the file.

Cindy stared right back at her. "No, I haven't. I don't know where he is."

"Are you sure?" Sally stopped her prowling, and turned to look at Thomas. "There was a man here this morning—a big guy, bodyguard type. What's his name, Thomas?"

Thomas consulted a small notebook. "Justin Stewart."

"I think Mr. Stewart was here to take your husband some stuff. Money, clothes, fake ID, a gun perhaps." Sally caught the panic that crossed the woman's face. She'd hit it right on the nose.

"And?"

"And I can have you arrested for aiding and abetting." She leaned towards an old picture of the two boys, a studio shot with a Christmas background. "What do you suppose would happen to your kids if you were in jail?"

Cindy closed her mouth. She glanced towards Thomas, who was going into the kitchen.

"You ever been in prison, Mrs. Markinson?"

Sally could see the blood drain out of the woman's face.

"How long have you two been married?" Sally asked as she picked up a wedding picture, even though she knew the answer. She saw Thomas move down the hallway, watching him with one eye, maintaining this conversation with the other.

"Twenty-three years."

"Twenty-three years is a long time to be with someone like him."

"What is that supposed to mean?"

Sally almost grinned at the angry reaction. "Nothing. I've been married almost eighteen years myself. No kids, though. I've been a little busy with my job." She studied the photo, marveling at how young the two people in it looked. The man was wearing a blue suit, his bride a simple dress. She looked into the camera with a nervous smile; he was just staring, as if posing for a mug shot. "Did you know what he was when you married him?"

"What is he?"

Sally put the picture down and turned to face Cindy. "A hired killer, right? That's the rumor anyway."

"Emphasis on rumor. Do you work on rumors? Go chasing after people based on what they might be?"

Sally shook her head. "I just chase fugitives. I don't care what he is or what he's done. He's running and that means I get to chase him." She stared right into the other woman's eyes. "It must be rough, with him on the run like this. I know I don't like being away from my husband for too long."

Cindy didn't answer. She compressed her lips, almost frowning.

"It'd go easier on him if he turned himself in. There are an awful lot of cowboys out there chasing him. You wouldn't want to see him dead, would you?" She paused, looking for sensitive spots. "He's not going to stay out for eight years this time. Not with me on his tail."

"You'd shoot him yourself if you had the chance."

Sally smiled. "Actually, I already had a chance. Couldn't get off a safe shot. But he might not be so lucky next time."

Cindy didn't respond, just pressed her lips together even tighter.

"If he's smart, he won't take any more chances like that. We both know he's smart, don't we?"

"You think you know him?"

Sally shrugged. "I'd like to know him better. Maybe you can tell me more about him. Tell me where he'd be hiding, where he's likely to go next."

"California."

Sally snorted and Thomas came back down the hallway, his boots clicking on the wood floor. The two boys followed him, and moved to their mother. Thomas met Sally's eyes and shook his head.

Cindy picked up on the signal. "You didn't really expect him to be here, did you?"

"Actually, I didn't. I know he's smarter than that," Sally moved towards the door.

"Are you okay, Mom?" Michael asked.

"I'm okay. You guys okay?"

Michael nodded. Andy just stood next to her, silent.

"Y'all let us know if you see him, won't you?"

"Fat chance," Andy said in a stage whisper, just loud enough.

Sally turned to look at him, noticing the resemblance. The long blond hair, the ice blue eyes. Then she spoke to Cindy again. "You'd better watch that one; he'll be taking after his father." She and Thomas headed back out to the car.

Sally leaned back in the passenger seat and let out a long sigh.

"You didn't think he'd be there, did you?"

She shook her head. "I don't think he's ever been there."

"So why are we wasting our time?"

"We're touching all the bases, Thomas. I have to keep him moving. He has to know we're looking. I can guarantee she's going to see him at some point today, and she'll tell him we were here. If I know anything about him, I know he won't like that. Especially if she tells him I threatened to bring her in."

"So what do we do now?"

"I need to make a couple of phone calls, and then we're going upstate again."

Thomas sighed. "We better fill the tank first."

CHAPTER 20

Kevin heard a muffled voice coming through the doorway. He rolled onto his back, opened his eyes, and saw Justin standing over him. "What?"

"Hey, I'm sorry. I didn't know you were asleep." Justin held up a duffel bag. "I got your stuff. How you feeling?"

"Lousy."

"Listen, I talked to Cindy. She wants to see you."

"Well, maybe we can work something out." He rolled out of bed, onto the floor.

"Uh, boss, I did work something out. Noon, at her work."

"Noon today?" He tried to stand up, lurching to his knees. "Little help, Justin."

"You need help, all right."

"Yeah. I know. Can we do it without getting caught? The doctor's office?"

"I think so." He reached out and took Kevin's arm. "How about some breakfast?"

Kevin got to his feet. "How about I take a shower first?" He looked down at his clothes, the same sweat pants and scrub shirt he had been wearing the day before, and then over at the bag. "What did she send?"

"I don't know."

"Look, can you go through the stuff while I clean up a little? Pick something out for me."

"Sure, boss."

Kevin left the bathroom door open a crack and called out as he started the water running, "She say anything?"

"She wanted to know how you were doing."

"What'd you tell her?"

"I told her the truth."

Kevin groaned.

"Liz?" Sally walked right on by her desk as she spoke.

"Yes, ma'am?"

"Do we have anyone watching Cindy Markinson's place of employment?"

Liz got up and followed Sally to her desk. "She works for a Dr. Andrew Williams. Out on Long Island."

"Do we have anyone watching the office?"

"Yes, ma'am. Locals."

"Are they obvious?"

"Yes, ma'am. Although the guys we had inside the building are gone. Andrews owns the building, and he claimed it was damaging his business. He got a judge to order a cease and desist."

Sally turned to look at her. "You're kidding."

"But we still have the locals watching the building. From outside."

"Good." She picked up the phone.

Kevin came back out into the living room rubbing his nearly non-existent hair with a towel. He was wearing what Justin had picked out for him, blue jeans and a large loose tee shirt with a picture of Bruce Springsteen on it, concert dates on the back.

Justin looked at him. "What'd you do to your hair?"

"Cut it and colored it. What'd you think?"

Justin rubbed his nose with the back of his hand. "It looks different."

"No shit, genius. Did you bring me a piece?"

"Yeah, just a minute." The bigger man reached into a pocket of his sport coat and brought out a handgun, which he handed off.

Kevin studied it. It was a tiny Smith and Wesson revolver—a thirty-eight, with a short barrel and wood grips. "Where did you get this?" He broke the weapon open. Five shots, fully loaded.

"Friend of mine."

"Friend of yours a Leo?"

"No. He might know some."

"Yeah." Kevin stuck the weapon into his front right pocket. The only good thing about something this small was its ability to fit in tight places. "He lift this off a plainclothes cop or what?"

"Don't know. I suppose he might have got it at one of those surplus property auctions. Cops are all switching to nines now."

"Pea shooters." Kevin snorted. "You got extra ammo?"

"Yeah, just a sec." Justin fished in his pocket again and came up with a couple of speed loaders, giving Kevin a total of fifteen rounds.

"Thanks."

Justin glanced at his watch. "We should get moving. You mind eating in the car?"

"I'm not hungry." He headed back into the bedroom. "Let me get my smokes." He grabbed his Camels off the dresser, and then dug through the duffel bag, coming up with his watch, his lighter, an ancient Mets cap, and a pair of sunglasses. He pulled the hat onto his head as he came back into the living room. "Okay, let's go. Maybe we can stop for coffee." He started to follow Justin, and then hesitated in mid stride. "You didn't bring your motorcycle, did you?"

"No."

"Good."

Justin brought the Caddy up in front of the doctor's office.

"Are you sure they're not watching this building?" asked Kevin, taking off the dark glasses and scanning the area.

"Yeah, they are, actually." Justin pulled the vehicle into the parking garage, and then got out. "Wait here a minute."

Kevin watched, slouching, as Justin walked across the garage to a brown sedan with two men in it. He couldn't hear any of the conversation, but he saw Justin hand over something. The man in the driver's seat nodded, and then he drove off.

Justin walked back and opened the passenger door for Kevin.

"What did you just do?"

"Those guys are willing to go take a break, if the price is right."

"They're not going to talk to the feds?"

"They're not going to talk to nobody. Hey, everybody's got to take a piss once in a while, right?"

Justin offered his arm and Kevin took it, struggling to get out of the car. He wobbled, leaning on the heavier man.

"I tell you, Justin, I feel old," he said, as he fought to keep his balance. He looked around. "Cindy hasn't seen anyone watching the office, out in the hall or anything?"

"Would you rather just go to a hospital?"

"No, you know that would be stupid."

"Then quit worrying and let's go." Justin supported his boss as they headed for the elevator. "I wouldn't bring you here if I thought it wasn't safe."

They rode up the two floors in silence, Kevin leaning against the wall, his balance off. He wobbled out into the hallway.

"Let me go in first," said Justin, outside the office. Kevin hung back, holding the wall for support. A moment later, Justin waved Kevin in.

He took a deep breath and limped through the door. Cindy came out from behind the counter.

"Your description was pretty accurate, Justin."

Justin nodded.

She looked at Kevin. "He told me you looked like—well, not so good."

"Yeah, that's how I feel." He looked at her, through the one eye that wasn't swollen shut. "I missed you."

She didn't respond. "Let's go in the back." She reached for his arm and he allowed her to lead him back to an examining room. "Can you take this shirt off?"

"Maybe, with some help."

Dr. Williams walked into the room at that moment. Tall, though not as tall as his patient, he wore cream-colored slacks and a navy golf shirt, with a stethoscope draped around his neck.

"Hi, Kevin. How're you doing?" He frowned. "Haven't seen you in a while." He pulled on a pair of exam gloves. "Tell me what happened."

Kevin cleared his throat. "Took a bullet last Thursday morning. Probably a large caliber rifle, but I think it went right through my left arm, up by the shoulder. Bled pretty good. Then I got hit in the arm by the same guys who did this to my face... uh... yesterday morning."

"Have you had any treatment?"

"Well, I was in the hospital for about forty-five minutes yesterday. They gave me some oxygen and started an IV, but it wasn't in very long. They also mentioned Demerol, antibiotics, a tetanus booster, and blood. They took an X-ray, but I didn't hang around to see how it came out. The doctor in the emergency room did look at my arm. Dressed it, but that was it."

"How are the vitals, Cindy?" the doctor asked.

"Blood pressure is low, but he tends to run low anyway. Pulse is about sixty, weak and thready." She paused for a moment. "He's breathing okay, a little fast, a little shallow."

"Still in a lot of pain, aren't you?" the doctor asked.

"Yeah."

"Well, I'd like to get an X-ray, but I don't think that's feasible." He peeled off the gauze and studied the wound. "Can you move the arm?"

"I'd rather not."

"Let me see you move it."

Kevin raised his arm, and moved it in a circle, gritting his teeth against the pain.

"I'm going to assume it missed the bone. You wouldn't be able to move it otherwise. You've lost a lot of blood; it's bleeding a little now, but you've always been a bleeder, right? At least since you ruined your liver."

"Yeah."

"I'd like to get some blood into you, but that's not really practical either, is it?"

"I can't go to a hospital."

"I figured. You can make up the loss with fluids and rest. Try not to move the arm too much. You need to stay quiet for a day or two, okay?"

"Yes, sir."

"All right, then. Let's wrap it up again, put your arm in a sling, and you'll just need to push the fluids. Rest and fluids." He paused. "But no booze, right?"

"I've been sober for eleven years. You know that, Doc."

"Just testing. You're still smoking though, aren't you?"

"Yeah, and I don't need you to give me a hard time about it." Kevin shook his head. He'd known this man for more than twenty-five years; longer than he'd known his wife. Doc was allowed to give him a hard time.

"Let me look at your face." He examined the swollen purple areas. "Just bruises."

"Yeah, that's what it feels like."

The doctor shone a penlight into Kevin's eyes and frowned. "They hit you hard enough to knock you out?"

"Yeah."

"You've got a mild concussion." He studied the bruise on the right temple, touching it gently. "Did they do a CAT scan or anything at the hospital?"

"I really wasn't there very long, Doc."

"You feel nauseous?"

"That's a pretty normal way for me to feel."

"Just answer the question."

"Yes."

The doctor took a deep breath and sighed. "I want someone checking on you on a regular basis." He looked at Cindy. "Is he staying with you, or what?"

She shook her head.

"You have someone keeping an eye on you?"

"Justin."

"Well, all right, then. I'm going to give you some samples of a painkiller. No driving and I don't want you taking more than three a day for three days. You know what I mean? Every eight hours." The doctor opened a cabinet, reached to the top shelf, and spoke with his back to Kevin. "If they bother your stomach just stop taking them. How is your stomach, anyway?"

"What?"

The doctor turned to face him, frowning. "Your stomach. How's your stomach?"

"Same old, same old. It hurts."

"Can you hear me?" the doctor lowered his voice.

"Of course."

"As long as I'm looking at you, right?"

Kevin shrugged his right shoulder. "I'm not deaf, yet."

"Getting there, though. Aren't you?"

"I've had high caliber weapons going off next to my ears for almost thirty years. Never wore any hearing protection."

The doctor wrinkled his nose, shook his head, and changed the subject. "The smoking doesn't help your ulcer."

"It's my only vice."

The doctor laughed. "Sure. Take whatever you find helps. Liquid antacids probably work better than the tablets. They're doing research now with antibiotics for ulcers; maybe we'll try that at some point. Put some ice on your face, too. Now I'm going to eat my lunch. Cindy, dress that with some antibiotic ointment, and put the arm in a sling." He started out of the room, and turned. "Take care of yourself, Kevin. And try to get some rest." He left.

Cindy wrapped the wound with gauze and taped it up. "I missed you, too," she said as she worked. "It's been hard this time. The kids are getting older. I'm busy at work." She looked into his eyes.

He leaned forward and tried to kiss her on the lips.

She turned away, and he lost his balance and had to step down off the table. She laughed as she got a sling out of the cupboard, helped him put his shirt back on, and then put the arm into the sling. "You'd better go. Celine will be back from lunch soon, and there'll be patients coming in."

"You know I love you," he said, pulling his ball cap back on.

"Yeah, whatever." She turned away and washed her hands. "Go on now. Get out of here."

He reached for the door.

"I love you, too," she said, staring at the sink. "Take care of yourself."

He stepped into the hall.

"Kevin."

He stopped, turning to look back at her.

"I'm worried about you."

"I'm okay."

"Stay that way, all right?"

He grinned, and bent to kiss her.

She met his lips, and then pushed him away. "You should go."

He straightened up and grabbed the door to keep from falling.

She frowned at him and shook her head. "Get some rest."

"Yes, ma'am." He wobbled down the hall and followed Justin back to the car.

Chapter 21

Monday morning Danny's mom announced she was taking some time off work. He wasn't sure if she was worried about him or didn't trust him. They hadn't talked about it all the rest of the day on Sunday; just kind of toyed around the edges. She'd actually climbed up a stepladder and patched the ceiling. Dinner was silent… and then the doorbell rang Monday afternoon. Danny hung back while his mom answered it.

"Hello, Mrs. Rutledge. I'm Deputy Sally Barnard." She flashed her badge. "I'm with the US Marshal's Service. I'd like to ask your son a few questions."

Danny watched his mom back up a step. "He's been through a lot. Is this really necessary?"

"I'm afraid it is." Sally had two men with her, the young man Danny had seen with her at the hospital and a local police officer as well. "I thought he might be more comfortable here than at the police station, but we can do it there if you want."

"No, come in. Have a seat; I'll go get him."

Danny came into the room and felt fear rising in his throat. He focused his attention on the familiar petite red-haired woman who was getting to her feet.

"Hello, Danny. I'm Deputy US Marshal Barnard. We help look for fugitives. I happen to be working right now on a specific case—a man named Kevin Markinson. You know him, don't you?"

"He's the man that saved my life yesterday. But he was caught," Danny replied, studying the woman's silver star, wondering how much she knew about what *he* knew.

"He actually took off from the hospital." She paused. "But that's not the reason I'm here. I want to talk to you about what happened before yesterday."

"What do you mean?" he asked, poking at the carpet with a toe, not wanting to meet her eyes. His mother had spent the morning scrubbing at the stains. It looked like they were going to have to just rip it up.

"Let's sit down." She waited while he sat, then she took a chair opposite him. She looked at him, but didn't force eye contact. "Danny." She paused. "It started out simple, right? You found this guy out in the woods somewhere. He was hurt and hungry, so you helped him. You didn't know who he was at first."

Danny stared at the floor as she spoke. His stomach was doing flips. He found himself biting his lower lip. He wondered how she knew so much. Had she talked to Duke? How could she possibly know what went on?

"But I think that by the time those three unlucky idiots burst in here yesterday morning, you knew full well who he was."

Danny didn't speak. He looked up at the woman.

"The reason he was here to save your life was because he was here. In the house. You knew who he was then, but it didn't matter anymore, did it?"

Danny shook his head and looked away again.

"He wouldn't do that. Would you, Danny?" said his mother. Danny could hear the pleading in her voice, the disbelief.

"I'm not saying it was premeditated, or even deliberate. But I am saying your son is going to be charged with harboring a fugitive." She paused, looking straight at him. "I've got three witnesses who will say he knew your name. He called you by name the minute he walked through the door."

"I didn't know who he was. He told me his name was Duke, that's all." Danny had hot tears in his eyes. He was ashamed to have finally lost the battle with the lump in his throat. "I didn't mean to do anything wrong."

She took a photograph out of a file folder. It was a family portrait, of a young man in a police uniform, his younger looking wife, with a baby in her arms. "This family was destroyed by Kevin Markinson. This little girl is growing up without a father because Kevin Markinson killed him."

Danny blinked and looked at her. "No, he didn't. He didn't do that." He paused, took a deep breath. "I didn't do anything. It's not like I busted him out of jail."

"You helped him though, didn't you?"

Danny shrugged and looked out the front window, trying to see something a thousand yards away.

"You brought him here; you let him in the house. You fed him, and you treated his wounds."

"Yes." He barely said it, and moved his focus to the floor.

"Why?"

"He needed help."

"He's an escaped murderer. You do understand that, don't you? You're not that young; you knew what you were doing."

Danny continued to stare at the floor. "He didn't do it. He told me he didn't do it."

"This man has made a career out of lying and you believed him." She sounded like she was getting impatient. "Don't you understand? He lied to you to save himself."

"Then why would he save my life? Tell me that." Danny raised his eyes and his voice now. "Tell me why this lying murderer would care enough to stay here and save my life! He had a chance to run. He was out of the house—he even had a gun—but he came back in here and he saved me." Danny hesitated, remembering the hours in the kitchen. "He practically made those guys beat him up. He kept getting them to hit him instead of me. He kept me safe."

She took a deep breath, held it for a minute, and sighed. "Did he tell you where he was going?"

He looked back down at the floor. "Home; back to the city. He wanted to see his wife and kids. That's all he talked about. His oldest son has a birthday coming up."

"I need to talk to the district attorney, Mrs. Rutledge, but I imagine he will want to charge your son with harboring a fugitive." Sally glanced at the police officer.

"It would be best if you just stay here, okay?" said the man.

She nodded.

"He really did save my life, you know." Danny could hear his voice cracking. The lump in his throat was back again, but he wasn't going to cry anymore. Not in front of these people.

"I know he did," Sally responded. "But it doesn't matter. I still need to find him." She paused again. "Do you still want to help him?"

Danny raised his head.

"You don't want to see him get hurt, right?"

"I guess."

"So where is he? Where did he go?"

"All I know is he wanted to see his family."

She nodded. "Thanks for your help."

Danny turned and left the room, feeling hopeless.

Sally's head was spinning as she walked to the SUV. *Utterly bizarre behavior.* She couldn't explain the kid's reaction; why he had helped the rabbit in the first place. Looking at this kid, his eyes wild and angry, all she could come up with was—why? *Why did this kid care? Stockholm syndrome, right? The kid was identifying with his captor, wanted to please the man he had been with for three days. But there hadn't been enough time for Stockholm syndrome to set in.*

And why did Markinson care? There certainly wasn't any Stockholm syndrome there. So what was it? She decided not to get any further into this. She refused to allow for the possibility that her quarry might be even remotely noble. Refused to consider that he had made the choice to stay there and help the kid when he had a chance to run. *Markinson wouldn't do that, despite the evidence to the contrary, and the witnesses whose statements corroborated it.*

He couldn't have run, because the house was surrounded by cops. His best shot was to take his chances in the house with the three idiots. So then, why didn't he beat those guys up instead of letting them beat him up? Why was this cop killer acting like a victim? Why did he step up for the kid? Why was the kid so convinced that Markinson wasn't a killer?

"So what was that for?" asked Thomas, as they walked to the car. "You already knew where Markinson was going."

She shook off her doubts. "I want this kid to be prosecuted for what he did." She paused. "Or at least charged."

"You just want to make the kid's life miserable?"

"You'll see. I have a plan."

"You going to let anybody else in on it?"

"Markinson gave up his freedom for the kid once, right?"

"I guess."

"Think he'd do it again?"

"I doubt it."

"Want to bet on it?"

"Okay. What are the stakes?"

"You buy me lunch, anywhere I want."

"Okay. Same here, then. Where to now?"

"Back to the office."

Dinner that night was rough. Danny didn't want to look at his mother.

"Did you help him, Danny?"

He looked at his plate, and swallowed hard, pushing the food around with his fork.

"Did he threaten you? Is that what happened?" His mother was insistent, probing. "Did he force you to help him?"

Danny shrugged.

"They can't prosecute you if he forced you to help him, you understand?"

Danny nodded.

"Did he force you?"

"I don't know."

"How can you not know? Did he have a weapon? Was it his idea to come to the house?" His mother shook her head. "They're not going to make those charges stick anyway; they've got to know that. I don't know what they're thinking. I'll talk to a lawyer tomorrow, but there is no way they can do this." She paused. "Your father wouldn't let them do this."

Danny looked up at his mom, hopeful. Maybe it would be all right. Maybe his mother would fix it. Even if his father wasn't here.

Kevin spent the rest of Monday alternating between sleeping, smoking, and channel surfing. He'd never been a big fan of television, and he couldn't find anything to change his mind this afternoon. He wished he had a book to read, but couldn't see any way to safely leave the apartment to get one. He had dinner delivered again, and then went to bed. He stretched out diagonally on the double bed and stared at the ceiling, wishing he could be at home with Cindy. He tried to picture home, but realized the place she was living now was a place he had never been. He hadn't lived with her in at least thirteen years.

He woke up Tuesday morning to the sound of the phone ringing. It took him a minute to figure out what it was and where it was coming from. He grabbed the receiver and glanced at his watch. Seven-thirty. *Who on earth would be calling him this early?*

"Yeah?"

"Kevin?"

He didn't recognize the voice, although the accent was familiar, almost British. "Who wants to know?"

"This is Roger."

That was a blast from the past. Roger. "Holy shit!" Kevin sat bolt upright.

Roger cleared his throat. "I'm doing you a favor; giving you a heads up. A friend of mine called me last week. I had to give him some information which will probably help them find you. I apologize."

"You talked to the cops?"

"No. I talked to a friend. I owed him a favor. I don't owe *you* anything, but I'm telling you out of the goodness of my heart."

"Roger, how did you get this number?"

"Kevin, if I want you, I have to know how to find you. Understand?"

Kevin snorted. "You haven't had any use for me since 1983."

Roger cleared his throat again. "Don't fall into your regular habits, Kevin. They'll be looking for that. This friend of mine, his wife is a deputy marshal."

"Fine. That's marvelous. Thanks a bunch, Roger." Kevin got to his feet and started to set the phone down.

"I told him you didn't do it."

"What?"

"I know you didn't do it. You didn't kill that cop."

"I know *you* know, Roger. You told me so fifteen years ago."

"I told him I knew that; I told him you were innocent."

"Why don't you call the DA and tell him?"

"He won't believe me. The only way we can convince the DA is to find Carlos."

"Yeah."

"An awful lot of time has gone. We probably can't find Carlos at this point."

"Right."

"So don't fall into your regular habits, Kevin. They're looking for that. Stay away from your associates."

"Roger, you're not making a lot of sense." But then, Roger never had made a lot of sense. Roger existed on a different level. In this world, Roger didn't exist at all. No family, no connections to anything that might be used against him; he was the ultimate spook. Kevin could see the man's face even now, after fifteen years. His white, spiky hair, the eyes a blue so dark they were nearly purple, the dimples. And the suit. Roger was always dressed in the same blue suit. Roger oozed charm, could talk anybody out of almost anything.

"Why do you care?"

"Kevin. You were my boy wonder, the best of the best. I don't want to see you end up dead in some gutter like a common thug."

Kevin was tempted to throw away the rest of the painkillers the doctor had given him, because now he was convinced he was just hallucinating. "Did you give your friend this number?"

"No."

"Thank God for that."

"I have to go."

"Roger, wait."

"Yes?"

"Do you know where Carlos is?"

"No."

"Can you find him?"

"I'll see what I can do."

There was a click, and a dial tone, and Kevin was standing in the room staring at the phone, wondering if he had really had the conversation he thought he had just had. He set it down, his hands shaking. Clearing his head with a cigarette, he grabbed the phone and punched in Justin's number.

"Justin."

"Yeah, boss?"

"I need you to do something for me."

"Right. Whatever you want."

"You know Harvey Longwood?"

"Your lawyer?"

"Right." Kevin paused, then added, "He should have all the evidence from the killing. You know, the whole Carlos thing. The thing I went to prison for."

"Was he your lawyer then?"

"Yeah, right out of school."

"Okay."

"I want you to look at that for me. Find out what they had for evidence; see if they found any prints aside from mine."

"Sure. The cops don't have that stuff?"

"I think the cops have the physical evidence, but I think they have to share what they have with the defense. What's it called, discovery? Harvey should have copies of reports, that sort of thing."

"I'll do what I can."

"Thanks, Justin."

That afternoon the phone startled him out of a nap. Kevin was starting to feel like taking the thing off the hook. "Yeah?"

"Kevin?"

"Charles?"

"Yes."

Oh hell. No telling what he wants, but it can't be anything good. Kevin cleared his throat. "What can I do for you, sir?"

"We need to talk. I have a matter that requires your attention."

Kevin sighed under his breath. This man was the one who had arranged this whole thing. He had paid for the escape. "I'm a little bit hot right now."

"I heard that."

Kevin thought about what Roger had said on the phone this morning. "I don't think you want me coming there."

"All right. How much time do you need?"

"I don't know. Couple of weeks, maybe? Will it keep that long?"

There was a long pause. "Yeah, okay. I'll put it on the back burner."

"Thanks."

"No problem. You'll be in touch?"

"Yeah, sure."

"Take care of yourself."

"Yes, sir." Kevin hung up the phone and stared at it. *Awfully easy, wasn't it?* He'd been gone for six years, but the minute he was out again the phone started ringing. He supposed it ought to make him feel good, to be in such high demand, but it made him feel sick for some reason. What had happened to him? He thought about all the stuff he'd been through in the last few days, the dreams and the flashbacks, and began to realize that something in him had snapped. Something had changed. Was he developing a conscience after all this time? Or was he just remembering one he had forgotten?

Kevin spent the rest of the day curled up on the threadbare couch in the little apartment, alone and lonely. He finally gave up and turned on the television again. The local news was all the usual. An accident on the Cross-Bronx expressway involving a tractor trailer full of chickens. A shooting in one of the drug-infested neighborhoods. And something else that made Kevin sit up and pay attention.

"While federal and state authorities continue to search for escaped cop-killer Kevin Markinson, prosecutors upstate are pressing charges against a thirteen-year-old boy whom they believe assisted Markinson after his escape. The boy is alleged to have provided Markinson with food and shelter for a period of several days. The charges are considered serious." A newer picture accompanied the story; one that looked like it had been taken from the hospital security system. He was looking up at the camera—it must have been in the elevator—and wearing the silly little cap and the scrubs. It had captured his new look—clean-shaven, the long hair gone.

Kevin got to his feet and paced for minute, watching as the news moved on to another story. "Fuck it." He picked up the phone again.

Chapter 22

Cindy walked into the fast food restaurant with the boys by her side and Justin hanging behind them. Kevin watched her as she figured out where he was, sitting in the back, wearing his Mets cap and sunglasses, watching the door. They headed in his direction.

Michael and Andy hung back, staying close to her, acting younger than their years. He was surprised at how tall they both were. Six years since he had last seen them. They probably weren't even sure who he was. He got to his feet as she approached the table.

"Kevin."

He nodded at her, leaned forward to kiss her. She turned and he pecked her cheek.

She sat down, Andy pushed to sit next to her and Kevin motioned to Michael, who was edging away from him.

"Sit."

Michael slid into the booth and Kevin sat beside him, keeping his right hand free. Justin pulled a chair over to the end of the table and perched on the edge, looking like he was afraid of breaking it.

"How are you?" she asked, studying his face.

"I'm okay. Justin—go get the food, will you?" Kevin took out his wallet and handed the younger man some cash. "Cindy, tell him what you and the kids want. I'll have a small fries and a chocolate shake."

"I'll just have a cheeseburger and a Sprite. Boys, why don't you go with Justin and help him."

Kevin slid out of the way and Michael got up, following Justin and Andy towards the front of the restaurant.

"You look a little healthier than you did Monday." She looked into his eyes. "How's your arm?"

"Sore." He sighed.

"You getting enough rest?"

"Yeah. Not doing anything else."

"That's good."

"I've got something I need to talk to you about."

"Okay."

"I..." he paused as Justin came back with the food. Got to his feet again and let Michael sit, watched as Cindy handed the kids their food and started on her sandwich. He took a sip of milkshake. "When I was upstate there was this kid who helped me out." He took another drink, and then squeezed a line of ketchup onto a french fry as he spoke. "They're going to prosecute him for it."

"What did he do?" asked Cindy.

"He just let me take a shower, gave me some food, you know, good Samaritan kind of stuff. He's a good kid. But they're going to charge him with a crime." He picked up another fry and balanced it between his fingers, wiggling it back and forth as he talked. "I need to go up there and tell them I threatened him, held him hostage, whatever." He focused on the table. "Get him off the hook."

Cindy put her sandwich down and stared at her husband. "You're going to turn yourself in? For this kid?"

He met her eyes, putting down the fry again. "Yeah."

Justin choked on his hamburger, coughing hard.

"Kevin." She reached across the table and took his hand. "I have to tell you the truth; there've been times when I wondered why I ever married you."

He tried to pull his hand away, but she squeezed it tighter.

"This has to be the noblest idea you've ever had."

He grimaced. "Yeah, well, don't tell anybody, okay? I don't want to ruin my reputation." This time he succeeded in pulling his hand away.

Justin coughed again, and Kevin turned to glare at him.

"Is there something you wanted to say, Justin?"

"No, sir. Just a bone in my burger or something." He took a drink.

Kevin turned now to look at his kids. "You guys behaving yourselves?"

"Yeah, Dad," Michael responded without looking at him, pushing himself further into the corner.

Andy stared at the table.

"Answer your father, Andrew," said Cindy.

"Yeah, whatever," the boy muttered.

Kevin raised his eyebrows.

Cindy looked down at the table and fingered her sandwich. "What do you think will happen?"

"I don't know. I guess they could try to get me for kidnapping or something. I hope they'll just let the kid go and leave it."

"Have you talked to Harvey?"

"No, I only just came up with this idea."

"He's a good lawyer. He's helped you before. Why don't you talk to him?"

"Okay, hon, I will. I have to go now." He stood up, picked up his shake and leaned over to kiss her.

"Let me know," she said, letting him kiss her on the lips this time.

"I'll call Justin." He limped away without looking back, sucking on the straw as he walked. He paused at the door, holding it open for an elderly woman, staring at the ground as she walked through.

"Our guys lost his wife tonight."

"What?" Sally looked up at Thomas, who was the only other person still in the office this late.

"The local cops tailing Markinson's wife. They lost her for a couple of hours."

"Well, one guess who she was meeting. How'd they lose her?"

"This Justin guy, the bodyguard. He loses tails all the time. They've pulled him over a couple of times too; but hell, he never exceeds the speed limit. Doesn't even run lights. He's just clever. He seems to have an unlimited supply of vehicles available. He's also generous with cash, I've heard."

"So he pays off the locals so they'll look the other way?"

"Apparently."

"I don't have the manpower to do this on my own."

"I know."

"So did she come home?"

"Yep."

"Without him, I suppose."

"Right."

"Thanks for the update, Thomas."

"No problem."

Wednesday morning, Danny got the mail. He felt his mother's eyes on him all the way down the driveway. It was still hard to tell if she was just anxious, or if she expected him to run or what.

There was a letter for him. No return address, but the postmark was from Queens. He opened the envelope as he walked down the driveway, eager to find out what it was. The only thing in the envelope was a twenty dollar bill. He stopped, smiled, and tucked the money into the pocket of his jeans.

Kevin dialed the lawyer's direct line Wednesday morning from one of the few pay phones left in the city.

"Harvey, this is Kevin," he said.

"Kevin, this line is tapped."

"Pay phone. I need to see you."

"Is it about what Justin's been doing here? The old case?"

"No."

"Kevin, I can't be party to this. I can't see you; I shouldn't even be talking to you. All I can do is tell you to turn yourself in."

"I want to turn myself in. I need your help."

"Okay." He paused. "What do you have planned?"

"I want them to kick the kid loose. That Danny kid, upstate. I'll trade with them. Me for him."

Harvey took it in stride, without hesitation. "All right, let me see what I can arrange."

"I'll call you back." Kevin hung up. Then he looked at the flyer in his hand, the one with his picture on it, along with a phone number.

He put another thirty-five cents in the phone and dialed.

"US Marshal's Service, Southern New York District."

"I'd like to talk to Deputy Sally Barnard."

"That may take some time. Who may I say is calling?" the pleasant female voice on the other end asked.

"Kevin Markinson."

"Can you hold, Mr. Markinson?"

"No. Tell her I'll call back in ten minutes." He hung up, leaned against the wall for a moment, and then limped down the street. Hesitating outside a bar, he looked through the dark windows, wanting to go in. *Just one little drink.* He could still taste it, after what, eleven years? The Jack Daniel's was calling him. He shook his head—causing a twinge of pain—lit a cigarette, and kept walking. He tried to remember where he was and if there might be a meeting somewhere nearby.

He found another pay phone after ten minutes, amazingly enough, dialed the same number, and got the same voice.

"This is Kevin Markinson. Is Sally Barnard ready to talk to me?"

"Yes, sir."

There was a click, and he found himself listening to instrumental Beatles music, then another voice, this one with a strong southern accent, said, "Mr. Markinson?"

"Yes, ma'am."

"This is Deputy Sally Barnard. What can I do for you?"

"I want to turn myself in, but I need a couple of guarantees. I'll have my lawyer contact you."

"Wait. What kind of guarantees?"

"I want the kid upstate released."

"I can't do that. But it might happen if you can testify as to what went on."

"I will." He glanced at his watch. "I have to go." He hung up the phone.

Sally turned and smiled at Thomas. "Well, Mr. Neelon, you owe me lunch."

He nodded. "I heard it, but I don't believe it."

"You didn't think this would work."

"I didn't believe the creep had a conscience. Why would he care more about this kid than his own freedom?"

"Have you read that file yet?" she said. "His commander in Vietnam hated him because he refused to help burn down a village full of women and children. He also single-handedly saved the lives of seven men in his squad by killing six enemy soldiers in close combat. Very much at the risk of his own life and freedom." She grinned. "I knew he wouldn't let that kid go to jail."

"So you set him up."

"Of course. The prosecutor and I agreed the kid probably didn't really do anything wrong, and it isn't likely to stick. But if he went after the kid, I knew Markinson would do his best to free him."

"You are devious."

"Well, he hasn't turned himself in yet, but it looks good."

Craig stuck his head in. "Somewhere in Queens, Sally. Couldn't get it any closer than that."

"Thanks, Craig. He says he's coming in anyway, but I'd love to turn the tables on him and nab him sooner."

Kevin limped along for another couple of blocks, glancing at his watch. He picked up another pay phone and dialed his lawyer again.

"Kevin." He paused. "You know they wouldn't be able to convict this kid, right?"

"What?"

"I tried to tell you when you called me earlier, but you hung up. There's no way they could make harboring charges stick against a thirteen-year-old kid. Seriously, even if he said he did it, he was obviously afraid of you. That's coercion. Any lawyer could get him off."

Kevin had to swallow hard. "Shit."

"You still want to give yourself up? You know that's the best thing you can do."

Kevin had to lean against the side of the phone booth, unsure of his footing. The sidewalk felt as if it was going to open up and swallow him. He glanced at his watch. He had to keep this conversation short. "I know."

"Let me talk to the DA up there and get back to you. How can I reach you?"

"You can't. Just give Justin the details."

"So we're still doing this, right? You're giving yourself up?"

Kevin looked at the second hand sweeping its way around the face of his watch. "Yeah."

Sally jumped on the phone when it rang twenty minutes later. "Who? Okay, I'll talk to him." She raised her eyebrows and put it on the speaker. "This is Deputy Sally Barnard."

"This is Harvey Longwood. I'm Kevin Markinson's attorney. How are you, Deputy Barnard?"

"I'm just fine, thank you."

"Good. My client will turn himself in Friday morning on the steps of the Dutchess county courthouse. We've already talked to the DA up there about this. The hearing is scheduled for ten-thirty. Mr. Markinson would like to be available to testify if needed. However, from talking to the DA, I believe the boy will simply be freed. It's my understanding that this case isn't really very strong anyway. We'll sit down and have a chat with a judge just before the scheduled time for the hearing. Do you have a problem with any of this?"

"No, sir. I'm simply responsible for turning your client over to the state. I think we can fudge that by a few minutes." She smiled. Thomas stood shaking his head. "I assume your client has enough sense to come unarmed, despite his flair for the dramatic."

"Well, Deputy Barnard, my client is a bit concerned about his personal safety."

"I will guarantee his safety, Mr. Longwood. As long as he's unarmed. I guess we'll see you on Friday, Mr. Longwood."

"Goodbye."

She cut off the connection.

CHAPTER 23

Kevin was lying on the couch as he spoke on the phone, feet up on the arm, staring at the yellowed ceiling. "Justin?"

"Yes, sir."

"See if you can get Cindy to take tomorrow off work. I really want to see my kids again."

"I'll do what I can, boss."

"Did you find out anything at Harvey's office?"

"Did you know about the other prints?"

"What other prints?"

"The car had three sets of prints. Yours and two unknowns."

Kevin sat up. "Two?"

"One turned out to be the owner of the car. It was stolen shortly before the shooting went down."

"Right."

"The other set of prints remain unidentified, as far as I know. They did a search at the time, but it can take a long time to find a match. We wouldn't know even if they had come up with a match now, because once you were found guilty, we wouldn't have gotten any updated information."

"Even if we knew the prints belonged to Carlos, that wouldn't prove he did the shooting. Was there any testing done to see if I had fired a weapon? You know, that skin thing?"

"Nope."

"And we've certainly lost the opportunity with Carlos."

"Your only hope is to get him back here and get a confession out of him. There's nothing in the evidence that's going to get you off."

"How do we find him?"

"Boss, I'm not a fucking detective."

"I didn't kill that cop, Justin."

"I know."

"We've got to find that little shit."

"Yes, sir."

"Don't call me sir." Kevin dropped the phone into its cradle even as Justin started to say something else. He stared at it and felt a sudden need for a drink. He could taste the whiskey, could feel it in his throat. Those thoughts led him almost as quickly to his memorized list of meetings in the borough, but that was ridiculous. How on earth could he go to a meeting if he couldn't even leave his apartment? He didn't have a sponsor anymore, nobody he could call. He picked up the phone book, set it on his leg, and thumbed through the yellow pages, wondering if any of the liquor stores would deliver. The book fell onto the floor, open to the beginning of the white pages, where the toll-free number for AA jumped out at him. That was just unfair. He pushed the phone book under the couch with his foot and stood up.

Justin made the arrangements and Kevin drove a rented car down to an amusement park in New Jersey the next morning.

He was waiting just inside the main gate. The boys recognized him, and this time they both went towards him without any urging from her. They stopped a few strides off, and he eyed them, tilting his head to get a better look. Andy's hair was too long, flopping into his eyes. Although considering the way he had been wearing his own hair up until recently he had no right to complain. Michael's hair wasn't as long. Both boys were wearing loose clothing, Andy had on black cargo pants and a black tee shirt, Michael loose cutoffs and an extra-large striped rugby shirt.

"How you guys doing?"

The boys just stared at him, and then turned back to look at their mother.

She came up behind them. He leaned around to speak to her. "It's good to see you again." He liked the way she was dressed. Tan shorts, sneakers, and a Hawaiian shirt, all reds and blues and greens. He stared at her bare legs, and licked his lips, feeling a stirring in his gut.

"Yeah, well, this was a good idea. The boys deserve to see their dad."

"You really think that's why we came?" asked Andy.

"What?" Cindy turned towards him.

"Nothing."

Kevin looked at the boys. "What do you want to do first?"

Michael perked up. "The roller coaster."

Andy just shrugged.

"Roller coaster it is, then. You guys won't mind if I take a pass, right?" They walked towards the line and as Kevin fell back he lit a cigarette with shaking hands.

Cindy glared at him. "I wish you wouldn't smoke around the kids."

He turned his head and blew the smoke away from her. "I can't go all day without one, okay?"

"We've only been here ten minutes."

"Let's not fight." He didn't want to waste the precious little time he had with her.

"I'm sorry. I'm just a little on edge."

"I know what you mean."

As they caught up with the kids, standing outside the pipe maze that defined the line, Michael turned towards his mother. "Hey, Mom. Why doesn't Dad live with us?"

"Aside from the whole prison thing?" Andy muttered.

Cindy glanced at Kevin, who was staring, open-mouthed, at the boys.

"Why, Mom?" Michael persisted.

"Because of your father's job."

"Nothing to do with prison, then?" Andy put in.

Kevin turned his glare on her.

Cindy shrugged.

Michael spoke up. "I think you're just a crook. I don't think you even have a job."

"Why would you say that?" Kevin responded.

"I'm not stupid, Dad. I saw the news; you just broke out of prison. That's where you've been for the last six years." He turned his back on his father and moved forward in the line.

Kevin bit his lip. He looked at Cindy, who gave him a "Let me see you get out of this one" look. Returning his attention to his younger son, he said, "I'm, um, I do have a job and someday, when we're in a more appropriate place, I'll tell you about it, okay?"

Michael responded without looking back at him. "You don't have to treat me like I'm seven. I already told you I'm not stupid. Besides, even if you were a crook, I wouldn't turn you in. I don't want to see Mom hurt."

Kevin found himself speechless.

Michael continued. "What about Justin?"

Justin, standing in front of the kids, swiveled his head to look at the boy.

"What about Justin, Michael?"

"Does he have a real job?"

"I do freelance security," Justin offered.

"Justin works for me." Kevin scratched his chin. "Sometimes."

"So what are you, like a spy or something?" asked Andy.

"Or something."

"So why were you in jail?"

"I screwed up."

"So you have to be a criminal, Dad, because you broke out." Michael was insistent.

Kevin took a deep breath, and lowered his voice. "Yes, Michael you're right. I was wrong to break out. I'm turning myself in tomorrow, okay?"

"Why'd you break out?"

Kevin hesitated. He broke out because his boss had something for him to do. It wasn't easy for him to understand it, never mind explaining it to someone else. He could feel a twitch starting in his left cheek. He wanted a drink. "I guess I just didn't want to be there anymore."

"Okay, Dad, whatever you say." Michael shrugged his shoulders.

"That's your reason?" Andy responded, his voice rising. "You just felt like it? What if you just felt like killing somebody?"

Kevin looked past his sons at the next family in line. The mother was staring at him, open-mouthed, and the father shifted his gaze as he shoved his two little girls forward.

"Uh, boys, can we talk about this some other time?"

The boys walked ahead and Kevin looked at Cindy as they followed behind them.

"You know that's only going to get harder as they get older."

"I know. I thought Michael was going to turn me in." He looked at Justin, and sent him on ahead with the kids.

"I don't want them to go through this," Cindy said. "The stuff I've had to go through. The sitting by the phone, the not knowing. This time, Kevin, the news said you got shot; then they couldn't find you. I thought you were dead in some swamp."

He cleared his throat, not knowing what to say in response.

"I hate that I can't see you. I hate that you've never even been to our house."

"I thought the kids would like the amusement park."

"It's not about the amusement park, Kevin. I'm not sure I want to go through this anymore."

"What are you saying? You want a divorce? You want to leave me?" He stopped, took off the sunglasses and tried to catch her eye, panic rising in his chest. "This is the last thing I need right now."

She looked at the pavement. "Why don't you just give it up? Quit the lying, stay in jail, serve your time, and get on with your life."

"Oh, right." He walked away. "You don't know what it's like."

"I know more about prison than I ever wanted to."

He turned and stood facing her. "And if I do that—quit working, stay in prison—what are we going to live on? You don't make enough money. We can't live on my settlement, not and send two kids to college. I don't have any other talents, other than doing what I'm doing now."

She shook her head. "I don't want to know what you do now. But there's always a way. You know we could do it. It might be tough, but we'd get by."

"I'm not going to have my family living in some cheap, smelly apartment while I rot in jail. I've been there. My life may not be perfect right now, but it's a hell of a lot better than what I had growing up."

"And what about the next time you break out, and get shot? You think I want to see you dead? What about the kids? Is that fair to them?" There were tears in her eyes now. "They're not stupid, you know; they know a lot more than you give them credit for. They've seen the news."

"Well, maybe you shouldn't be letting them watch so much television."

"Maybe you should just stay put and think about somebody other than yourself for once." She took a deep breath; let it out in a long sigh. "This isn't what I thought I was getting when I married you."

"What did you expect? You went into this with your eyes open."

"That's not true. I didn't know who you were, what you were."

He glanced around, checking to see if anybody was paying attention. He lowered his voice, struggling with his anger; trying to see things from her point of view. "You had your pick of the guys, Cindy. You didn't have to marry me; you wanted me. You liked what you saw."

"I wanted what I thought you were. I liked the long hair and the tattoos, the cigarettes and the combat boots. I thought I wanted a rebel, somebody different. Not a criminal." She lowered her voice to the point where he could hardly hear it. "A murderer."

That hurt. "I don't need this right now, Cindy. I'm going back to prison tomorrow. I don't want to go, but I will, and this is my last chance to be with you and the kids for a while. So let's just enjoy the time, okay?" He put the glasses back on and started to walk towards where the boys and Justin were standing, waiting in line.

Without looking at her he said, "If you want a divorce, I won't fight it. It's not what I want, but if it's really what you want, then you go ahead. If I'm not what you want, not what you thought you were getting, then just do it. Just leave."

"Kevin." She raised her voice.

"What?" He turned, twisting on his heel, ready for a fight.

"I don't want to divorce you, I want to live with you. I love you. I just would have liked a normal life."

He softened, very nearly melting. He walked back to her, put his good arm around her, and hugged her. "A normal life. Wouldn't that be nice?"

"Why'd they hit you in the face?" she asked, running her fingertips over the bruises.

"Just those kind of people. It's an intimidation thing." He looked at the boys. They were about halfway through the line.

"Were you scared?"

"When?"

"When you were in that house, going through this. Getting beat up."

He hesitated and stepped away from her. "Yeah. They were scary people."

"Take those glasses off again."

He took them off, blinking in the sunlight.

She studied his face. "Nasty shiner."

"Goes good with my nose."

"Can you get Justin to take the kids for a couple of hours?"

"Why?"

"Why do you think?" She started walking towards the boys again. She looked over her shoulder towards him. "What do we usually do after a fight?"

"I can't remember," he said, putting the sunglasses back on. "It's been six years."

"Maybe I can refresh your memory." She walked back to where he was standing and kissed him hard on the mouth.

"I think my memory is coming back. Can you do that again?"

"Not here, you idiot. People are staring."

"Let them stare." He pulled her close and held her tight. Then he let her go and half trotted off towards Justin and the boys.

He made the arrangements with Justin. Finish the park together, and then Justin would take the boys out to their favorite pizza place. Let them play some pinball and video games and take them home. Kevin would take Cindy back to his apartment in his rented car, maybe order some takeout food.

"You know the boys are at an age now where they're just starting to realize the world is not always black and white." Cindy was standing with him next to yet another fast ride Kevin didn't want to go on. "Andy doesn't like it."

"Doesn't like what?"

"He wants the world to be right or wrong. No gray areas."

"So?"

"You don't fit into that. You're his father, but you're not a good guy. You don't wear a white hat. He thinks you should. He doesn't want to love you because of what you've done, but he wants to love you because you're his father."

"He doesn't love me at all."

"Of course he does. He just doesn't like you, or trust you. He doesn't like what you do."

"So he'd like me to be a spy. Someone who can do what I've done without being a bad guy. Except I don't know any spies who believe the world is black and white. They all live in a gray world." He sighed. "Like me."

"You know the difference between right and wrong."

"I do?"

"You just choose to ignore it."

Kevin nibbled at a hot dog and watched his kids eat, marveling at the way they looked. They were so big, so old. It had been way too long.

"When do you boys go back to school?"

Andy just looked the other way.

"End of the month," Michael answered.

"What grade you guys in?"

Andy set his jaw and picked up his can of soda.

"I'm going into seventh, Dad." Michael nodded towards Andy. "He'll be going into ninth."

"You get good grades?"

Michael shrugged. "B's, mostly."

"Shit!" Andy dropped his soda and jumped from his seat as a yellow jacket buzzed by his face.

Cindy held out a hand.

"Come on, Mom, I was about to get stung."

She wiggled her fingers. Kevin tried to figure out what she was doing.

Andy reached into a pocket, pulled out a quarter, and handed it to his mother.

Kevin looked at her. "What was that?"

"The boys have to pay a fine if they swear."

He glanced at Justin, who shrugged. He focused back on Cindy, eyebrows raised. "You're kidding me."

She glared at him. "You're not here to raise them. I'm going to raise them the way I think they should be raised. I don't want my kids using that kind of language."

"Shit?"

"Give her a quarter, Dad," Andy said, laughing.

She glared at the boy, and then turned the look on her husband. "It has to do with manners and respect, Kevin."

"There're lots of worse things they could be saying."

"Just let me handle this, okay?"

He decided it wasn't worth getting into, shrugged, and instantly regretted it. He could feel the blood drain out of his face, and he bit his lip.

"Does your arm hurt a lot, Dad?" Michael looked at him with a frown.

"It does." He nodded.

"You screwed up again, didn't you?"

"What?"

"You didn't set out to get shot, did you?"

Kevin looked around, to see who was listening. "I'd rather not talk about it right now, Michael."

"When will you want to talk about it, Dad?"

Kevin fidgeted in his seat. "You can't talk about this kind of thing with people around."

"Why?"

God, was the kid stupid? Kevin eyed the boy, trying to figure out why he was questioning everything. "How do you know who these people are? How many of them are off-duty cops? How many of them read the papers? Or watch the fucking television?"

"You're paranoid."

"I am not. I'm careful. I didn't stay alive this long by being stupid."

Both boys blinked.

He hissed under his breath. "Don't you know that's what it comes down to? My life, okay? Staying alive; keeping my life. You know how many of the people I have after me would like to kill me? And now you guys have a problem with me?"

"I don't know," Andy said, looking down. "I don't think I know you well enough to have a problem with you."

"What?"

Andy shrugged, didn't lift his eyes.

"You have to look at me. I can't hear you unless you look at me."

Andy shook his head.

"If I was around more, would that make you guys happy?"

Michael shrugged and Andy just stared at the ground.

"And if I got caught or killed because I was around, would that make you happy?"

Cindy glared at him.

The rest of the day the boys kept their distance, not bothering to talk to him.

Chapter 24

He held her close with his good arm the minute he closed the door. Pulled off the hat and sunglasses and tossed them towards the couch. Then he buried his face in her hair, losing himself in her smell. A simple, clean smell. That was something he had always liked about her. She didn't wear perfume, rarely wore makeup. She had a sort of baby powder smell about her, something clean and fresh and new. It brought memories with it. He could still picture her when he first saw her. She was twenty-three or so, standing in the doorway of the diner in her nurse's uniform, smiling at him while he leaned in the kitchen doorway, soapsuds clinging to his arms. She was the first woman he had ever fallen for. The only woman he had ever fallen for. She taught him to love.

"Six years," he muttered, then turned her face up to his and kissed her.

She pulled away, looking around the apartment. "This place is awful. Who did the decorating?" She sniffed. "What have you been doing, chain smoking for the last three days?"

"Less talk, more sex."

"Easy, big guy." She led him towards the bedroom.

"Oh, are you one of those loose women?"

She laughed. Then she pushed the bedroom door closed behind them, and walked over to where he stood in the middle of the room. She took his coat off, helping him get his arm out of the sling, and the shirt off. He was naked from the waist up now, except for the gauze and tape on his shoulder. She shook her head. "You're a mess, you know that?"

"If you're trying to seduce me, madam, you're doing a good job." He pushed his sneakers off with his feet. It felt like the whole lower half of his body was throbbing, ready.

She stepped closer, and traced the scars with her fingertips. He shuddered. It bothered him, her fascination with his old injuries, but not enough to ask her to stop.

"How's your arm?"

"What arm?" he replied, leaning towards her, kissing her on the neck.

She backed up, and took off her shirt and bra, then her pants.

All the blood was rushing out of his head and he felt dizzy. He sat down on the bed, too fast. Damn.

"You've lost weight." She walked towards him.

"You're talking again. Mmmpf." He couldn't finish his thought because her mouth was on his. He moved his hand to her breast, feeling her reaction.

She was unbuttoning his pants.

He wanted her, wanted her now. He slipped out of his jeans and sank down onto the bed, rolling onto his right side and pulling her to him, his mouth hard on hers.

"You're different, you know. Sometimes." She was lying beside him, with his right arm wrapped around her, tracing the scars again.

"What do you mean?" His heart was still pounding.

"You're desperate, wilder, in a hurry. Like you're afraid somebody's going to come through the door blasting." She smiled, a sly smile that he liked.

"Is that okay with you? I wasn't being selfish, right?"

"Sure. No, it's just different, that's all. I know when you're on the run just by the way you behave in bed."

"I've been on the run for the last twenty years, haven't I?"

She laughed, and ran her fingers over the scar on his chest.

He had to swallow hard. She shifted her attention to his right arm.

"This is new," she said, probing the long scar on the underside of the forearm.

"Yeah."

"But it didn't just happen. It's what, a month or so old?"

"Yeah."

"So what happened?"

He stared at the ceiling. "I got into a fight."

"Really? You?"

"Yeah."

"Tell me about it."

He took in a deep breath and let it out in a long sigh. "I was up to Clinton. You know, Dannemora."

"You were there for six years, right?"

He nodded. "Clinton's a weird place. They've got this hillside in the yard. Used to be a ski jump there, believe it or not. Anyway, they've got these little plots of land; they call them courts. The guys can buy them, or I guess lease them, so you've got some ownership. Guys'll set things up, like cook stoves, or little rock gardens. I was growing vegetables."

She rolled towards him. "You were growing vegetables? Do you even know how to plant seeds?"

"I had some help."

"You got into a fight over vegetables?"

"It's a little more complicated." He closed his eyes for a second and the images appeared—the big guy with the knife, stomping on Kevin's pea plants, as Kevin came to the defense of the youngster the big guy was after. "It was a gang thing."

"You're in a gang?"

He laughed, and reached for his cigarettes, pulling himself up a bit, and leaning against the pillows as he lit the Camel. "It was between two other guys. One of them was my new roommate. I got stuck in the middle."

"And you got cut."

"You should have seen the other guy."

"You cut someone?"

"No. I don't…" He had to pause. "I follow the rules when I'm in. I didn't have a weapon. The other guy, my roommate, took a pretty good slash to the chest, he was bleeding out."

"You helped him, didn't you?"

"Yeah." He leaned over to the bedside table and tapped the ash off. "I got transferred down to Hudson after that."

"Was that a reward?"

"I didn't ask for it."

"Do you think they'll send you back there? Back to Hudson?"

"No. Hudson is medium." He sighed. "They'll probably send me back to Dannemora. That's where they send the guys they don't like. Not violent enough for Attica; Sing Sing is too close to home. They'll be sending a message, by moving me away from my family."

She was quiet for a minute, snuggled up against him. Then she rolled away from him, stood up, stretched, and padded into the bathroom. "Do you have a bathrobe I can borrow?"

"I don't know. Did you send one?"

"What do you want to do for supper?"

"I'm not hungry."

"How long do you think Justin will want to watch the kids?" She walked back into the bedroom, wearing one of his dress shirts.

He licked his lips. "How about the next six years?" He set the cigarette down, stood up, and walked towards her, naked.

She sidestepped him and walked to the phone, picking it up and punching the buttons. "Let me see how long he can stay."

He crossed the room in a hurry and put his finger on the switch hook. "You can't call home from here."

She looked at him, and her face crumpled. "I'm so sorry, Kevin. I forgot." She sat down on the bed.

"It's okay."

"How can you live like this? How can I live like this?" Tears started in her eyes.

He sat beside her and put his good arm around her. "You get used to it."

"I don't want to get used to it." She pushed him away and stood up. "You know, this crummy apartment reminds me of something you were saying earlier. What was it? Oh yeah, you didn't want to live in a smelly little apartment like you grew up in." She looked into his eyes. "Is this the way you want to live? Is this so much better than prison?"

He licked his lips. "The sex is better."

She glared at him.

That joke was a bomb. He sighed, got up, and slid his boxer shorts on.

"How am I supposed to get home? You can't very well take me."

"I'll call Justin's cell phone." He pulled on his jeans.

While they waited for Justin, he sat and put his arm around her again. "Where would you like to live? If you had your choice?"

She looked at him. "You're going back to prison, Kevin."

"I wasn't talking about me. You. You and the boys. Don't think about me. Think about yourself for once."

"I'd go home."

"Back to New Hampshire."

"Yes."

"Would you do that, if it didn't matter to me? If I didn't matter? If I was out of the picture?"

"You're not going to run again, are you? Or get yourself killed?"

"No, I'm going back to prison. I'll be out of circulation, and you don't visit me anyway. So why do you need to be around here?"

"I'd visit you if you'd let me."

"I know." He wouldn't look at her. "I don't want you to see me like that." He moved his eyes back to hers. "Do you want to move to New Hampshire? Take the boys and go?"

She shrugged her shoulders. "I guess."

"Let's see what we can do to make it happen, okay?"

"Are you serious?"

"Of course." He stood up and stretched his right arm. "Justin can help. Put this house on the market; find one up there. I know people who can do things with identity—get you a new name, and get the kids into schools up there. You won't have to think about cops anymore." He walked over to the refrigerator and got out a bottle of water. "You want a drink?"

"What do you have?"

He eyed the shelves. "Water."

She walked over. "Have you been eating?"

He shrugged.

"Kevin."

"Enough to live on."

She opened the garbage and examined the contents. "What, once a day?"

"I'm not hungry." He walked back to the couch and sat down.

"You remember what happened the last time you didn't eat."

"I know. I don't let it go that far." He didn't even like to think about that—the vitamin deficiency that had developed when he drank instead of eating.

She eyed him and changed the subject. "I like what you did to your hair."

"You do?"

"Have you ever had it this short before?"

"Parris Island."

She frowned.

"Marine boot camp."

"Oh. Is that why you kept it long; you didn't want to be reminded?"

He shrugged. "I guess I started letting it grow as a sort of protest. I wanted to prove I had control over some segment of my life. I got into the habit. Just never thought about cutting it short." He grinned. "My commanding officer hated it."

"I like it short. Although the color is disturbing." She touched the bristles. "I always liked your blond hair."

"I think it will grow out. The color, that is. I'll keep it short if you like it that way. Doesn't matter to me." He paused. "What does Andy want for his birthday?"

"You remembered?"

"Yeah."

She shrugged. "He likes computer games."

"If I give you fifty bucks will you buy him something from me?"

"You could just give him the fifty bucks."

"Come on, can't you just help me out here? Buy the kid something he'll like?"

"Okay. You want me to drive you upstate tomorrow?"

"No."

"Can I be there?"

"No."

"Why? You going to do something stupid?"

"Nope."

"Then why can't I come?"

"Cindy. I don't, I can't…" He let his voice trail off. "You don't want… I don't want you to see me like that. In chains."

She turned her head, avoiding his eyes. "I love you, Kevin. I can handle it."

"It's not that. I know you're strong. I'm not the same." He struggled for the words. "I'm different. I have to be different. It's not you." He couldn't explain it to her, the shell he had to grow when he was away from her, when he was dealing with cops. When he was in prison.

"I could be there to support you."

He almost told her he didn't need her support, but he bit the words off before he got them out. "I'll be okay."

There was a knock on the door. Kevin got to his feet, grabbed his handgun, and stationed himself beside the bedroom door. Cindy swallowed hard, looked at him, and then moved to open the front door.

"Are you ready?" asked Justin from the hallway.

"Yeah."

Kevin walked over to her and gave her a peck on the cheek. "I'll see you sometime."

"I love you."

"I know." He smiled as she shook her head. "I love you, too."

"Take care of yourself."

"I will."

"Don't do anything stupid."

He shook his head. "I won't."

"You come back to me in one piece."

"Yes, ma'am."

Justin cleared his throat. "I don't want to break this up, but I have to get moving."

Cindy turned and followed the big guy. Kevin stood, watching until the door closed behind them.

CHAPTER 25

Thomas perched on the edge of Sally's desk. "So, what's the plan? How are we going to do this?"

She looked up from her paperwork. "Do what?"

"This thing with Markinson."

She looked over the top of her reading glasses towards Craig and Liz, who were listening in from their own desks. She didn't want to disappoint anyone. "I don't think we'll need a whole team. I've already talked to the sheriff's department up there. We don't want to spook Markinson. We don't want a bloodbath, so we do it low-key."

"No SOG?"

"The last thing we need is those bozos." She looked over at the next desk, at a deputy who happened to be on the Special Operations Group team. "No offense, Phil."

Phil ignored her.

"From what Bob has told me about this guy, he reacts to force with force. We go in loaded for bear and we'll have to use it. We go in treating him like a human being and he'll behave like one. We give him the benefit of the doubt."

"Sure." Thomas didn't sound convinced.

"Of course, I've alerted the sheriff's department, so they know what time we're coming. They're going to keep the area as clear as they can without making it too obvious. We don't want to scare him. And we'll go in ready to rumble."

"Without looking like it though, right?"

"Right. You've got it, Mr. Neelon." She glanced over at Craig, debating who to take with her. "And you've earned the right to drive me up there to bring him in."

"Thanks for the vote of confidence." Thomas said with sarcasm.

"I could take Liz instead."

"I'll go."

"Thanks, Thomas."

Thursday night at dinner Danny's mother dropped the bomb.

"They can't get a conviction. They're going through the motions to get the man to give himself up."

Danny sat and stared at his mom, his food forgotten. Then he jumped up from the table and ran upstairs to his room, throwing himself face down on the bed. His mother was there a moment later.

"You can't tell him, you understand me? You can't get in touch with him."

"How could I?" he shouted back. "I don't even know where he is." He rolled over and stared at the ceiling. Bait. That was what he was reduced to. Just a piece of cheese in a giant game of Mouse Trap.

"It's too late anyway. He's turning himself in tomorrow."

Danny could almost detect a note of triumph in his mother's voice. The good guys win again. He wondered how long she had known the truth. Probably since Tuesday morning. And she had allowed her son to suffer through the last few days, convinced he was going to end up in jail for it. But what hurt even more was knowing that Duke was going to jail instead, knowing that the man had given himself up for him. For nothing.

"Thomas, we need to drive up to Poughkeepsie now."

"Okay. Is this going to be a media event?"

"I guess we'll find out when we get there, but I kind of doubt it. Markinson is not fond of publicity. Why do you ask?"

"Well, you are dressed a little nicer than usual."

Sally glanced down at the neatly pressed chinos. "I probably will end up talking to the press at some point today," she said. "I just want to make a good impression."

"I'll bring my sport coat. So what's going on?"

"We're going to take Mr. Markinson into custody, escort him to his hearing, and then deliver him to the state."

"That's unusual."

"Yeah, I know. We got special permission. I don't want to be transferring custody more than once. Didn't want to hand him off to the county and then have them transfer him to the state. After what happened at that hospital, I'd rather keep him in sight."

"So do we have to drive him up to whatever prison they're sending him to?"

"Yeah, after the hearing. He's probably going back to Clinton."

"That's a long drive."

"I know. We can decide when we get up there if we want to stay overnight up there or just come home."

Kevin took Harvey's advice and wore a pair of tan chinos, with a tweed sport coat over a short sleeve shirt and a tie. That had been a real struggle, figuring out how to tie the stupid thing with one hand. It wasn't as if he made a habit of wearing a tie anyway. It surprised him that Cindy had even packed one for him, a blue and gold striped model he didn't even remember owning.

Harvey drove, timing their arrival thirty minutes early. Kevin wanted to make sure there wasn't an army of cops. The steps of the old brick courthouse were empty, although there were a few people walking by.

"Let's do it," said Kevin with a sigh as he unbuckled his seat belt. He pulled the little revolver out of his jacket pocket and dropped it in the glove compartment.

"What is that?"

"That was my insurance, in case someone decided to keep me from coming up here."

"I told the marshals you'd be unarmed."

"I am now."

"And what am I supposed to do with it? I assume it's illegal."

"Call Justin, he'll take care of it. You never saw it; never touched it."

Harvey shook his head, maneuvered himself into his wheelchair, and got out of the van.

Kevin walked up the steps while Harvey rolled up the ramp. Kevin turned and faced the street, watching.

"Oh, hey, Harvey, would you mind taking this?" Kevin slipped his heavy watch off his left wrist and handed it to the lawyer. "Make sure Cindy gets it back. I've had it a long time."

"No problem. You going to hang onto your ring?"

"Yeah. They'll let me keep that. Cindy'd kill me if I took it off." He didn't want to think about what he was facing; that where he was going he couldn't have a wristwatch.

The man cleared his throat. "She couldn't be here today?"

"I didn't want her here."

"You're not going to do anything stupid, right?"

"I'm not going to do anything. No worries."

"I heard about the stunt you pulled, drawing down on a bunch of cops, wanting to get shot."

Kevin turned his head, taking his attention off the street to stare at the man in the wheelchair. "You won't tell her about that."

The younger man met his client's stare. "I just don't want to be party to something like that, you understand?"

Kevin shifted his gaze back to the street. "Don't worry about it."

"You want me to come up and pick up the rest of your stuff?"

"Yeah, if you don't mind. I don't know where I'll be going."

"As far as I know, you're going back to Clinton."

"You don't mind making that drive?"

"No, I don't mind. It's billable time."

Kevin nodded.

Sally and Thomas also arrived ahead of schedule.

"Is that him?" asked Thomas, pointing out the tall, thin man with his arm in a sling and a face full of purple bruises.

"Has to be. I can't believe he got here before us. You cover me."

They parked in front of the courthouse, right next to a blue van with handicapped plates on it. Sally got out of the SUV. Thomas also got out, leaving his door open and bringing his shotgun onto the hood of the Suburban.

"Mr. Markinson?" she asked as she came up the steps, left hand on her weapon, staying wide, making sure Thomas had a clear shot.

"Yes, ma'am," he replied, his eyes shifting from her to the man with the shotgun.

"Would you mind just keeping your hands where I can see them? My partner has an itchy trigger finger."

He held his right hand out, well away from his body. He held the left hand out as much as he could.

"Are you armed?" she asked.

"No."

"Do you mind if I check? I'm Deputy Marshal Sally Barnard, by the way. Would you turn around, please?" She frisked him. "Okay." She motioned to Thomas, who put the shotgun in the car and started up the steps.

"I wish I could say it was nice to meet you," Kevin said in a low voice as he turned around again.

"I know it's a big thrill for me," she replied. "I know you've got a bit of rabbit in you. Just in case you feel like taking off, I want you to know I've got this nifty semi-automatic here." She held open her blazer so he could see the holster. "I'm a pretty good shot, too. And I can shoot you if you're running, whether or not you're armed." She pulled out her handcuffs. "So, Mr. Markinson, what made you decide to turn yourself in to me? Did you think I'd be a softy?"

"No, ma'am. I called you because you were the one I saw on television; you looked like you were doing the most work. You were the one I ran into at the hospital. I figured you deserved the collar."

She snapped the handcuff onto his right wrist, snugged it down tight, remembering he was double jointed or something. She felt him pull back, and almost regretted it. "You trying to change your rep? Going to be Mr. Nice Guy now?"

Thomas snorted.

She started to bring his right arm behind his back, and then frowned at the left arm in the sling.

Kevin cleared his throat. "I also figured you probably set up the kid, so you could get him off."

Sally was surprised, but didn't let it show. "I don't suppose you can bring that arm behind your back?"

"No, ma'am, I can't."

The lawyer cleared his throat. "My client has a documented injury, Deputy Barnard."

She sighed and considered shackles. Was there any reason to humiliate the man? Did she have any other choice? "I'm going to have use shackles then, because I know how much you like to run. Thomas, would you go down to the car and bring up my shackles?"

Thomas nodded and trotted down the steps.

"I'm not going to run," Kevin muttered.

"Sure you're not. I remember what you did at the hospital. I still can't believe that. Out cold my ass."

Kevin pursed his lips. "Opportunity presented itself."

"Well, there isn't going be any opportunity here, you understand?"

"Yes, ma'am."

She took the shackles from Thomas when he returned. "You gonna behave while I put these on?"

He closed his eyes and moved his head in an almost imperceptible nod.

She put the chain around his waist first, marveling at how thin he was, then crouched and fastened the cuffs around his ankles, brought the chain up and snapped the handcuffs, moving his left arm as she did. She caught the noise in his throat and glanced at his face, saw a quick flicker of pain cross through his eyes.

"Hurts a bit, does it?"

"I can handle it."

"Occupational hazard, ay?" put in Thomas.

The taller man twisted his head to glare at him.

"Let's go on in, okay?" said Sally. "It's got be cooler in there, and we won't attract quite so much attention."

They went into the courthouse and sat down on a bench outside the judge's office to wait.

Sally looked at her prisoner. He was staring into space, his face set in a frown. He really looked beat up, and it wasn't just the fresh bruises standing out against his pale skin. This guy looked like he'd spent his whole life getting beat up. She brought her hand up to her chin, concentrating. He did look different from the pictures; that was for sure. The hair alone was enough for the average person. She had a hard time matching up this neatly dressed man with the short hair with the mug shots she'd seen, all long hair and mustache.

"Markinson."

His head swiveled towards her. "What?"

"Did you do what they said you did?"

"What?"

"D'you kill that cop?"

He shook his head, and half-snorted. "You're a fed, lady, you expect me to answer that?"

"Forget who I am for the moment. You convinced the kid you didn't do it. Convince me."

"He was a kid. He was easy to convince."

"So you are what they say you are?"

"What do they say I am?"

"An assassin. A cop killer."

She was sure she saw something flicker in those cold blue-gray eyes.

"I didn't kill that cop. I don't kill cops; I don't kill civilians. I killed soldiers. I am not what they say I am."

"How do you account for your rep?"

He shifted his gaze. Wouldn't meet her eyes. She wasn't ready to believe him.

"I tried to save that cop's life. I caught a bullet trying to stop his murder. I did not kill him. That's not my style." He looked at her again.

She still didn't believe him. She narrowed her eyes, thinking. "Yeah, I heard it wasn't your style. But you were in a tight spot, you had just started your run, and here was this young cop trying to send you back."

"Think about it. If he had caught me, what's the worst that would have happened, a few more months on my sentence, right?"

She nodded.

"It made no sense for me to kill him. You've read the file, right? You know one of the other things they say about me is that I'm smart, right?"

She nodded again. "IQ off the charts."

"So why the hell would I kill a cop? If I am the other thing they say about me, if I am an assassin, or was one—a very successful assassin—why the hell would I jeopardize that by killing a fu… uh, a cop? I'm not stupid."

"So why didn't you stay and do the time? After you were convicted? You could have been out on parole in eight years."

"You ever been in prison?"

She cocked her head sideways. "Sure."

"No you haven't. You've never done time. You've been in a prison, sure, but that's not the same as being in prison." He looked down for a moment, staring at the floor. He raised his hands, pulling against the cuffs, rolling his shoulders.

Thomas tensed up. "Watch it."

Kevin glanced in his direction, and then looked down again. "I couldn't do it."

"But you just did six years before this escape. Up in Little Siberia, right?"

"I'm getting old. I think I'm mellowing with age." He paused, raised his eyes, and met her gaze again. "I also don't have to worry as much about my family. You know I got a lot of money from getting beat up."

She nodded.

"Plus I've got a rep in prison now. When I first went in I had to prove myself. Now everybody knows who I am. Nobody messes with me."

"So you going to stay put this time?"

He shrugged his right shoulder, looked straight ahead again. "Probably."

She raised her eyebrows. "Probably?"

"I'm sick of getting shot." Kevin lifted his hands, reaching towards his coat pocket.

"What the hell are you doing?" Thomas put a hand on the older man's arm.

"Cigarettes."

"Not in here, buddy. No smoking."

"How much longer do we have to wait?"

"You're the one that showed up early," replied Sally. She glanced at her watch again. "It's getting there."

CHAPTER 26

When Danny walked in with his mother, he saw Duke sitting on a bench outside the courtroom, between two people he recognized as the Deputy US Marshals he had met on Monday. He looked at Duke, trying to catch his eye, but the man avoided his gaze. Danny wanted to talk to him, to tell him to run, that there was no reason for him to be here, but he couldn't see any way to do it.

The courtroom was empty of spectators when the gray-haired judge motioned for Kevin to step forward. "Mr. Markinson?"

Kevin shuffled up the aisle and stood in front of the bench. "Yes, sir."

"It's my understanding that we already have a plea arrangement worked out in this case." The judge was looking over the tops of his glasses in the direction of the DA, who nodded. "So, do you have something to say, Mr. Markinson?"

"Yes, sir."

"How do you plead to the charge of escape?"

"No contest."

"And regarding the prosecution of the minor," the judge looked down at his papers. "Daniel Rutledge. You have something to say in that case as well? Did you coerce the boy into helping you during your escape?"

"Yes, sir. I forced him to take me to his house."

Danny jumped to his feet. "He did not!"

The judge looked at the kid, his hand on his gavel. "Sit down, Mr. Rutledge." He returned his attention to Kevin. "It's my understanding you got into a bit of a mess while at the boy's house. You killed a man—a Mr. Paul Sandisfield."

Danny jumped to his feet again. "You can't blame him for that! I saw the whole thing. It was self-defense. He saved my life; that guy would have killed me!"

"Danny, sit down." His mother grabbed him by the arm.

"Paully had a rifle; he was shooting at the cops. He would have killed him. Probably would have killed me, too. He saved my life." The boy twisted away from his mother's grip, running up the aisle towards Kevin, who stepped closer to the bench. This brought a quick reaction from both deputy marshals and the court security officer, all of them converging on Kevin. The court officer stepped in front of Danny, who leaned around him to try to speak to Kevin. "Tell them. You tell them what really happened."

Kevin swallowed, staring straight ahead, not looking at Danny. The judge looked at Danny, and then at the prosecutor.

"We can't have this sort of behavior in my courtroom, do you understand? This is all unusual—this whole request—and I won't tolerate this."

The DA nodded. "We elected not to charge him with it, your honor."

"Settle down, son." The judge looked at Danny again and sighed. "This is not the forum for any of this."

Danny sat down, shaking.

"Mr. Markinson. I'm sentencing you to three years for the escape. That's the minimum under the guidelines."

Kevin nodded without lifting his eyes from the floor.

"I appreciate your testimony on behalf of the boy, but he wouldn't have been convicted anyway."

Kevin lifted his head, thinking about another three years in Clinton. Three years he didn't deserve.

The judge smiled. "Prisoner is remanded to the custody of the state."

As they walked out of the courtroom, Kevin clenched his fists, tightening his wrists against the cuffs. "So this was all for nothing?"

"We talked about this." The lawyer turned his face up towards his client. "Don't make a scene, Kevin."

Thomas put a hand on Kevin's right arm. "Let's go."

Kevin pulled against the man, stepping back, trying to throw the marshal off balance, to get the upper hand. He moved towards his attorney, towering over the man, glaring down at him. Harvey Longwood went pale. Kevin struggled to free his arms, tried to raise a hand, to do something, anything. His ears were ringing again and his vision was narrowing.

"Markinson!" Sally barked at him.

Thomas grabbed Kevin's right arm with both hands and set himself against the older, lighter man, keeping him from moving. Kevin tried to twist away from him.

Sally raised her voice. "Deputy Neelon is a whole lot stronger than you, Mr. Markinson. I suggest you mellow out."

"Do I need to get out the stun gun?" Neelon growled through clenched teeth, feet braced.

"Kevin, this kind of behavior is not helpful for your case," the lawyer tried.

Kevin twisted his head, looking up and down the hall, trying to place the exits, trying to figure out if he could actually run with shackles on, wondering if he could get a hand on Neelon's gun. If he couldn't run, he could at least shoot himself.

It was at that moment Danny and his mother stepped out of the courtroom into the narrow hallway. Sally motioned towards them with her right hand, her left hand on her Glock. "Can you folks hang on just a second and let us clear out of the hall? I'd sure appreciate it."

She turned her attention once again to her prisoner. "You ready to grow up and behave, Mr. Markinson?"

Kevin looked at the boy then, for the first time that day. Their eyes met, Kevin registered the pain in the kid's eyes and turned away, his shoulders drooping.

Neelon gave him a good shove. "Goddamn idiot."

Kevin stumbled, his left leg buckling, but recovered and shuffled out into the courthouse lobby.

Danny hurried forward, towards the man in the wheelchair near Duke. "Excuse me, Mr. Longwood."

Kevin tried to push the man he was next to towards the exit, but Thomas stopped. "Quit shoving. Did I mention the stun gun yet?"

Kevin's lawyer looked at the boy, and held out his hand. "Harvey Longwood." He looked short, although it was hard to tell for sure with the man seated in his wheelchair. He had red curly hair, which was still curly despite the short cut.

"Daniel Rutledge."

"It's nice to meet you. What can I do for you?"

"Can we go?" asked Kevin.

"No," said Thomas. "I'm waiting for my boss."

Sally was standing with her head tilted sideways, listening to the conversation between Harvey and Danny.

Kevin sighed, shrugged, and shifted from foot to foot.

"Mr. Longwood, he saved my life."

Kevin turned his head, glancing at the boy.

"I know," the lawyer answered.

"He shouldn't get in trouble for that." Danny looked at Duke again, but the man had turned away, staring out the glass door, chewing on his lower lip.

"I need a cigarette," Kevin said to Thomas.

"You'll have to wait," Thomas growled.

"It's okay, he's only being punished for the escape, and the judge gave him the minimum sentence. He didn't get in trouble for any of what he did at your house," said Harvey.

"Okay." Danny looked at the floor, poking at the marble tiles with the toe of his shoe. Then he looked up at the man who had saved his life. "I didn't know. They didn't tell me."

Kevin narrowed his eyes and frowned down at the kid.

"I wouldn't have let you do this. I wouldn't have wanted you to do this. I didn't know they were going to trap you."

Kevin set his mouth in a hard line now, all the color gone from his lips. "I know."

"I'm sorry."

"It's not your fault. You did the right thing."

Danny straightened up. Turned and walked out of the building.

"Can I have a smoke now?"

Thomas shifted his gaze from the kid to the prisoner. "Sally?"

She sighed. "Yeah, what the hell. Let him have a cigarette. Outside."

It took him three tries to light a match, between the shackles, the sling, and his shaking hands, but he finally managed to get a Camel lit. He pulled on it, letting the smoke out in a long breath.

"Tell me what went on in that house, Markinson. Tell me why that kid worships the ground you walk on." Sally didn't look at him, just stared out over the street from where they stood next to the parked Suburban.

"Fuck you."

"What?"

"You heard me."

"I really want to know. Is it just Stockholm syndrome, or did you look out for that boy? Cause you really seem to be an asshole, and I can't picture you taking care of anybody other than yourself." She paused. "But then again, you've got all those medals. You must have been looking out for someone besides yourself to earn that Bronze Star." She turned her head and looked at him. "Tell me about it, Markinson. Tell me how you got to be a hero."

He let the cigarette dangle from his lip as he replied. "I'm not a hero. I never wanted to be a one. I was in the wrong place at the wrong time."

"You were out of the house; you went back in. The kid told me about it. He told me you were home free. You had a shotgun and you came back in to get him."

"And you still think I'm a cop killer?"

Sally couldn't answer that.

Chapter 27

Kevin sat in the middle of the back of the SUV, still shackled, staring out the window. "You're not that different from me, you know."

Sally twisted around in her seat to look at him. "What?"

"You used that kid. You had him scared, thinking he was going to go to jail, all so you could outfox one old fox."

"The means justify the ends."

"I've heard that one before." He snorted. "That's what they used to tell us before they sent us in to burn villages. 'We've got to kill them to protect them, don't you see? It became necessary to destroy the village in order to save it.'"

Sally blinked.

"At least I'm honest," Kevin muttered.

"Hey, asshole. Why don't you shut up?" Thomas craned his neck to look at Kevin in the rearview mirror.

"Yeah, or you'll get out the fucking stun gun. I know."

"It's all right, Thomas." Sally looked at her associate, and then back at her prisoner. "You don't think I have the right to do whatever it takes to bring in a fugitive?"

"Do you really think you have the right to ruin this kid's life?"

"You already did that. You compromised the kid; led him to believe you needed his help."

Kevin looked out the window. "I'll admit that. I did need help. But I never intended that the kid should get into trouble."

"You didn't think."

Kevin lowered his chin in what could pass for a nod. "I was in a tight spot."

"And you did what you felt you had to do. Because the end justifies the means." She stared straight into his eyes.

He swallowed, and she turned back around to stare out the windshield.

She paused for a moment, thinking. "So this has got to be the shortest time you've been out, right?"

He looked in her direction, but not at her. "No. I was out for about an hour that time the cop got shot."

"At least you didn't get hurt as bad this time."

"Sure." He snorted a feeble laugh.

"What happened anyway? This run wasn't your style, either. You wouldn't have just gone for the gate without a plan."

He shifted his eyes, looked at her again. She could see the wheels turning in his head as he considered whether or not to talk to her.

"Oh, what the hell." He sighed. "I paid somebody enough to take care of the right people and he took off with the money without taking care of the tower guards."

"And you got shot."

"Right."

"You want to name names, get some time off your sentence?"

"Do I look like a rat?"

"You look like a smart man with a family. Someone who might not want to spend the rest of his life behind bars."

"Sorry. You seem to have seriously misread me."

"Okay, so you got shot. After that, though, what went wrong?"

He snorted. "Everything. I was supposed to ride the train a lot longer than I did. I was supposed to get off in the state forest, hike out to a ride. It was a good plan, but I couldn't do it. I ran out of gas. I jumped off to keep from passing out and falling under the wheels."

"But you still walked after that."

"Yeah. I felt better moving."

"Did the kid help you from the beginning?"

"No. I found the pipe on my own."

"How'd you keep the kid from calling the cops? Before you convinced him you weren't a killer."

His eyes shifted again. "Told him I'd slit his throat."

She didn't believe that. "You ever kill a kid before?"

"You've seen my file. There's nothing in there about me killing little kids, right?"

He was staring into her eyes again now; she felt like he could see all the way into her soul. She was starting to understand why the kid had believed everything this man had said.

"What about during the war, over in the 'Nam?"

He blinked. Sucked in his breath and averted his eyes before answering. "The kids over there weren't kids. God, there were children wearing bombs, walking booby traps. Some of the soldiers were twelve, thirteen years old. That doesn't mean I liked it."

She was almost sorry for bringing it up, his reaction was so obvious. She cleared her throat. "But you told the kid you'd kill him if he called the cops."

"Had to do something. I needed help. I didn't want to die in the swamp. I told the kid he had to help me; forced him to take me to the house."

"And he did."

"Right. But only because I forced him."

"What would you have done if he was less cooperative?"

He looked away. "I guess you would have found me sooner. Although I might have been in worse shape."

"Wouldn't have bothered me." She was quiet for a minute. He was staring into space, shutting down.

"How come you didn't shoot the other two assholes in the kid's house?"

He almost jumped, brought his focus back to her, looked at her. "What?"

"Why didn't you shoot all the guys who took you hostage?"

"Didn't have to."

"I put the fear of God into one of them, the one called Al. Told him who you were, that you'd probably come after him."

Kevin shrugged. "Not worth bothering with."

"He beat you up pretty good, didn't he?" She tilted her head sideways, examining the bruises on his face.

"Wasn't him that did it. Was Paully, the one I killed. Self-defense, though." He glared at her.

"Did you really pull a gun on the cops?"

"Yeah. But I wasn't going to shoot anybody. The gun wasn't even loaded."

"Not loaded? What were you trying to do?"

He shrugged. "Suicide by cop."

She frowned. "Why?"

"I was having a bad day."

She narrowed her eyes and stared at him. "A bad day?"

"Yeah. I got to feeling a little depressed; couldn't really see a way out. I let myself get to the point where I just didn't care."

"And you were ready to die?" She was finding this hard to believe. Then it occurred to her that this man, this war hero who supposedly had no fear of death, might really be that way. Might not care whether he lived or died. That made him a lot scarier. It was the ones with this attitude—the who-gives-a-fuck attitude—who were the most dangerous.

He shrugged.

"Just like that?"

He looked at her again. She met his eyes, looking into the ice, searching for some sign of life. She didn't see any.

He raised his right hand and snapped his fingers. "Just like that."

"That kind of talk is going to get you a trip back up to that Mid-Hudson Forensic whatever it is place."

He eyed her. "I know better than to say that sort of thing in front of the shrinks. You think I want to spend the rest of my life shuffling around in slippers and a bathrobe?"

Sally frowned at him. "So what about after you walked by me and out the door at the hospital? Where'd you go?"

He raised his eyebrows. "You found the car. I saw it on the news."

"Yeah, we found the car. How about after that?"

He shook his head. "You don't want much, do you?"

"You get a chance to see your wife? You give your kid a birthday present?"

He glared at her now. "I'm here. You won. You don't need to rub it in."

"I wasn't rubbing anything in. I was just curious, that's all. So when you saw her, she tell you I saw her?"

Something flared in his eyes then. Something that almost scared her. He clenched his jaw; she could see the muscles working, almost hear his teeth grinding.

"I didn't see her."

"Sure you didn't. She tell you I was going to bring her in? Let her sit in federal prison on aiding and abetting?"

He worked his jaw now, the cords in his neck standing out. When he answered her, it was through gritted teeth. "I didn't see her."

"Did you see that Justin Stewart guy? He's a real hotshot, isn't he? Thinks he's clever. We couldn't keep a tail on him. Unlimited funds, this guy has."

"You ought to bring that up with internal affairs, not with me."

"Yeah, well, what're ya gonna do?" She paused to look at her watch. "You've got a couple of nice looking kids. They're getting pretty tall, aren't they?"

"I wouldn't know, since I haven't seen them in six years." He was staring out the window at the trees whipping by as they drove north.

"Your family doesn't come visit you in prison?"

"Nope."

"That's not very nice. You think your wife fools around on you?"

She saw a flush of red creeping up his neck.

"Nope."

"So why doesn't she visit you?"

"I won't allow it."

"You don't miss her when you're in?"

He turned towards her and she saw his whole face relax at that, melting. His eyes drifted away, and the angry spark disappeared. Maybe he was human after all.

It took him a minute to answer her. "You harassing me on purpose?"

"Am I harassing you? I'm not even asking questions relating to any crimes. Hell, you can just shut up any time you want."

"Do you miss your husband when you're working? Like when you were upstate chasing me?"

She hesitated. "Yeah."

"Why would I be any different?"

She laughed. "You miss her, then."

"Yeah. I do. I'm a normal human being."

Thomas snorted. "Fucking psychopath, that's what you are."

"Actually, I think the term you're looking for might be sociopath. I am not a psychopath. I'm not nuts. The state spent a lot of money proving that a few years ago."

Chapter 28

Sally stayed with him until she signed him over to the custody of the correctional officer in charge. They handed her the shackles and she watched the tall man disappear down a narrow hallway, still bent and shuffling, even though he was no longer shackled.

"You'll watch that one, right?"

The CO looked up at her with a bored expression. "What?"

"He's escaped from custody four times."

"Yeah, lady, don't worry about it."

As they exited the prison, Sally spotted a red-haired man in a wheelchair heading towards the door.

"Hold on a sec, would you, Thomas?"

"Sure."

"Excuse me, Mr. Longwood?" She was walking towards the man now.

He stopped and turned his head towards her. "Deputy Barnard. What can I do for you?"

"Can we talk for a minute?"

He glanced at his watch. "Sure."

"They need you in there?"

"No. I'm just here to pick up Mr. Markinson's personal belongings."

"That gives you a little time." She looked around. "Maybe we could chat over there, out of the way." She pointed towards his van, and the empty spot next to it.

"Sure." Longwood followed her. "So what do you need, Deputy?"

"Well, Mr. Longwood, it's nothing really, just curiosity. I can't figure your client out, and I thought maybe you could help me with that. I mean, for one thing, I can't even figure out what the hell you're doing representing someone like him. You're not the typical mob lawyer. You've got a pretty respectable business. No ties to any of the families—not even the one he's tied to."

"If you're inferring, Deputy Barnard, that my client is somehow connected with organized crime…"

She interrupted. "Oh no, Mr. Longwood. I'm not inferring anything."

"Good, because I don't think you have any proof of that at all."

"My point, Mr. Longwood, was that you don't seem the type to have a client like him."

The man lowered his eyebrows, but didn't speak.

"So why?"

"Why what?"

"Why are you working for him?"

He shifted in the chair. "The man saved my life."

"What?"

"You heard me."

"No, what do you mean? Did he like pull you out of the line of fire in Vietnam or something?"

"Do I really look old enough to have been in Vietnam, Deputy Barnard? I graduated high school in 1975." He took a deep breath and looked over towards Thomas, who was leaning against the Suburban and contemplating something on the ground. "Don't you have some fugitive to chase or something?"

"No, I just caught one. Tell me how he saved your life."

"He taught me to play wheelchair basketball."

"Really?"

"That's it. It was what I needed. He was actually teaching my older brother, who *was* in Vietnam and lost both legs to a land mine. But I tagged along, recovering from a gang shooting, thinking I was never going to do anything again as long as I lived, ready to drop out of school. Kevin taught me to play ball, to keep going, to live again. He saved my life."

"So you went to law school to get him out of jail?"

"I went to law school long before I knew what kind of trouble Kevin was going to get himself into. I'd always wanted to be a lawyer. Kevin just put me back on the tracks."

"You're serious, aren't you?"

"Why wouldn't I be? You think I'm faking this?" He waved an arm at his useless legs.

She licked her lips. "You think he killed that cop?"

"I know he didn't kill that cop."

"Why didn't you get him off?"

Longwood looked at his lap for a moment. "I was young, right out of school. Just passed the bar. Kevin's wife came to me, scared to death, saying that Kevin wanted me to represent him. He wouldn't take anybody else; he had to have me. I saw what the state had for evidence; it was pretty compelling. Kevin was telling the truth; I knew he was, but I couldn't prove it. They were talking about life—thank God there was no death penalty then—but first degree murder. I mean, it was a cop, on duty. That's life. Kevin was only thirty years old, and his wife had just had a baby. I could just see him going down if I couldn't prove he didn't do it, and it would be all my fault. They weren't willing to bargain. I had no choice but to take it to trial, but we just didn't have enough evidence." He shook his head.

"So, they found him guilty."

"Yes, ma'am."

"But you don't think he did it."

"He didn't do it."

"Why doesn't he just stay in jail?"

"I wish I knew. The man has travelling bones, I guess. He won't stay put."

"Maybe his boss breaks him out. This Marconi guy."

His voice went cold. "I have no idea what you're talking about, Deputy Barnard."

"You think he's going to stay put now, like he said he would?"

Longwood let out a long sigh. "If there's one thing I've learned over the years, Deputy Barnard, it's that I have some clients I can't trust to tell the truth. Kevin will tell the truth when he thinks it will benefit him. Other than that, the man can't be trusted. He's not a bad guy; I'm not saying that, but he learned very early on in life to avoid telling the truth unless it was to his benefit. If a lie is better, he tells a lie. Sometimes, I'm not sure he knows whether or not he's telling the truth." Longwood paused. "He has some issues."

"But you still think he's a good guy."

"I would trust that man with my life. But I wouldn't believe him."

"Sounds like an alcoholic."

"Actually, I think you're right. He used to assure people he wasn't drinking, but he'd drink right in front of them. Tell them it was ginger ale."

She turned to stare at the entrance to the prison again and sighed. "Well, thanks, Mr. Longwood."

"You're welcome." He turned around and headed back up the ramp towards the door that led into the prison.

She sat silent in the SUV as Thomas drove back to the city, didn't even load a CD.

"What's with you, Sally?"

She shook her head. "Nothing, just a long day. What'd you think of that guy?"

"Markinson?"

"Yeah."

"He's like all the others, isn't he? A really good liar. Slit your throat if you turn your back on him."

"I didn't see that in him."

"You getting all psychological on me?"

"I didn't believe a lot of the stuff I read about him—the hero stuff, the noble stuff. I was actually surprised when he let those kids out of the car he stole, regardless of what I said to you. But there's something there."

"It's just a job, Sally. We catch 'em; we don't analyze them."

"Just the same, Thomas. I've been thinking about doing something else with my life."

He turned his head. "What?"

"Watch the road, will you?" She sighed. "I'm ready for a change."

"You're not going to retire, are you?"

"No. I'm going to see if I can pick up a witness security rotation."

"Really?"

"Yep."

"I'll miss you," Thomas said.

"Hah. You'll be fine without me. You're a real star, up and coming; you'll do well. It's time for me to step aside. I haven't got it in me anymore. I don't care about the chase the way I used to."

"Sure you do. This guy was just a tough one, that's all. We'll get a new one on Monday and things'll be back to normal."

She shook her head. "Thomas, I don't want to be taking bullets anymore. I don't want to be point on the door anymore. I'm tired. It started before we took this case; he just confirmed it."

Thomas licked his lips. "You'll be good at whatever you want to do, boss. You've got talent."

She laughed, and they rode in silence the rest of the way back to the city.

CHAPTER 29

Danny felt as if his life had changed. He found himself unsure of what he wanted, where he was going, what he was doing. Nights were the hardest. He would lie awake, dreading the sound of the doorbell. When he did manage to sleep, he would wake up screaming, the images of Paully and his pals fresh in his mind.

Subjects he'd always loved in school were suddenly hard for him. He felt alone, as if his mother and his friends didn't understand him anymore. He wasn't sure he understood himself anymore.

The first week back at school Danny got a hint of what things might be like. He wasn't happy to be there. He wouldn't have been anyway, but he was exhausted, feeling like he hadn't slept in weeks. It was bad enough when he was yanked out of class to talk to the school psychologist, a dumpy man of at least sixty with a gray beard who chewed gum the whole time he talked. He wanted to know what had happened, wanted Danny to talk about the "traumatic event" as he called it. Danny didn't want to talk to him, so he didn't. He spent the twenty minutes staring out the window, wondering what Duke was doing now.

He was just getting his bearings in the new school when the same old gang of bullies surrounded him in the stairwell between the first and second floor. But he wasn't going to let it happen. He looked up, and met their eyes, one after the other. Eddie was missing. There was a replacement, another kid Danny didn't know, but who fit the same greasy mold.

Randy started. "So you decided to help out a serial killer, huh?"

Danny opened his mouth.

"Shut up," said Terry, and pushed at Danny.

Danny blinked, swallowing the fear that started to rise in his throat. His vision was getting fuzzy, black around the edges. He didn't understand this. He'd never felt anything like this in his life. The fear was melting away, replaced by rage. He was suddenly angry at every person who had ever screwed up his life. Why should he take this from these jerks? Only the word in his brain wasn't jerks. It was a swear word he had heard from Paully, or maybe Duke. He dropped his backpack on the floor and heard himself screaming. It felt as though he was outside himself, watching. He could hear a steady stream of profanity, but didn't realize it was coming from him.

He launched himself at the nearest person, who happened to be Randy. He began beating the bigger, older boy with his fists, landing blows on his face, his belly, his groin. The older kid backpedaled, and fell backwards down the stairs. The other two boys fled. Danny stood there, staring, wondering what had happened.

He was still in a daze when the teacher led him away, when he sat in the principal's office, waiting for his mother to arrive from work.

He continued to just sit and stare as his mother talked to the principal and the gray-haired psychologist. He heard bits and pieces. Words like "press charges," and "Stockholm syndrome," that he didn't really understand. Then he heard something he did understand, when the principal started talking about posttraumatic stress disorder. He turned his head and concentrated for a moment on what the man was saying. "Psychiatrist or psychologist, we'll get a court order if we have to."

"I'm sure it won't come to that," Danny heard his mother respond. He tuned out again as the principal said something about suspension.

"Would you like to talk to someone? Like a doctor?" She brought it up right away, in the car on the way home, as if he hadn't been there in the office.

"No. Nobody understands. It's like everybody thinks I either did it—you know, helped him—and I ought to be in jail. Or they think he forced me to help him and they feel sorry for me."

"So which is true?"

"Neither. Sort of. I don't know." He turned towards her. "Oh, Mom, what if I did do it? I helped this guy avoid capture. I would never do anything like that, never even dream of doing something like that. So why did it happen?" He looked out the window, and thought for a moment. "Maybe I could talk to someone."

"I know someone at work whose son is a psychologist. He's young, just out of school. I'm sure he'd talk with you." His mom sighed. "You've been through a lot, you know. It's okay to feel confused."

As Danny and his mom sat in the waiting room, a man walked in. He looked like he was about nineteen. Danny assumed he was just another patient. He wore blue jeans and a leather jacket. His black, curly hair stuck out of a baseball cap.

"Hi, I'm Lucas. You must be Danny." He held out his hand.

Danny shook it.

"Let's get started." Lucas led the way to his office. It was a small room, with a metal desk, and bookshelves made of cinder blocks and boards. The shelves were crowded with books. Danny looked at some of them while Lucas took off his coat. He was surprised to see some of his favorite crime novels on the shelf.

"Have a seat, Danny. Is that what you like to be called?"

"Yeah."

"Why are you here?"

"My mother and teachers seem to think I need to talk about stuff."

"Do you think you need to talk about stuff?"

"I don't know."

"Why don't you tell me what happened last summer?"

Danny related the story, from the time he discovered Duke in the pipe, through his speaking at Duke's sentencing.

"Wow." Lucas leaned back in his chair. "That sounds like an adventure."

"I guess. It wasn't boring, that's for sure."

"So why are you here?"

"They told me I had to come here." He paused. "Well, I guess I've been having a hard time. I have a lot of feelings that are mixing me up. I don't know what to believe anymore. I mean, this guy was a criminal, and I helped him, and that should be wrong. But it didn't feel wrong. That worries me."

"You helped him because he was hurt, not because he was a criminal. You didn't know he was a criminal, right?"

"Not at first. By the time I knew, I was in too deep. I couldn't just throw him out, or call the cops. By then I knew him, and I didn't believe the things they said about him."

"Do you think he could have led you to believe things about him that weren't true? Made you think he was a better person than he really is?"

"How? By being nice to me? By saving my life? By treating me like a person instead of a kid?" Danny shook his head. "You should have seen it. Every time those jerks started to pay attention to me, he got them to focus on him. He kept them working him over so that they wouldn't touch me."

"There're lots of cases of hostages becoming attached to their captors. It's called Stockholm syndrome. It has to do with stress. He made you think he needed you; led you to believe that he was an innocent man."

"No, he didn't."

"Did he tell you who he was?"

"Not really." Danny hesitated. The man *had* tried to tell him, hadn't he? "He wouldn't let me give him money, and he said I'd get into trouble if I did."

"Was it fun? Is that why you did it?"

"I don't know. He said the same thing; kept asking me if I was having fun, if it was all a game. He didn't really want me to help him."

"Would you do it again?"

"I don't know. If he walked up to the front door and asked to come in and hide, I wouldn't do it. If he came and asked me for money I wouldn't do it. I don't know if I would call the cops, but I wouldn't help him."

"But if it was last August again, and you climbed into that pipe and saw that man, would you help him?"

"I don't know. If I hadn't helped him, he would have died."

"Maybe. Or you could have called the police, or an ambulance."

"So, was it wrong to help him?"

Lucas put a finger in his mouth and chewed on the nail. "It was wrong, and it was right." He tilted his head sideways and looked hard at Danny. "Did he scare you?"

"Yes. But not deliberately. He wasn't trying to scare me, but I found him frightening, I guess. Not as scary as the other guys, though."

"Just the fact that he scared you was enough to intimidate you, keep you from the calling the police. He didn't have to threaten you. Just his presence was enough to keep you from turning him in. It's called implied coercion." Lucas paused. "Think about it. This guy is like, what, six and half feet tall. Scary looking, right? He would scare me, and I'm not thirteen years old. He was in charge, and you knew it, even if you didn't realize it. You would have done anything for him."

Danny looked at Lucas. Blinked a couple of times, and realized that the man was giving him an out. He was off the hook. Even if Duke hadn't directly threatened him, he still had power over him, and used that power. Danny nodded. "I get it. I didn't really think I was scared, but I was. You're right."

"You're okay. You know that, right?"

Danny nodded.

"We're going to need to spend some time talking about what happened."

Danny shifted in his chair. "Why?"

"If you want to get over the flashbacks, the nightmares—if you want to sleep again, you need to learn to deal with it." Lucas paused. "It's called posttraumatic stress disorder."

"No way."

"Yeah. You've heard of it."

"My dad had some of the symptoms, I guess. And that man, the man I helped…"

"Markinson."

"Yeah. I saw him have a flashback. He said things; he was a Vietnam veteran. But how could I have that? I wasn't in a war."

"You went through something traumatic."

"Not like that."

"Danny, Markinson killed a man in front of you. You saw somebody die. It doesn't get any worse than that."

Danny felt the burning in his eyes again, the lump in his throat.

"Tell me about it."

"He held a gun to my head. I thought I was going to die."

"Markinson?"

"No." Danny shook his head. "He wouldn't; he didn't hurt me. He kept me safe."

"So who held a gun to your head?"

Danny closed his eyes. He didn't want to bring it back. He began to talk, to tell the story, and he began to cry.

When he left, still sniffling, he realized he actually felt better. He felt as if he was starting to get some control over it. He had talked about it and nothing had happened. He was okay.

It took him weeks to get comfortable in school again, to stop jumping every time someone slammed a locker.

"Danny." His mother approached him just before Halloween, when he was feeling really low. She sat on the bed as he lay stretched out, staring at the ceiling. "How are you doing?"

"I'm okay," he replied.

"Would you have done anything differently?" She stood up, and walked over to the window.

He sat up, swung his legs over to the floor, and said, "I don't know, Mom. I just don't know." He paused. "Life used to be so simple. Good guys and bad guys. Black and white. Everything is all blurry now." He stood up, and stretched. "What's that line from that movie you like so much? Oh yeah, Jimmy Stewart says 'I know what I'm doing tomorrow and the next day and next year and the year after that'; and then the guy's dad has a stroke, and it all changes." He scratched his head. "I feel like everything has changed for me. Like I can never go back to who I was. As if I grew up all of a sudden."

Danny actually found himself getting along better with other kids at school. He didn't have trouble with bullies anymore; for some reason, they seemed to treat him with new respect. He figured it had something to do with Randy's trip to the hospital after the stairwell incident. He made more friends, got involved with more activities, and didn't spend as much time alone. He didn't want to be alone.

"So, what are you going to do after high school, Danny?" Jessie Saxby stretched as she spoke, flipping her blond hair out of her face.

"I'm going to college. Don't know where yet; I'll apply at a few different places." He fired the basketball at the net, remembering to keep it on his fingertips. His sneakers squeaked on the polished wood floor as he caught the rebound when the ball bounced off the rim. He tossed it towards the girl.

She caught it easily, with a laugh, and tossed it through the hoop. She was taller than he was, lean and long-legged. "You're not going to get a basketball scholarship, that's for sure."

"So far, my grades are good enough that it doesn't matter. I imagine I'll get some help with a scholarship for that, depending on the school." He wasn't lying now; he was proud of that. His grades had come up again.

"What are you going to do after college?"

"Promise you won't laugh?"

"You know I wouldn't laugh at you."

"I'd like to go into the Secret Service. It's what I've always wanted to do." At least it used to be. He had never questioned it before, almost as if it was destiny.

"No way. That's cool. I've never known anyone who wanted to do that." She paused. "That's like protecting the President and all, right?"

"Yes. They do other stuff, too, like chasing counterfeiters."

"So, what do you have to study in college?"

"I'm looking at law enforcement, politics, criminal science. That sort of thing." He shrugged his shoulders.

"That is so cool. Your dad was a cop, right?" Jess fired off another shot at the hoop. "Swish! Nothing but net."

"Yeah, he was." Danny wanted to change the subject. "You going to college, Jess?"

"Probably. It's a little early to be thinking about it." She looked around. "You ready to take a break?"

He was sweating, although she looked like she wasn't even breathing hard. "Sure."

They sat together on the top of the bleachers, sucking on water bottles, and watching other kids shooting baskets.

"I remember the time last summer you were in trouble for helping out that escaped murderer." She ran a towel over her largely dry forehead.

He didn't answer right away. It was too much, too close to real. Too many memories, too recent. He really wanted to just forget. "I wish I could stop remembering," he said softly.

"Was it scary? I mean, did the guy threaten you?"

"No. He wasn't that bad. He never really threatened me. It was Eddie and his cousin and his friends that were scary. Duke didn't do anything to me." Danny sat on the edge of the seat, elbows on his knees, chin in his hands.

"Didn't he kill somebody?"

"Yeah."

"That must have been wicked scary. I would have been out of my mind. I can't imagine somebody like that. Somebody who could just kill a person."

He looked away. "I was intimidated by him, but I didn't think I was afraid of him. I know now that I must have been. That must have been why I didn't turn him in."

"That's so cool. You really got to meet this murderer. Like Al Capone, right?"

"Actually, I don't think he would appreciate being compared to Al Capone. But he was a killer. Is a killer, I guess. Although he denies it." He thought for a moment. The man he had met, the man he had helped was not a killer; at least not in the sense the police used the word. At least he didn't seem like he was. "He must have killed people. Actually, he said he had killed people, but he couldn't go out in the woods and shoot at defenseless animals."

"But he killed someone right in front of you."

"It was self-defense, Jess. The guy was about to shoot him."

"What was he like?"

"I don't know; it's hard to talk about. He wasn't like anybody I've ever met before. He treated me like an adult, instead of like a kid. He was polite. He didn't tell me what to do, you know?"

"Was he mean?"

"No. He kept me safe, protected me from the other goons. He was screwed up though, I'm sure. I couldn't really tell, but nobody could be that kind of person and not be screwed up, right?"

"I don't know. I know Eddie's dad is wicked screwed up."

Danny knew that Eddie's father had been in and out of jail repeatedly for the last five years. "He's using drugs, isn't he?"

"Yeah, that's the rumor. He's wicked mean, too. He hits Eddie and Eddie's mother, too. I don't think he's ever killed anybody, though."

Danny found himself actually feeling sorry for Eddie. "Does it take a special kind of person to kill somebody? Are you born without a conscience? And what keeps someone like Eddie's dad from killing people? He's not half the man Duke is, but is that it? And how come this killer saved my life?"

"Lot of questions."

"Yeah, that's pretty much the way my life has been since then. I would love to sit down with this guy for a couple of hours and pick his brain. Find out why he did what he did. Why he cared about one little kid enough to give up his freedom—freedom he would have killed to get."

"Are you sure you want to be a Secret Service agent? You're talking about the possibility of having to kill people."

"I know. I'm not quite sure, you know. I don't know if I could ever do that."

"I think you ought to be a psychologist or psychiatrist, something like that."

"Why?"

"I like to talk to you; I'll bet other people would, too. Besides, wouldn't it be fun to explore the criminal mind, like you just talked about?"

"Yeah, I guess." He glanced at Jess, and then looked back down at the court. "My dad was so proud when I told him I wanted to go into law enforcement."

"So you're doing this for your dad?" She snorted, poured some water into her mouth, and shook her head.

"It's not just that. I've always been interested in this kind of stuff. You know, I love mysteries and suspense and all that."

"So, do you really want to be a cop?"

Danny shrugged. "You know the cops tricked him into giving himself up."

"I didn't know that."

"They let me think they were going to send me to jail. Let him think that they were going to send me to jail. That was why he turned himself in."

"What do you think about that?"

"It seems pretty rotten to me."

"You couldn't do something like that, could you? Could you deceive him to the point where he would turn himself in?"

"I don't know."

"I don't think you're cop material."

He turned his head to stare at her. "My dad was a cop."

"I know. I'm sorry. I didn't mean anything by it." She shrugged, dropped her towel on the wooden bench, and trotted down to the gym floor, leaping easily from seat to seat.

He watched her go, thinking hard. She was right; he knew it. There was no way he could go back to what he had been before it all happened. There was no way he could just become a cop, federal or not. His life wasn't what it had been. He wasn't the same person. He wasn't normal anymore; there was no normal anymore.

Epilogue

That hot day in August, Kevin had walked into the cell with nothing, just the prison-issued clothes on his back. The black man in the cell was younger, but most everybody was. He was also probably seventy-five pounds heavier. He was sitting on the bottom bunk, flexing his muscles. Kevin looked back at the CO, who grinned.

"Enjoy."

Kevin climbed to the top bunk and stared at the pink cement block walls, thinking about a way out.

"Yo, what's your name?"

Kevin rolled over and met the man's eyes, which were right at his eye level as he stood next to the bunks. "Duke."

"What the hell kind of name is that? It's a dog's name."

"So I've heard."

"I'm George. What you in for?"

"I killed a cop."

George took a step back. "Really?"

"No."

The youngster narrowed his eyes. "What the fuck is up with you?"

"What are you in for, George?"

"Armed robbery."

Kevin nodded as he studied the cell. George had a translucent boom box on the metal desk, along with some pictures of a young woman. Or maybe more than one young woman. He figured it wasn't worth asking George if he knew when the library was open. He spent most of the first night awake, listening to the noises of several hundred men in small spaces.

A different CO came by the next day, just after lunch. Kevin was doing some stretches.

"Markinson."

He looked up at a young black woman. "Yes, ma'am?"

"You need to go over to the infirmary and see the doctor."

"Okay."

"It's in another building, so we need to do shackles."

"Yes, ma'am." Kevin stood while she fitted the chains.

The corrections officer waited until they were in an empty hallway before she started a conversation. "You came with a reputation. Guys say you were here before. Last year. You got transferred to medium and went rabbit."

"Yes, ma'am."

"I don't need you trying nothing with me, you understand?"

"Yes, ma'am." Kevin kept his head down as he walked, but he paid attention to where they were going.

"Just 'cause I'm a girl doesn't mean I'm weak."

"I understand that, ma'am."

He sat on an examining table and waited for the doctor, who turned out to be a very young woman. She held out a hand. "Good afternoon, Mr. Markinson. I'm Dr. Mara Anderson."

He shook her hand and nodded.

She motioned to another, older woman behind her. "This is Sheila Baker; she's our nurse for today. You're here for follow-up on an injury you received earlier this week?"

"It was last week, actually. Last Thursday."

"Let's take a look."

He pulled off the tee shirt and shifted so that she could look at his arm.

She pulled off the dressing. "No stitches?"

"No, ma'am."

"How's your range of motion?"

He raised the arm as high as he could. She took his forearm and pulled upward, causing him to wince.

She frowned. "Sheila, can we make a note that Mr. Markinson needs to see a physical therapist? If we don't keep these muscles loose, you're going to lose a lot of motion."

He nodded.

She turned to the nurse. "Dress this back up." Then to Kevin. "We'll see you next week."

"Yes, ma'am." He watched her walk away, and then focused on the nurse, who was dabbing at his arm with some sort of sudsy cotton. "What is she, like eighteen?"

"She's right out of school. Government forgives your student loans if you come and work in a place like this."

He flinched as she poked at his arm. "Take it easy."

"You don't need to be talking back to me, old man."

He eyed her, and then glanced at the CO, who was grinning.

He decided to try a little conversation during the walk back. "How long have you been working here?"

"I've been here eight months. Transferred from Attica. Trying to work my way up to a minimum security women's prison."

"I guess I didn't think about women working men's prisons."

"There aren't enough women's prisons for everybody who wants to be a CO. A lot of the guys with seniority will request a women's gig; it's easier."

They were walking down a long hallway at that point, and she tightened her grip on his arm. He looked up. Three big white guys at the other end of the hall. No CO in sight. "Are those guys supposed to be there?"

"No." She keyed her radio. "What's up in the hallway, admin building?"

He lifted his head at the sound of a siren. "What's that?"

The CO came to a stop, reached for her radio mic. "What's going on?"

"We've got some sort of trouble in the visitor center; going into lockdown. Where are you?"

"I'm on my way back with a prisoner."

"You gone by the visitor's center yet?"

"No."

Kevin kept shuffling, head up now, scanning.

"Markinson, hold it." She keyed the radio again. "What do you want me to do?"

The anonymous voice on the other end of the radio replied, "Don't get near there. Get your boy somewhere else; lock him in a conference room or something."

Kevin turned to look at her now. She looked scared.

He swallowed. "Sounds bad."

"Yeah, you want to turn around for me? We'll go back the way we came."

"Sure." Just as he started to turn, a door about a hundred yards further down opened into the hall and three more big white guys poured through it.

"Shit." The corrections officer was backpedaling, keeping an eye on the crowd. She pressed the button on her microphone again. "We got company. Hallway outside the visitor's center. It's just me. Alone."

"Yeah, we all got problems," the voice crackled back at her.

Kevin looked at the other prisoners and stepped between them and the woman. "Get that door open, we'll get in there and lock them out. Can we do that, lock the door from inside?"

"I don't know. I don't think so." Her reply was shaky.

"What's this?"

Kevin wasn't sure which of the guys said it, but it didn't matter. They were all the same. Big white guys with nasty prison tats and muscles from lifting weights all day.

"Take off the shackles," he hissed at her, pushing her back down the hall.

"I can't do that," she shot back in a whisper.

"You got a better idea? I can't even defend myself like this, never mind you."

"How do I know you won't just join in with them?" She almost sounded like she was going to cry.

"You'll have to trust me."

"Oh, great." She tried the radio again. "I've got six AB guys coming after me and my prisoner. What do I do now?" No response. The alarms were louder now.

"You're going to have to take the fucking shackles off." Kevin kept his back to her, watching the group.

The big guys were advancing now, spread across the hallway. Smoke was oozing out of the doorway they had come from, smoke or tear gas, or something.

"Here." She opened the door to a conference room.

The guys began to move faster, maybe figuring out what the plan was.

"Give me the keys."

"What?"

"Get in there and give me the keys."

"Here, take this too." She handed him her baton and the keys and he locked her in. Then he unlocked the shackles, starting with his feet. He dropped the keys into his pocket as the cuffs and chain fell off. Then he stood his ground in front of the door.

The biggest of the group, nearly as tall as Kevin and probably a hundred pounds heavier, stepped into his space. "Okay, old man. Give us the keys and you can walk away."

"No."

"The fuck you say?"

"No."

The big guy snorted and looked around at the other five guys. They were all wearing the same green pants and the same green tee shirts, which made them look like some sort of cleaning crew. "This ain't your fight, old man."

Kevin wished for something bigger than the small baton in his left hand. His right hand closed on the keys in his pocket. "Okay, boys. Who's first?"

The leader laughed. Kevin watched him, waiting, sliding the keys out of his pocket, clenched in his fist with the biggest, sharpest key sticking out through his fingers. *Let the guy get in close. Stay up as long as possible. Keep them away from the woman.*

He stepped forward into the guy, knee to the groin, keys to the eyes. *One down.* The other guys hesitated for a moment, and then came at him all at once. *Baton to the nearest knee, keys to any eyes he could reach. Keep his hands up; protect his head. Hold onto the keys; hold onto the keys.*

Kevin woke up in the prison hospital. He opened his eyes and focused on the young doctor.

"You saved her life, you know."

He didn't answer. His whole face hurt and he wasn't sure he could say anything.

"You kept those guys busy long enough for reinforcements to arrive. Kept that CO safe."

Kevin didn't think he could nod either, but he blinked.

The doctor touched his right shoulder. "I'm going to make sure you get some sort of recognition for this."

This he had to respond to. The last thing he needed was attention. "No." He could barely squeak it out; his throat felt like sandpaper.

"Just relax and concentrate on getting better." She walked away.

He watched her go. This was really going to mess things up.

Kevin Markinson
will return in

- Frostbite -

More Kevin Markinson
Now Available:

Lead Poisoning
(Kevin Markinson Series, Book 1)

Blackbird and Other Stories:
A Kevin Markinson Anthology

Also From J.E. Seymour

Lead Poisoning
(Kevin Markinson Series, Book 1)

Blackbird and Other Stories: A Kevin Markinson Anthology

"Mickey Takes a Dive," short story in *Live Free or Die, Die, Die,*
an anthology of New Hampshire noir

"Lights Out," short story in *Quarry,*
an anthology of crime fiction by New England writers

"The Big Bash," short story in *Deadfall,*
an anthology of crime fiction by New England writers

"Life's a Beach," story story in *Windchill,*
an anthology of crime fiction by New England writers

Coming Soon From J.E. Seymour

Frostbite
(Kevin Markinson Series, Book 3)

WWW.JESEYMOUR.COM

J.E. Seymour

J.E. Seymour lives in a small town in seacoast New Hampshire. Her first novel, *Lead Poisoning* was originally released in November 2010 and reissued in May 2014 by Barking Rain Press. Ms. Seymour has also had a number of short stories published in anthologies—*Live Free or Die, Die, Die, Windchill, Deadfall,* and *Quarry,* as well as *Thriller UK* magazine, and in numerous ezines including *Spinetingler, Shots, Mouth Full of Bullets, Mysterical-E, A Twist of Noir, Beat to a Pulp, Yellow Mama* and *Shred of Evidence.* The markets coordinator for the Short Mystery Fiction Society, Ms. Seymour is also a member of Sisters in Crime and Mystery Writers of America. Find out more about J.E. Seymour at her website, Facebook page, or on Twitter.

WWW.JESEYMOUR.COM

About
Barking Rain Press

Did you know that five media conglomerates publish eighty percent of the books in the United States? As the publishing industry continues to contract, opportunities for emerging and mid-career authors are drying up. Who will write the literature of the twenty-first century if just a handful of profit-focused corporations are left to decide who—and what—is worthy of publication?

Barking Rain Press is dedicated to the creation and promotion of thoughtful and imaginative contemporary literature, which we believe is essential to a vital and diverse culture. As a nonprofit organization, Barking Rain Press is an independent publisher that seeks to cultivate relationships with new and mid-career writers over time, to be thorough in the editorial process, and to make the publishing process an experience that will add to an author's development—and ultimately enhance our literary heritage.

In selecting new titles for publication, Barking Rain Press considers authors at all points in their careers. Our goal is to support the development of emerging and mid-career authors—not just single books—as we know from experience that a writer's audience is cultivated over the course of several books.

Support for these efforts comes primarily from the sale of our publications; we also hope to attract grant funding and private donations. Whether you are a reader or a writer, we invite you to take a stand for independent publishing and become more involved with Barking Rain Press. With your support, we can make sure that talented writers thrive, and that their books reach the hands of spirited, curious readers. Find out more at our website.

WWW.BARKINGRAINPRESS.ORG

Also from Barking Rain Press

LEAD POISONING — J.E. Seymour

CABIN FEVER — James M. Jackson (A Seamus McCree Mystery)

DANGEROUS DENIAL — Amy Ray

EINE KLEINE MURDER — Kaye George (A Cressa Carraway Musical Mystery)

SPEAKING OF MURDER — Tace Baker

RIVER BOTTOM BLUES — Ricky Bush

VIEW OUR COMPLETE CATALOG ONLINE:

WWW.BARKINGRAINPRESS.ORG

**Make Your Mark Here
So You Know You've
Read this Book**

Made in the USA
Charleston, SC
21 August 2014